"I need you, C[illegible]"

He slo[illegible] his hat to look at her. "[illegible]rough this. We're n[illegible]r. A man doesn't ta[illegible]t a woman like you—unl[illegible]ke her his wife. I don't plan to m[illegible] wife, Patience."

"C[illegible] right now I don't care how you feel about me. I'm lonely . . . and I'm beginning to wonder if I'll ever be able to make a man happy. I *need* you to hold me, to love me. I need someone to care just for *me,* even if it is only for tonight."

"Patience . . ." He *did* want to hold her, make love to her—but he knew it wasn't right. He could never promise her commitment.

Sensing his growing weakness, she leaned over and brushed his mouth persuasively with her lips. "Cass, please. Just for one night. Teach me how to be a woman . . ."

"You are so lovely," he whispered. "So very lovely." Desire had a razor's edge that seared through him, mingling pain with pleasure. He let his hands explore and tease through the thin fabric of her gown, bringing from her a moan of pleasure. "Come with me," he whispered. "Don't be afraid . . ."

There was no denying passion now.

OTHER BOOKS BY *LORI COPELAND:*

Avenging Angel
Passion's Captive

SWEET TALKIN' STRANGER

Lori Copeland

A DELL BOOK

Published by
Dell Publishing
a division of
Bantam Doubleday Dell
Publishing Group, Inc.
666 Fifth Avenue
New York, New York 10103

ISBN: 0-440-20325-2

April 1989

Printed in the United States of America
Published simultaneously in Canada

10 9 8 7 6 5 4 3 2 1

KRI

To the three Copeland sons:
Randall, Richard, and Russell,
Your papa and I are right proud of you.

Prologue

Kansas Frontier: 1868

The early morning wind had a sharp bite to it, but the sun shone brightly in the eastern sky. Guess a man couldn't ask for much more than that on the twenty-sixth day of December, Cass Claxton thought contentedly.

As the old wagon rattled along the road, a smile pulled at the corners of his mouth. He set the brim of his hat lower on his forehead as his cobalt-blue eyes surveyed the endless expanse of Kansas sky.

The visit with his brother Beau and Beau's new wife, Charity, had been good, but he was eager to get back home before a storm set in. Winters in Missouri were contrary, but he didn't think they could hold a candle to the full-blown blizzards of Kansas.

His face sobered as he recalled how Beau had nearly lost his wife and baby daughter the week before when they'd gotten stranded in a sudden blizzard.

The newly formed Claxton family had been lucky. Cass remembered the solemn way Reverend Olson had reminded them that it had been nothing short of a miracle that Charity and Mary Kathleen had survived after having been buried beneath the snow for half a day.

Cass's smile returned as he thought of how happy his brother was now. And it was about time. Beau had had a hard time getting over the death of his first wife, Betsy, but it looked like he'd make it just fine now.

The way Beau had loved his first wife and now Charity sometimes puzzled Cass. As far as women were concerned, Cass could take them or leave them. And he'd done just that, more times than he cared to admit.

There was no way a woman was going to hog-tie and brand him. He'd never met a woman he'd want to be around much longer than a week—with maybe the exception of Wynne Elliot.

Now there was a woman. The image of her crimson hair and dancing sea-green eyes came back to haunt him. He probably should have married her when he'd had the chance four years ago, but there was no use crying over spilled milk. Cole, his eldest brother, had married Wynne, and Cass had to admit he'd never seen a happier couple.

Of course, Beau's wife, Charity, wasn't all that bad either. She'd sure make Beau a fine woman—Cass couldn't argue with that. But taking a wife was the last thing on Cass's mind. He wasn't anywhere close to settling down and raising a family. He had a peck of wild oats to sow before any woman got him to the altar—if one ever did.

Cass gave a sharp whistle and set the horses into a fast trot. The old buckboard rumbled over potholes as he began humming a jaunty tune.

Directly ahead, he could see four riders approaching. Their horses were coming fast, and Cass wondered where they were headed in such a hurry.

As they drew nearer Cass frowned, noting that one of the riders was that infuriating Patience McCord.

The woman had been nothing but a thorn in his side since the day he'd run into her in Miller's Mercantile. He'd hoped to leave Kansas without encountering her again, but it looked like his luck had just gone sour.

Well, he'd tip his hat politely and ride on by, he thought, and was about to do just that, when the foursome reined up directly in his path. Caught by surprise, Cass hauled back on the reins, bringing his team to a sudden halt.

Leviticus McCord; his daughter, Patience; Reverend Olson; and a large man wearing a tin star sat stiffly in their saddles, staring back at Cass.

Cass tipped his hat. "Morning, Reverend."

"Good morning, Mr. Claxton."

The horses danced about, breathing frosty plumes into the brisk morning air.

"What brings you out this way so early in the day?" Cass carefully avoided looking at the young woman on the dappled-gray mare. He still seethed whenever he thought of how Patience McCord had hauled off and hit him below the belt with her purse during their unpleasant encounter a week ago. Then the silly twit had had the gall to look him up a few days later to offer him the exorbitant fee of five hundred dollars to escort her back to her aunt in St. Louis.

Cass has refused promptly and none too nicely. He wouldn't take Patience McCord to a dog fight, let alone ride all the way back to Missouri with her, and he'd wasted no time in telling her so.

But by then it had grown dark, and Patience had started to cry. She'd pleaded that she felt too faint and frightened to find her way back to town. Cass had had no recourse but to let her stay that night; he'd sent her packing first thing after breakfast the next morning.

But here she was again, looking down at him with that superior smirk of hers that made his blood boil.

"We're looking for you!" Leviticus roared.

"Me?" Cass's grin began to fade. Why would

Leviticus McCord be looking for him, he wondered.

"Mr. Claxton, would you mind climbin' down off that buckboard?" The man with the double-barreled shotgun and tin star motioned for Cass to comply.

"Well, I don't know . . ." Cass glanced back to Reverend Olson expectantly. "What's going on?"

"I believe you've met . . . uh . . . hummruph . . . uh . . . Miss McCord?" Reverend Olson met Cass's gaze apologetically.

Cass glanced toward Patience dispassionately. "I've met her."

Patience nodded from beneath the veil of her ostrich-plumed hat, her violet eyes mocking him.

"Met her! Met *her!*" Turning scarlet, Leviticus shouted louder, "I should hope to heaven he's *met* her!"

Cass's eyes snapped to Leviticus. "Yes, I've met her!"

"Cass . . . uh . . . this is very difficult," Reverend Olson said in an uneasy tone. "Would you care to step down from your wagon for a moment?"

Cass obediently wrapped the reins around the brake, and in a lithe motion landed on the ground beside Patience, who was sniffling loudly into her lace handkerchief.

As she began to sob, her mass of blond ringlets trembled against her back like strands of spun gold in the morning light.

Something was wrong. Cass could feel it. "What's the problem, Reverend?" he inquired hesitantly.

The men dismounted and stared at Cass for a moment. Then Leviticus exploded: *"What's the problem?"*

Cass could sure see where Patience had inherited her volatile nature. The little retired circuit judge was now hopping around in the road with his fists balled into tight knots. *"What's the problem?"* Leviticus repeated in utter disbelief, pausing just long enough to draw an indignant breath before shaking his finger under Cass's nose. "I'll tell you what the problem is, you . . . you young whippersnapper! You sullied my daughter, and you're going to be held accountable!" He stomped angrily, nearly dislodging his felt bowler.

Cass shifted his stance and eyed the judge sourly. "I've what?"

"Sullied my daughter!" Leviticus shrieked. "Disgraced, soiled, *tarnished!*"

Cass's eyes narrowed. "I know what the word means, sir."

"I should hope so!" Leviticus shouted.

"Now, now, gentlemen, let's all calm down," Reverend Olson advised. "I'm sure we can settle this matter without hollering to raise the dead."

"What is he talking about?" Cass demanded calmly.

Reverend Olson glanced cautiously at Patience, then back at Cass. "Well, it seems that you and . . . you and Miss McCord spent a night together last week. Am I correct?" Reverend Olson sincerely hoped that he wasn't. He didn't know Cass all that well, but what he was here to carry out, he wouldn't wish on any man.

"Spent the night with her?" Cass shot a reproachful eye toward the lady. "No, I didn't spend the night with her."

"Oh, yes, you did!" Patience accused. Then she sniffed again.

Cass shifted his weight, and the blue of his eyes pinpointed her angrily. "I did not." Cass knew as well as anyone what her accusation could lead to.

Patience sighed tolerantly and dabbed at her welling eyes. "I told you he would take this attitude, gentlemen."

"Now just one minute." Cass turned to Reverend Olson. "I don't know what she's told you, but nothing happened that night—"

"So, you *did* spend the night with my daughter!" Leviticus accused indignantly.

"I didn't spend the night *with* her," Cass responded.

"She was gone all night!" Leviticus bellowed. "How do you explain that?"

"I was there . . . but so was my brother Beau and his wife. If you won't take my word for it, you can ask them . . ." Cass's voice trailed off as he began to realize that the more he tried to explain, the more he seemed to incriminate himself.

Leviticus glanced at the sheriff pointedly. The entire town of Cherry Grove knew that Cass's brother had lived with the widow Burkhouser for months before he'd married her. Did this young whippersnapper think he and the sheriff were foolish enough to take Beau Claxton's word about such an impropriety?

"Daddy"—Patience turned her watery eyes toward Leviticus—"don't you think it would be a waste of time to ride all the way to the Claxton soddy? You know good and well Beau Claxton would lie to protect his no-good brother." Her voice trailed off to a whine. "Can't we just settle this matter quickly?"

Cass shot her a scathing glare. "Patience, this is *not* funny," he warned. The seriousness of the situation was beginning to sink in, and Cass was feeling downright scared. "Nothing happened the night you stayed with me, and you know it. I should have sent you packing, and I would have if you hadn't lied to me when you said you were feeling faint."

Cass turned to Leviticus imploringly. "Sir, your daughter approached me that night and offered me five hundred dollars to take her to St. Louis." Cass straightened proudly. "Of course I said no." He didn't mind telling on the silly twit. Now Leviticus would see how rotten through and through his daughter really was.

Leviticus leveled his gaze sternly on his daughter. "Did you do that, Patience? Did you offer this man five hundred dollars to take you back to St. Louis?"

Patience gasped, batting her huge damp eyelashes. "Heavens, no, Daddy! Where would I get five hundred dollars?"

Leviticus turned to Cass. "Where would she get five hundred dollars?" Leviticus knew his daughter's penchant for lying, so he felt obliged to ask.

"I don't know!" Cass snapped. "She offered me money; she didn't say where she was going to get it!"

"Mr. Claxton." Leviticus stretched to his full five-feet two inches. Though his comical pose wasn't all that intimidating, it struck the proper respect in Cass. "I'm inclined to believe you, but I know for a fact that Patience doesn't have five hundred dollars. Good Lord, man! I barely have five hundred dollars! That's a fortune!"

"I know, sir . . ." And he did know! The little schemer had been lying about the money too! "But that's what she offered me—five hundred . . ."

Cass felt a sinking sensation as he began to realize that he was in deep trouble this time.

"No, if my daugher says she didn't offer you the money, then I must assume she's telling the truth," Leviticus decided.

"But she's lying!"

Leviticus shot his daughter an exasperated look but continued, "Whether she offered the money or not, she says you took advantage of her that evening, and I can't risk the possibility of her coming up with a little blue-eyed bastard after you return to Missouri."

"Now, wait a minute—"

"No, you wait a minute," Leviticus said, his eyes narrowing. "You're about to take a wife, son."

"The hell I am!" This conversation had slipped beyond the point of reason. Cass whirled and was about to climb onto his wagon when he felt the cold barrel of a shotgun tapping him on the shoulder.

"You want to take a few minutes to reconsider your hasty decision, boy?"

Cass froze. The clear implication in the sheriff's voice made him pause.

"Son!"—Reverend Olson laid his hand on Cass's shoulder reassuringly—"I think you'd better think this thing through."

"But Reverend"—Cass looked at him helplessly—"I haven't touched Patience McCord."

Reverend Olson nodded sympathetically. "I'm sorry, but we have no way of proving your side of the story. In Cherry Grove, we tend to take the woman's word in matters of this delicate nature. I'd suggest you marry the girl, then try to resolve the matter in a more satisfactory manner later on."

Marry Patience McCord? Cass would prefer they throw a rope over the nearest tree and get it over with.

Leviticus helped his daughter dismount, and she rested her slender hand upon his arm. "You do believe me, don't you, Daddy? I wouldn't lie about a terrible thing like this. I warned Mr. Claxton he'd surely be facin' my papa's wrath. That's what I said . . . but I do declare, he just wouldn't listen . . ." She broke off tearfully and covered her eyes with her lace handkerchief.

Leviticus wrapped his arm protectively around her trembling shoulders. "I believe you, daughter," he soothed. Then he lifted his chin. "Sheriff," he prompted in a righteous tone.

The sheriff stepped forward, and Cass looked at Reverend Olson pleadingly. "Are you actually going to let them do this to me?"

Reverend Olson sighed and opened his Bible. "Do you, Cass Claxton, take Patience McCord to be your lawfully wedded wife?"

"Hell, no, I don't!"

Reverend Olson turned patiently to the bride.

"Do you, Patience McCord, take Cass Claxton to be your lawfully wedded husband?"

"I suppose I'll just have to, under these dreadful circumstances. Don't you agree, Daddy?" Her lovely amethyst eyes peered at Leviticus woefully.

He patted her hand. "You just relax, darlin'. Papa will see to it that your virtue is protected."

"Virtue—that's rich! She doesn't know the meaning of the word!" Cass accused.

"Oh, Daddy. He's just dreadful. Do I really have to marry him?" Patience peeked out from behind her handkerchief at Cass.

"You don't have to marry me," Cass insisted through gritted teeth. "All you have to do is tell the truth!" He'd never raised a hand against a woman in his life, but given half a chance, he'd gladly have strangled Patience McCord at that moment.

"Do you promise to love, cherish, and obey, till death do you part?" Reverend Olson droned on, hoping to complete the unpleasant ceremony as soon as possible.

"Wellll . . . I . . . I suppose I can . . . if I must . . ." Patience glanced at Cass. "I *do*."

Reverend Olson turned back to Cass. "Do you promise to comfort, honor, and keep her, in sickness and in health—"

"I wouldn't pull a mad dog off of her!"

"—forsaking all others, till death do you part?"

Cass glared at his bride heatedly.

The sheriff lifted the barrel of the gun a notch higher. "Say you're gonna forsake all others till death do you part, boy, or I'll blow a big hole through your chest."

"I will not!"

The sheriff pressed the shotgun between Cass's shoulderblades.

Cass darted a frantic look at Reverend Olson.

Reverend Olson sighed. "You must say you'll take her for your wife, son. The marriage won't be legal otherwise."

The gun nudged him again. "Wanna live to see thirty, boy?"

"I do, but—"

Reverend Olson snapped the Bible shut. "I now pronounce you man and wife." He lifted his brows hopefully. "I don't suppose you'd want to kiss the bride?"

"*No,* I don't want to kiss the bride!"

Reverend Olson sighed. "I didn't think so."

Five minutes later Leviticus was placing the last of Patience's baggage in the back of Cass's wagon.

He knew he should be worried about his daughter's fate, but strangely enough he wasn't. Reverend Olson had assured him that the Claxtons were good people, and he could see for himself that Cass was a big strapping fellow who would hold his own with Patience McCord.

Lord knew she needed such a man.

"Take care of my daughter." Leviticus reached up to meekly shake his new son-in-law's hand. Cass sullenly ignored the gesture.

Leviticus laid a small pouch filled with several gold pieces on the wagon seat beside Cass. "She's a good girl," Leviticus told him in a hushed whisper. "Just a mite bull-headed at times."

Cass thought that had to be the understatement of the year.

Reverend Olson, the sheriff, and Leviticus remounted. With a nod, they prepared to leave the newlyweds alone.

"You be sure and write your daddy the moment you reach St. Louis," Leviticus reminded.

"I promise, Daddy. You take care now."

The small party turned their horses and trotted off toward town.

Cass whistled sharply, and the wagon lurched forward as the horses began moving. "You are not going to get away with this," he warned.

"I believe I just did, dear husband."

"Don't call me that."

"Why? I'll grant you permission to call me your wife . . . but only until we reach St. Louis." She laughed merrily.

"I'll be calling you a lot of things before we reach St. Louis," he promised.

"Tsk, tsk, such a sore loser! You should have accepted my gracious offer the other night," Patience pointed out, adjusting her skirts primly. "You'd have been much better off—five hundred dollars richer and still single."

"You don't have five hundred dollars!"

"But you don't know that for certain," she pointed out.

"Your own pa said you didn't."

"My own pa doesn't necessarily know everything," she reasoned sweetly. "You'll discover, Mr. Claxton, it's much easier to let me have my way."

"And you'll find your lying little fanny dumped on your aunt's porch so fast it'll make your head spin," Cass snapped. "I'll take you to St. Louis, but once we're there this absurdity is over. I want this so-called marriage annulled. Immediately."

Ignoring him, Patience turned and waved her handkerchief at Leviticus. "Bye-bye, Daddy. I'll write real soon!"

Leviticus waved back fondly.

"And you'll find"—Patience turned back to resume the conversation—"all I wanted in the first place was to go back to St. Louis." She sighed happily. "I'll be glad to have our marriage annulled, darling, just as soon as I reach my Aunt

Merriweather's. However,'' she said, pausing to smile at him, ''it was truly a touching ceremony—wouldn't you agree?''

Rotten. Cass had no doubt about it. The girl was just plain rotten.

1

St. Louis, Missouri, 1874

A sharp crack of thunder resounded along the quiet residential street. A young woman hurried on her way, her hand placed strategically on top of her head to prevent the gusting wind from carrying off her plucky straw hat.

Patience McCord didn't mind the rain, but she did wish it could have held off for another thirty minutes. Fat drops began to pepper down on the cobblestone streets, filling the air with the tangy smell of summer rain.

Her shoes skipped gingerly over the gathering puddles as her eyes hurriedly scanned the numbers printed on the towering houses. The three-story frame dwellings nearly took her breath away with their lovely stained-glass windows and hand-carved doorways.

When lightning flashed as brightly as a noon-day sun, she peered at the address scrawled on a scrap of paper that was fast becoming soggy in her hand.

Her feet flew purposefully up the walk as the heavens opened to deliver a torrential downpour. Pausing to catch her breath, Patience stood for a moment under the shelter of the porch eaves, watching the rain pelt down. She smiled as she saw an old lamplighter, already soaked to the skin, hastily making his way down the street.

She called out to the man, inviting him to take cover with her. He turned and scurried up the walk, his head bent low against the driving rain.

"Terrible, isn't it?" Patience commented as the white-haired gentleman removed his top hat and shook the rain off.

" 'Tis for certain, little lass." As he smiled his wizened face broke into a wreath of wrinkles. He set his lantern down and extended a friendly hand. "Thaddeus McDougal here."

Patience returned his smile as they shook hands. "Patience McCord. It looks like we're in for a good one." Patience had never acknowledged her married name, nor did she ever plan to. Since their journey from Kansas to St. Louis, she'd never seen Cass Claxton again. They had parted on bad terms, with Patience declaring she would see him again when hell froze over.

Thaddeus sighed. "Aye, it does at that, lass."

"Well, we can always use the rain."

" 'Tis true, 'tis true." Thaddeus glanced about the massive porch with mild curiosity. "Wasn't aware the old house had finally been sold."

"Oh, I don't think it has." Patience noticed that the house was not in the best of repair. The porch sagged; the paint was peeling; and several shutters flapped haphazardly in the blowing rain. It didn't matter though—it looked beautiful to her. "I'm here to see about acquiring the use of it."

"Eh? Well . . ." Thaddeus's pale gaze roamed over the peeling rafters. "Old Josiah would be real upset if he could see his house now. Used to brim with love and laughter, it did." His eyes grew misty with remembrance. "Josiah never had children of his own, you know, but he took in every stray he could find. Fine man, he was. The world lost a bit of sunshine when Josiah Thorton was laid to rest."

"I never knew him," Patience admitted.

"He was a good man." Thaddeus sighed again. "Well now, little lass, why be you tryin' to acquire such a big old barn of a house?"

"I'm looking for a place big enough to be a home for nine children."

"Nine children!" Thaddeus took a step back. The chit didn't look old enough to have nine children!

Patience smiled at his obvious bewilderment. "I'm overseer of a small orphanage. The bank has been forced to sell the home we're presently living in, and someone mentioned that this house was empty. Since I've looked unsuccessfully for weeks for somewhere to move the children, I hurried over to obtain the name of the owner." Her forehead wrinkled in a frown. "I'm sorry to hear he's passed away."

"Josiah died about a year ago."

"Then I suppose his family will be disposing of the property?"

Thaddeus frowned. "Josiah didn't have any family, leastways, not that I know about. Rumor has it he had a business associate though. Could be he can tell you what's to be done with the house."

"And how might I contact this business associate?" Patience hoped that wouldn't prove to be another time-consuming delay. The orphanage had to be out of its present location by the end of the month.

"Well . . ." Thaddeus stepped over to the legal notice nailed to the porch railing and peered through his wire-rimmed spectacles. "It says here that anyone wanting information about this property should contact a Mr. Daniel Odolp, Attorney-at-law."

Patience took a small pad from her purse and prepared to scribble down the attorney's address.

"Does Mr. Odolp reside here in St. Louis?"

"Yes, his office is close by." Thaddeus read the address aloud for her.

"Oh, that's not far."

"Just a wee jaunt."

"I wonder if Mr. Odolp would still be in his office?"

Thaddeus reached into his waistcoat and withdrew a large pocket watch. He flipped open the case and held the face of the watch toward the receding light. "Depends on how late he works. It's nigh on six o'clock."

Six o'clock. Patience doubted Mr. Odolp would be working this late, but since she'd be passing by his office anyway, it wouldn't hurt to check. "Thank you, Thaddeus." Patience replaced the pen and pad in her purse and reassessed the inclement weather. It wasn't raining too hard, just a nice, steady drizzle. "I'll just go by and see if Mr. Odolp is still in his office," she announced.

"But it's still raining."

Patience shrugged and gave Thaddeus a bright smile. "I won't dissolve."

She looked as if she might, to him. She was an unusually pretty piece of fluff with flaxen hair and the softest violet-colored eyes Thaddeus had ever seen. If she had wings, she'd look like an angel, he thought wistfully.

"It's been nice talking with you, Thaddeus." Patience reached down and quickly removed her shoes and stockings, then her hat. It was senseless to ruin them. Her toes peeked out from under the hem of her skirt, and Thaddeus had to grin. A barefoot angel.

"Nice talkin' to you, lass." Thaddeus reached down and picked up his lantern. "Guess I should get about my work. It'll be growing dark soon."

The old lamplighter and the young woman moved off the porch to go their separate ways.

One set out to light man's path, the other to find a home for nine children.

St. Louis, Missouri, was the gateway to the West for adventurers, explorers, traders, missionaries, soldiers, and settlers of the trans-Mississippi. It was founded in 1764 by Pierre Laclede Liguest, a French trader, as a settlement for the development of the fur trade. One hundred and ten years later the area had developed into a thriving waterfront town where cotton, lead, pelts, gold from California, and silver from New Mexico poured through shipping lanes along the busy Mississippi levee. It was said that St. Louis was admired for her hospitality, good manners, high society, virtue, and the sagacity of her women.

One such woman hurried through the night, intent upon her mission. Patience could hardly believe her good fortune as she rounded the corner leading toward the landing and saw the faint lantern glow spilling from a window on the second story.

Prominently displayed in bold black letters across the window was DANIEL R. ODOLP, ATTORNEY-AT-LAW.

Quickly, Patience covered the short distance to the building and began climbing the steep stairs leading to the second floor. A few minutes later she tapped softly on Mr. Odolp's door.

"Yes?" boomed a deep voice that brought nervous flutters to Patience's stomach. The man sounded like a giant.

"Mr. Odolp?"

"Yes!"

"I . . . I wonder if I might speak with you?"

Patience heard a shuffling, then the sound of chair legs being scraped across a wooden floor. Heavy footsteps approached the doorway.

She swallowed and her throat went dry. The narrow hallway was dark and foreboding, with only a small tallow candle splitting the shadows.

She suddenly wished she'd decided to wait until morning to make her visit. Just as she was turning to leave, the door abruptly flung open.

"Yes?"

The man standing in the doorway was indeed a giant, at least six feet five. Bushy dark eyebrows nested over his beady black eyes. His face was pockmarked, and his jowls hung heavily on his neck. Sweat beaded profusely on his ruddy forehead. Patience thought he was the most unattractive and intimidating-looking man she'd ever encountered.

"Mr. Odolp?" she asked meekly.

"I am Mr. Odolp!" he barked. "Good Lord, woman, are you deaf?"

Patience drew herself up stiffly, perturbed by his appalling lack of gentility. "No, sir, but I shall be if you continue to speak to me in that tone."

"You called my name," he boomed, "and I answered. You implied you wanted to speak to me, and when I opened the door, you asked *again* if I was Mr. Odolp. Naturally, one would assume you have a hearing problem."

Patience jumped as he bellowed again, "*Yes*, I am Mr. Odolp!"

"Well, you needn't keep shouting." She lifted her skirts and brushed past him irritably.

He closed the door and stalked back to his desk, his eyes grimly surveying her bare feet. "Where are your shoes and stockings, young lady?"

Patience glanced down and blushed. Her shoes were still in her hand, along with her hat and stockings. She must look as strange to him as he did to her. "I'm sorry . . . it was raining."

"What brings you to my door at this hour?" he demanded, curtly dismissing her stammering explanations. He sat down and reached for a wooden box filled with cigars. He selected one, bit off the end, and spat the fragment into the wastebasket as his chair creaked and moaned with the burden of his weight.

Patience flinched at his lack of manners, but her demeanor remained calm. "I understand that you're handling Josiah Thorton's estate?"

"I am." The lawyer held a burning match to the cigar and puffed, blowing billowing wisps of smoke into the air.

The humidity in the room was stifling, and Patience fanned the smoke away from her face. "I was wondering if Josiah's house is going to be sold?"

"Which one?"

"Does he have more than one?"

Daniel turned his face upward and hooted uproariously.

" 'Does he have more than one?' You're not serious!"

"I'm afraid I didn't know Mr. Thorton personally."

"I'm afraid you didn't either." Daniel fanned out the match, propped his feet on top of his desk, and took a long draw on his cigar. "Exactly which house did you have in mind, honey?"

Patience felt her hackles rise with his growing insolence. "The one on Elm Street. And my name is Miss McCord, sir."

"Well, what do you want to know, Miss McCord?"

"Some details about the house. For instance, who will be disposing of the property?"

"The house was jointly owned."

"By whom?"

"Josiah and his business partner." Daniel brought his feet back to the floor and stood up. He lumbered to the files and rummaged for a few minutes before extracting a thick folder. "Since Josiah had no immediate family, we're waiting to see if anyone comes forth to put a claim on his estate." Daniel grinned as though he knew his next remark would certainly shock her. "Josiah's partner wants to be sure there aren't any little Thorton bastards waiting in the wings."

Patience wasn't shocked by his speculation, merely annoyed at his continuing audacity. "And if there aren't?"

"Then the Thorton estate goes to Josiah's partner." Daniel sighed, and Patience detected a note of envy. "A sizable fortune, I might add. The partner will then decide what he wants to do with the property."

"Exactly how long will it be before a decision is made?"

"Six months or longer."

Patience walked to the window and looked down on the rain-slicked streets. She pursed her lips thoughtfully. The house was exactly what she was looking for. Undoubtedly there were others available in town, but none so well-suited for her purpose.

She'd hoped to stay in the house longer, but six months would be sufficient. If she could persuade Josiah's partner to lease the house to her for six months, it would alleviate her immediate problem. At least she and the children would have a roof over their heads until she could make other arrangements.

"Would it be possible for me to speak with Mr. Thorton's business associate?" Patience requested.

"I see no need to bother him. What is it you want?"

Patience turned from the window, and her violet eyes met his beady ones. "I would prefer to speak to the partner in private, Mr. Odolp."

"And he would prefer you speak to me."

"Then let me phrase it differently." Patience's eyes grew noticeably cooler. "I *insist* on speaking to Josiah Thorton's business partner."

"You can't."

Patience arched one brow. "Does the name Silas Woodson ring a bell with you, Mr. Odolp?"

"The governor?"

"Yes, the governor of Missouri." Patience tapped her finger on her cheek thoughtfully. "You see, Uncle Silas would be quite distressed to learn of this conversation—"

Daniel Odolp's eyes began to widen. "Now, now, let's not jump to conclusions. I'll help you if I can." If the governor was the chit's uncle, then he'd better be a bit more cordial. "It's just that I don't like to have my clients bothered . . . but in this particular case I'm sure I can bend my rules a bit."

He reached hastily for a pen and paper. "Now, I'll just jot down the name and address of Josiah's partner. There's no need to tell him where you got this information, of course—"

"None at all."

Daniel slapped the piece of paper into her hand. "How is your uncle these days?"

"Oh, very busy."

"I can imagine."

Patience nodded. "He and my dear mama are brother and sister, you know."

"No, I didn't know."

"Well, I must be off, Mr. Odolp." She folded the paper carefully and slipped it into her bag. "Thank you for your cooperation."

Daniel rose and extended his hand pleasantly.

"So happy to oblige you, Miss McCord. Must you be going so soon?"

Patience smiled. "I do wish I had time to stay and chat."

"Just stop by any time."

"I will."

Patience clutched her shoes, stockings, and hat as she walked to the door. She'd pulled it off! Aunt Merriweather would have disapproved of her tactics, but under the circumstances even she would tolerate this one tiny deception.

"Good evening, Mr. Odolp."

"Good evenin', ma'am. You say hello to the governor for me."

"I will. He'll be ever so pleased to hear from you."

Once safely outside, Patience hurried down the steep stairway and out onto the street, still grinning from her victory.

Pausing to catch her breath under the streetlight, she reached into her purse and carefully unfolded the paper the attorney had given her.

Her eyes widened, and she felt a hot flush creep up her neck as she read the name printed in bold black letters.

CASS CLAXTON.

Cass Claxton! She had to force back a rush of hysteria.

Great day in the morning! Her *husband* was Josiah Thorton's business partner.

2

The late afternoon sunlight clung in dappled ridges to the foot of the cherry four-poster bed. Golden rays bathed the man and woman who lay entwined in each other's arms in a warm, intimate glow. The storm of fiery passion was slow to subside as the couple stole a few more precious moments together.

"It is getting late," the woman drawled. The sound of her soft voice, heavy with a French accent and her still unsated passion, caused the man's arm to tighten around her possessively.

"So it is." His mouth took hers again, and she spoke his name softly as her fingers curled into his thick mass of coarse dark hair. Her small firm breasts, damp with perspiration, pressed tightly against the wiry mat of hair on his chest as they were caught up in a renewed fire storm of ecstasy.

The shadows had lengthened and turned to a rosy hue when Laure Revuneau finally summoned the strength to leave his arms. She slid quietly from bed, wrapped the sheet snugly around her slender frame, and walked to the small washbasin.

"*Mon chéri,* you will make me late for the party," she reproached.

Cass Claxton smiled up at her lazily, dimming her hopes of serious reprimand. "Laure, my love, I can think of a hundred things I'd rather do with you than attend another one of your Saturday soirees."

Stung by his honesty but accustomed to it by now, she began to gather her clothing, which had been earlier discarded in haste. "*Chéri,* I do not understand you at times. They are not merely *soirées*. As the daughter of the French consul, I have many responsibilities, not the least being to uphold Papa's image."

Cass reached out and caught the hem of the sheet as she brushed past the bed petulantly. Drawing her back into his arms, he kissed her until she became warm and willing again.

"*Mon pauvre chéri,*" she whispered when their lips finally parted. She sympathetically traced the tip of her finger around the outline of his sensual lips. "Do you truly hate my parties so?"

"Absolutely. So why do you insist I attend?"

"Because, it . . . it is something a man of your importance should do."

Cass threw back his head and laughed heartily at her simplistic reasoning.

"Do not laugh at me, *mon chéri*. Someday we will be called upon to host many parties in our own home," she said, pouting.

Cass tensed at her thinly veiled reference to marriage—her hints were coming up with unnerving regularity. "I'm sure having your social responsibilities must be burdensome, but may I say you handle it with an elegance and charm that other women can only envy," he soothed.

"Oh, *merci, chéri*. I have wondered if you'd noticed." Laure smiled seductively into his blue, fathomless eyes that were growing heavy with desire once more. Cass began to ease her back onto the bed when she thwarted his move effortlessly.

"*Non, non, non*. It is after six, *mon amour*. I must be going now. Papa will be worried."

She moved gracefully across the room to the small dressing area as Cass sighed and reached toward the bedside table for a cheroot. A match flared, and a moment later he lay back on the pillow to watch her dress.

"Would it honestly upset you if I failed to attend the party tonight?"

She was distressed but not surprised by his inquiry. Since she'd known him, he'd never enjoyed social functions. She lifted a delicately shaped leg to carefully pull a silk stocking over it. "You have other business?"

Laure knew better than to press the matter. She'd discovered months ago that he was not a man she could easily manipulate.

The sun's sinking rays formed a halo around her hair, making it appear as rich as black velvet. Watching her slip into her lingerie pleased Cass. He smiled as she diverted her attention to the satin corset. A tiny frown appeared on her flushed features as she studied it.

"Are you really going to put that thing back on?"

She turned and smiled. "It would be most improper of me if I did not."

"Since when have you ever been proper?" Cass said in a suggestive tone.

"Oh, yes, you are right!" She tossed the corset at him teasingly. "You may keep it to warm you on a cold winter's night!"

Cass chuckled as he caught the garment in one hand, then mockingly saluted her. Although there had been many women in his life, none could match Laure Revuneau's beauty, charm, and playfulness.

"I don't have other business," he said, returning to the subject. "I'm just not in the mood to socialize."

She tilted her head coquettishly. "But what are you in the mood for, *mon chéri?*"

Cass drew deeply on the cheroot as his eyes met hers hungrily.

She laughed softly, continually delighted—yet amazed—by his voracious appetite. Her eyes roamed over his broad shoulders, his wide chest with its dark springy hair, his lean waist, and she sighed wistfully. "You are a temptation, but I fear I would be delayed another hour if I were to stay."

"That's a strong probability." Cass sat up and stubbed out the cigar. "But the choice is entirely yours."

Laure finished dressing and walked over to the large looking glass. She peered at herself critically for a moment, then began to pull the pins from her tangled hair. "I wish you would change your mind about tonight. Many of your business associates will be there."

"I thought it was to be a charity function," Cass remarked absently as he lay back on the pillows and closed his eyes.

"*Vraiment*, truly, but the guest list is quite impressive," she encouraged. "I've invited everyone having the tiniest bit of social prominence—"

"And money," he speculated.

She laughed softly again. "*Oui,* most assuredly those who have *nichesse.*" Not only was she in love with the handsome, charismatic Cass Claxton—considered to be the most eligible yet the most unobtainable bachelor in town—but it didn't hurt that he was a highly successful entrepreneur with valuable connections to the wealthiest people.

Cass had contacts that Laure drew upon regularly. Because of his various holdings in shipping, cotton, lead, and even silver from Mexico, Cass could be a real asset for a man in her father's position.

Laure's candid admission of where her values lay annoyed Cass. The last thing he wanted this evening was to mingle in a smoke-filled room with the idle rich. "Why don't I make a donation to whatever it is you're supporting and let it go at that?"

Laure turned, and Cass noticed that her lower lip was close to pouting again. "Please, *mon chéri* . . . say you'll come . . . for me?"

Cass hated it when she—or any woman, for that matter—tried to pressure him. "Laure, I don't want to argue about this," he warned.

"But papa will wonder where you are . . . and so will my friends." She crossed the room and knelt beside the bed, grasping his hand. "Please!

It will be the last party I will ask you to attend this week." She stared up at him pleadingly.

"This week?" Cass shook his head with amusement. It was Friday.

"Say you will come, *chéri,*" Laure caressed the palm of his hand imploringly.

"Laure . . ."

"S'il te plaît?"

Cass sighed, realizing she was going to be stubborn about it. "All right, but I won't promise to stay the evening."

"Merci beaucoup, mon chéri!" Laure wrapped her arms around his neck and kissed him breathlessly. "You will not regret it, *chéri* . . . I promise."

Cass wasn't optimistic, but it was difficult to refuse her when she looked at him with her wide turquoise eyes.

"I will instruct Mozes to prepare your bath." Laure rose and leaned over to kiss him fiercely. "Try to arrive before dinner. It will please Papa."

Blowing one final kiss, she hurried from the room, leaving a faint trace of her expensive French perfume in the air.

As the door closed behind her, Cass lit another cheroot and lay back against the pillow. He didn't plan to hurry.

He toyed with the idea of going back on his promise to attend the party, but after mulling over the ramifications such a reversal would bring, he concluded it wouldn't be worth all the tears and accusations.

He viewed the white satin corset lying next to his pillow, and a smile played at his lips. Her scent still lingered on the sheets, causing an ache deep within his loins at the memory of her satiny body next to his. He'd rather have Laure in a giving mood than a sullen one, so he would attend the party, but only briefly.

Afterward he would stop by the club for a game of cards and a bottle of his favorite brandy.

Having convinced himself that his concession was the only way to keep peace, he finally slid out of bed and went in search of the waiting bath.

It was growing dark as the carriage carrying Patience drew to a halt in front of an impressive rose-red brick home. The railing of its charming cupola matched the one along the length of its wide veranda. A beautiful rose garden on one side caught her eye. She had debated whether to postpone her business until morning, but had decided that since she was in the vicinity, she would approach Cass on her way to the charity function she was about to attend.

She sat for a moment staring at the lovely old two-story home, wondering when her estranged husband had become so prosperous.

She realized she knew nothing about Cass

Claxton other than the bits of information she'd been able to extract when he'd escorted her to St. Louis six years ago.

Six years. It hardly seemed possible that the days and months had passed so swiftly. Patience felt a familiar prick of guilt as she thought about the way she'd tricked the man into marrying her. Now she was deeply ashamed of what she'd done when she remembered the selfish lengths she'd gone to get her way, but at the time she'd been desperate. She had been sure she couldn't have stood another moment in Cherry Grove, Kansas, and since Papa wouldn't hear of letting her return to St. Louis alone, she'd thought her only alternative was to use Mr. Claxton as a pawn.

She winced as she recalled the pall of black silence that had hung between them as he escorted her back to St. Louis. He had been justifiably furious and had spoken only when absolutely necessary, to bark a warning or issue her a brusque ultimatum. Then, on her Aunt Merriweather's front lawn, he had dumped her—and that was the most charitable way Patience could describe it—and tossed to her the small pouch of money Leviticus McCord had given him following their shotgun ceremony.

He had issued one final, tight-lipped decree: Have this outrage annulled!

A nagging twinge reminded Patience that she had never gotten around to it.

Not that she had taken her vows seriously, far from it, but she had just never filed for the annulment. She'd assumed there was no hurry. Cass had returned to his home in River Run, and she'd felt certain that she'd never see him again. A real marriage, a binding one, to Patience's way of thinking, began with a snow-white wedding gown, a church, flowers, and a host of well-wishers, not with an embarrassed minister, a sheriff carrying a loaded shotgun, and a bewildered groom—little more than a stranger—pleading for mercy in the middle of a dusty road. But she supposed she *should* have kept her promise before now. . . .

Stepping down from the carriage, Patience instructed the driver to wait, then turned and proceeded up the flagstone walk.

A lovely dark-haired beauty about her age was just coming out the front door. As Patience approached, the woman greeted her softly, "*Bon soir, madame.*"

Patience returned her smile. "Good evening. Is Mr. Claxton in?"

"*Oui.*" Curiously, Laure paused to study this stranger who was wearing an exact copy of a dress Laure had admired only that morning in the latest edition of *La Modiste Parisienne*. The pale rose dinner dress, with its off-the-shoulder neckline, cuirass bodice, lace trim, and long train of fine, pleated silk was breathtakingly beautiful. Rosebuds were entwined in the woman's shiny mass of blond hair, swept high at the crown to cascade down her back in golden ringlets. The stranger was simply exquisite.

"Thank you . . . *merci.*"

Patience continued up the walk as the young woman replied distractedly, *"Pas de quoi . . ."*

Moments later Patience stood before the brass door knocker fashioned in the shape of a lion's head, trying to bolster her courage. She knew that what she was about to do would not be pleasant. Cass would not be happy to see her again, and she couldn't blame him.

But the needs of nine homeless children were far more important to her than a bruised ego.

She turned slightly to watch the pretty young Frenchwoman enter the hansom cab waiting at the side entrance.

Who was she, Patience mused. A maid? She seriously doubted it. One of Cass's lady friends? Patience smiled. Apparently her dear "husband" was managing to amuse himself in his wife's absence.

She smothered a laugh, recalling her unusual marriage to Cass Claxton.

The philistine brute!

She drew a resigned breath and reached for the brass knocker. Cass Claxton be damned! Whether he was pleased to see her or not, they had business to discuss.

"Excuse me, sir, there's a young lady in the drawing room who wishes to see you." Mozes's giant frame dominated the doorway to Cass's bedroom.

The black man's height of six feet seven inches was a foreboding sight for all who were not acquainted with his genteel ways and impeccable manners. His hands were as big as ham hocks and his features were pinched and far from attractive, but anyone who knew Mozes could attest to his kindness and gentle heart.

For the past three years the tall black manservant had run Cass's household with a tenacious spirit and a firm hand. Cass commonly referred to Mozes as his right arm, and Mozes had more than earned Cass's trust and respect.

"What young lady?" Cass kept his attention centered on the stubborn cravat he was trying to tie.

"She says her name is McCord, sir."

"McCord?" Cass sighed and irritably jerked the cravat loose. The name failed to register with him. "Can you do something with this damned thing?"

Mozes stepped forward, and within a moment the task was effortlessly completed.

"I don't know how you do that," Cass reflected absently. "Would you hand me my jacket?"

"About the young lady, sir?" Mozes retrieved the double-breasted topcoat and held it as Cass slipped it on.

Reaching for a hairbrush, Cass tried again to control the springy mass of dark hair still damp from his bath. "Tell the lady I'm indisposed. She'll have to make an appointment to see me on Monday."

"Are you feeling ill, sir?"

"I feel fine, Mozes."

"The lady was quite insistent about speaking to you this evening," Mozes felt obliged to convey.

Cass laid the brush down on the dressing table. "That's too bad. It's growing late, and my business for the day has been concluded. If the lady wants to see me, she'll have to come back Monday."

"I'll tell her."

"Oh, and have the carriage brought around, Mozes." Cass reached for the black top hat lying at the foot of the bed. "I'm ready to leave."

"Yes, sir." Mozes bowed politely. "Will you and your lady want a bite to eat when you return, sir?"

"No. Miss Revuneau won't be returning with me. I think I'll stop by the club later." Cass glanced up and flashed Mozes a perceptive wink.

"You and Sarah Rose can find something to keep you busy all evening, can't you?"

Mozes's grin spread guiltily across his face. "Yes, sir, I'm sure we can."

Closing the bedroom door, Mozes returned to Patience, who was waiting in the downstairs hallway.

"I'm sorry, madam. Mr. Claxton is not receiving guests at this time."

"Oh?" Patience lifted her brow with surprise. "Did you tell Mr. Claxton that *Patience McCord* wishes to speak to him?"

"Yes, madam, I informed Mr. Claxton of your wishes."

"And he refused to see me?"

"Mr. Claxton requests that you make an appointment to see him Monday morning."

"Oh, he does, does he!" Patience shot a reproachful glance up the stairway. Did she dare try to sidestep this giant and force her way into Cass's bedroom?

She measured the manservant with a critical eye. He was twice, three times, her size. No, there was no way she'd be able to make it up the stairs without his stopping her.

"Then I suppose I have no other choice but to bow to Mr. Claxton's request." She nodded coolly. "Good evening."

Mozes opened the door for her. "Good evening, Miss McCord."

About the time Patience was leaving by way of the front entrance, Cass was leaving from the side entrance of the house.

He paused momentarily to light a cheroot and enjoy the early evening air. The temperature was beginning to cool as a dark bank of clouds gathered in the west, hinting of rain before sunrise.

His attention was suddenly drawn to a young woman just entering a carriage at the front entrance.

A flash of rose silk, and the door to the carriage closed. Moments later the carriage disappeared in the growing dusk.

McCord. Cass frowned as the name Mozes had mentioned earlier popped unexpectedly into his mind.

McCord? Patience McCord?

Oh, damn! He shook away the alarming thought hurriedly. It couldn't be her again.

3

The French consul's elegant mansion was ablaze with light as Patience emerged from her carriage a short time later. She was in a decidedly foul mood.

Her husband's lack of cordiality hadn't surprised her, nor had his insolence. See him Monday, indeed! She didn't have the time or tolerance to play silly games with him.

Gathering her skirt in her hand, she started up a walk lined with towering hickory and walnut trees. The air was heavily perfumed with the scent of roses, and the occasional streaks of lightning in the west gave hope for relief from the insufferable heat the city had been enduring lately.

Patience dolefully recalled how Slader Morgan had asked to escort her to the party this evening. When she'd explained to him that she wanted to make a brief stop before the party, Slader had consented to meet her later. As it turned out, her stop had been so brief that he could have accompanied her easily, she thought irritably.

She nodded to a young couple who strolled past her arm in arm as she hurried up the walk.

Patience found herself wishing again that tonight's festivities were being held to benefit Maison des Petites Fleurs, or House of Little Flowers. But the small group of homeless waifs had been Aunt Estelle Merriweather's personal crusade, so the hodgepodge flock rarely received attention from outsiders. The nine children were viewed as less than ideal youngsters—street urchins who had stolen for survival, had eaten their meals from garbage cans, and had fought tooth and nail for the right to exist in a sometimes cold and callous world.

The memory of dear, colorful Aunt Estelle Merriweather brought the first smile of the evening to Patience's lips.

Estelle had had a heart as bottomless as her renowned brandy bottle. Patience fondly recalled how her aunt, without a word of recrimination, had welcomed the frightfully overindulged daughter of her baby brother into her home six years ago.

Over the years Aunt Merriweather had managed to channel Patience's zest and eagerness for life in more sweet-natured directions. She taught her niece the rewards of asking politely instead of demanding rudely. She had shown Patience the wisdom and power of a twinkling eye and a gracious smile. Gradually the young woman had given up the habit of stamping her foot and petulantly tossing her head of golden curls. No longer headstrong, she had become a lady. Estelle had watched proudly as a lovely, levelheaded woman had risen from the shell of the original Patience McCord, like a beautiful butterfly emerging from its unattractive cocoon.

Estelle had shown the same zeal and enthusiasm with the nine orphans. She saw them not as thieves and misfits but as needy children crying out for love. Society's lack of compassion toward those children had haunted her.

So one cold, snowy morning she had gone out into the streets, gathering the town's homeless lot to her ample bosom, telling them something miraculous, something they had never, ever heard before in their young lives: They were loved.

The dark eyes that had stared back at her with open skepticism had seemed forbidding; however, one by one, their small, dirty hands had clutched the material of her skirt, and like the Pied Piper, she'd led them down the street, past the shops and doorways of the town's most respectable and prominent citizens and into the first real home they had ever known.

She had secured an elderly couple to attend to the children while she personally handled the children's religious training and the financial burden. It had been a rigorous undertaking, born of love, but she declared it had been worth her every sacrifice to ensure the boys and girls a decent childhood.

When Estelle had passed away a year ago, the awesome responsibility of keeping the small group intact had fallen to Patience. At times, keeping the wolves from their door had seemed nearly impossible. Estelle had not been a rich woman, and she had left too little money to keep the orphanage operating.

Leviticus McCord had sent what money he could spare, but it was not enough. Estelle's house was heavily mortgaged in order to pay the orphanage bills. Finally the bank had been forced to sell it in order to settle her estate.

Patience had been able to keep food on the table by first depleting the small inheritance her mother had left her, then by working as a seamstress. But now that they'd lost the very roof over their heads, she wasn't sure how much longer she could manage to hold on.

Harlon and Corliss McQuire, the elderly couple who had always helped look after the children, refused wages, saying that they were so old they needed very little. Patience knew the two of them had grown to love the children as their own, but she felt guilty about their working for nothing.

Just one fund-raiser like tonight's, and the children would be secure for a whole year, Patience thought wistfully as she stepped onto the large veranda. However, she would settle for the lease to Cass Claxton's rose-bricked house.

Slader Morgan was waiting in the shadows of the portico. As Patience approached he stepped forward and bowed graciously to kiss her hand. "How lovely you look this evening, my dear."

Patience's face broke into a radiant smile. The charming, debonair riverboat gambler managed to capture the attention, as well as the hearts, of most women. He had an easygoing manner and a silver tongue that rendered most women hopelessly smitten. His effect on Patience was no less stimulating. She had met Slader four months ago when he'd come to the shop to have a dress made for his mother. Since then, they had seen each other often.

She curtsied demurely. "Sir, you're ever so kind."

Slader gazed back at her fondly. "Kindness has nothing to do with it. You are, without exception, the most beautiful woman here tonight."

"May I take that to mean you have already examined the other ladies in attendance?" she bantered, knowing with full well that he had.

"Only in passing." He grinned.

"Of course, only in passing." Patience was content with their informal relationship. She wasn't involved with Slader—or with any man for that matter. She wasn't sure she was happy with her present state, but between working and looking after the orphanage, there was little time to dwell on it.

Patience looped her arm through Slader's and smiled up at him as he guided her through open French doors into a large ballroom where elegantly dressed men and women were whirling around the floor to the strains of violins and harps.

The ballroom was splendidly opulent. The French-cut glass chandeliers flickered brightly overhead, their gaslight fixtures illuminating the rich red tapestries draped artfully at the great long windows. There were massive bouquets of summer flowers atop carved stone pedestals and priceless paintings on every wall. The marble floor was magnificent, having been polished until it reflected the pastel images of the ladies' gowns like a shimmering rainbow.

Patience found herself thinking that she could care for her nine homeless children for the rest of their lives with just a small portion of the money represented in this room.

"It's marvelous," she whispered under her breath.

"They're all stuffed shirts," Slader confided. "But I thought you might enjoy the change."

Didier Revuneau spotted Slader and Patience as they entered the ballroom. Taking his daughter's arm, he gently moved her through the crowd to greet the late arrivals.

"*Bienvenu,* my good friend, *bienvenu!*" The French consul reached out to grasp Slader's hand warmly.

"Good evening, Consul."

"You have met my lovely daughter, Laure?"

"We've met." Slader's eye ran over the dark-haired temptress with lazy proficiency. He bowed. "Good evening, Miss Revuneau."

Laure acknowledged the greeting graciously, her wide turquoise eyes openly admiring the handsome gambler. "*Monsieur* Morgan."

"Ah, such a lovely young flower you bring with you tonight." Didier's eyes were warm as he bowed and lifted Patience's hand to his mouth, lightly kissing the tips of her fingers.

Patience curtsied. "It is an honor to meet you, sir."

"Ah, but the honor is all mine, *ma chère*."

"Who is this lovely young flower, *Monsieur* Morgan?" Laure asked as she demurely slipped her arm through Slader's with such a familiar ease that it made Patience wonder exactly how well they knew each other.

It was rare for a man of Slader's reputation to

be invited to such a prestigious gathering, but then Patience knew that he was widely accepted in the community, despite his questionable occupation.

Laure's smile was cordial, effectively covering the surprise she felt at seeing the same blond beauty she'd encountered earlier at Cass's.

Slader glanced down at Patience affectionately. "Miss Revuneau and Consul, may I present Miss Patience McCord."

Laure inclined her head demurely. "I believe Mademoiselle McCord and I share a mutual acquaintance."

"Yes, I believe we do." Patience had the distinct impression that the consul's daughter might be better acquainted with Cass than she.

"*Monsieur* Claxton," said Laure.

"Monsieur Claxton," Patience confirmed. So here was the reason—and a decidedly lovely one—her husband had been indisposed earlier.

"Did you see Cass?" Laure asked.

"No," Patience admitted, waiting to observe Laure's reaction.

"Oh," Laure's full lower lip formed into a pretty pout. "I am sorry."

"So was I."

"You are good friends with *Monsieur* Claxton?"

"I was there on a business matter."

Laure's expression was noticeably more

guarded, but the tone of her voice remained pleasant. "Perhaps you will be granted another chance. Cass promised to come to the party. He should arrive very soon."

Patience felt her pulse take an expectant leap. "Oh?"

"Yes . . ." Laure's attention was momentarily diverted by the brocade gown Patience was wearing. "I was admiring your lovely dress earlier. Is it not the one shown in the recent issue of *La Modiste Parisienne?*"

"Oh, my, no. I could never afford to purchase such a gown. I'm afraid I only copied it," Patience admitted.

"You *made* this dress?" Laure's brows lifted.

"Yes. I'm delighted you like it."

"It is exquisite," Laure complimented, then returned her attention to Slader. "You must promise me a dance later."

Slader inclined his head politely. "Of course. I would be honored."

"Enjoy the evening," Didier said. Patience detected a merry twinkle in his dark eyes. "And your lovely lady."

"Thank you." Slader glanced at Patience again. "I'm sure I'll enjoy both."

Moments later the consul and his daughter merged into the crowd, leaving Patience and Slader free to mingle.

"She is lovely, isn't she?" Patience's gaze

still lingered on the consul's daughter as Slader swept her onto the dance floor.

"Laure?" Slader chuckled. "Indeed, she is quite a woman." The tempo of the music shifted to a slow waltz, and Slader drew Patience more closely into his arms as they whirled beneath a canopy of shimmering lights.

"Slader . . ." Patience was annoyed to discover that she was actually curious about Cass's relationship with the French beauty, though she hadn't the vaguest idea why. She had never considered Cass appealing.

"Yes?"

"I was wondering about Miss Revuneau's friendship with Cass Claxton."

Slader's eyes met hers with a look of amusement. "Friendship?"

"I was on my way to speak to Mr. Claxton earlier, and as I was coming up his walk I saw Miss Revuneau leaving."

Ordinarily, Patience would have felt ill at ease prying like this, but she knew Slader wouldn't think her boorish—they always felt free to discuss their thoughts.

Slader lifted his left brow inquisitively. "Why would you be going to see Cass Claxton?"

"I told you, I had business I needed to discuss with him."

"And Laure was leaving?"

"Yes."

Slader's smile, overflowing with male perception, confirmed the obvious. "I would guess they'd spent the afternoon together." Slader felt a rush of envy as he recalled the many afternoons he had spent in bed with the hot-blooded young Laure.

"Oh . . . are they seeing each other?" Patience deliberately kept her inquiry casual. It was really none of her business . . .

"Yes, I believe you could say that." Slader smiled at her innocence.

It was Patience's brow that lifted this time. "Seriously?"

"If Laure has her way. Cass has been a difficult man to get to the altar, but Laure is a determined young lady." Slader leaned closer and whispered conspiratorially, "I've heard she's hoping for a Christmas wedding."

Patience glanced at the dark-haired belle whirling around the floor with one of her many admirers. "Oh, really? How interesting." How *very* interesting, she added silently.

Around ten, Slader suggested he go in search of something cool for them to drink. Patience agreed and drifted toward the veranda for a breath of fresh air while she waited.

She strolled along the railing, listening to the peaceful voices of nature blending in muted harmony. A full moon shone overhead, and she was disappointed to see that the earlier promise of rain had vanished.

She allowed her thoughts to drift. She was feeling relaxed and more optimistic about the children. Somehow things always had a way of working out, she assured herself. If worse came to worst, she could always take the children to her father in Cherry Grove. Leviticus had mentioned in his last letter that he would be willing to provide a home for the orphans, but Patience feared Harlon and Corliss were too old to make such a long trip, and she didn't have the heart to leave them behind. The children had become like family to her, and so had the elderly couple. It would be best for all if she were able to keep her flock in St. Louis where Harlon and Corliss could remain a part of their lives.

Directly ahead, Patience saw a man step onto the veranda and pause to light a cheroot. Her footsteps slowed as the light spilled out from the ballroom, and she recognized Cass Claxton's familiar figure.

For a moment she could do nothing but stare, taking in the head of curly dark hair and incredibly broad shoulders. The years had added an attractive, virile maturity to him. In fact, he now possessed devilishly good looks. He had been heavier when she'd last seen him, almost stocky from what she remembered, and now he looked leaner, older, wiser . . . more forbidding, for some reason. He was fashionably dressed, looking every bit the successful young entrepreneur he was reported to be.

Patience stood quietly in the shadows, not ten feet from him, afraid to breathe. What would he say when he saw her? She was afraid she knew. He would be none too happy.

He cupped his hand to the flame of the match and drew on the cheroot. The tip glowed a bright red in the darkness as he tossed the match away.

And their eyes met.

For a moment it seemed as if even the cicadas and tree frogs were holding their breath with strained anticipation as the couple stood staring at each other.

His eyes, even more of a vibrant cobalt blue than she remembered, narrowed as they coolly ran over her slim body.

Patience remained immobilized, holding her breath as she prepared herself for what was to come. Would he explode with pent-up anger? Or would he turn and walk away without a word? She hoped he wouldn't walk away. She didn't want to cause a scene, but she would if necessary.

Keeping his gaze centered on her, Cass calmly removed the cheroot from his mouth. In a voice as casual as if they had last seen each other only yesterday, he murmured, "As I live and breathe, if it isn't Miss McCord. I gather hell must have just frozen over?''

Patience swallowed hard and tried to summon her most charming smile as she responded, ''Only temporarily, Mr. Claxton.''

4

Ooh, the insufferable brute hadn't changed one bit! Patience seethed, but wisely refrained from saying anything rude.

"I'm glad to see you're here," she greeted in an even tone. *Move carefully, Patience,* she warned herself. *You don't want to spook him.*

Cass drew on the cheroot as their gazes remained locked.

She was prettier than he'd remembered. Her once too slim body had rounded gently to form lush, ripe curves. Only her eyes were familiar, a defiant deep violet lined with long, sooty lashes. She was wearing her hair differently; it looked more refined and sophisticated than it had six years ago. But he'd be willing to wager she was still the devious little schemer she'd always been.

"Looks like the rain has passed us by," he remarked, hoping he could keep this unexpected encounter as impersonal and brief as possible. He hadn't seen Patience McCord or thought about her in years, but her appearance suddenly brought back the black day six years ago when, at the wrong end of a shotgun barrel, he'd been forced to marry the spoiled twit. It was a memory Cass did not hold dear. He had no idea what Patience McCord was doing here at Laure's party, but he didn't intend to stick around long enough to find out.

With a sinking heart, Patience realized that Cass intended to avoid her. His same casual, cocksure air of dismissal was there; it was just as infuriating as it had been years ago. She forced her voice to remain amiable, though she could see that he was already beginning to ease toward the doorway: "We certainly could have used a good rain."

Surreptitiously, she edged toward him.

She debated whether she should block his way to the ballroom. Such a move would undoubtedly upset him, and she didn't want to make him angry. He'd be impossible to deal with then, but she could see no other way; she had to talk to him sooner or later.

She would force herself to remain tolerant and

cool, even though she was aching to inform him that she wasn't any more enamored of him than he was of her.

Taking another step closer, she decided to try cajoling him. "Cass, I'm glad you're here. I'd like to talk—"

"Sorry," he interrupted. "If you want to talk to me, Miss McCord, you'll have to make an appointment." He flicked his cheroot into the darkness, and with an insufferable smile and a mock salute, he turned and started back into the ballroom.

She gasped, hardly able to believe his impertinence. The deplorable swine!

After a second of indecision she bolted forward to thwart his escape, sensing that he would do everything within his power to avoid seeing her on Monday—or the day after or the day after that.

Cass caught her abrupt movement out of the corner of his eye and sidestepped defensively, his hands moving reflexively to shield his manhood from what he assumed would be another one of her brutal onslaughts.

He hadn't forgotten the misery she had dealt him when he'd angered her by deliberately blocking her path in Miller's Mercantile six years ago. Out of the blue, she'd ruthlessly brought him to his knees with one swift, retaliatory blow of her purse. He wasn't about to let that happen again.

Facing her, he narrowed his eyes menacingly. "Just try it, lady!"

"Try what?" Patience's footsteps faltered as she watched him cover himself defensively.

"Try hitting me again in the . . ." His voice trailed off, then returned full force, "because this time I'll overlook the fact that you're a woman."

Though appalled that he assumed she would try such a thing again, Patience was determined not to let him rattle her. If there was even the smallest hope that he might lease Josiah Thorton's house to her, it was imperative that she remain calm. She fought to check her rising temper, even though her cheeks were flaming with embarrassment. "I wasn't going to strike you!"

The sharp exchange between the couple was beginning to attract attention.

Cass glanced uneasily at the growing cluster of curious onlookers. "What do you want?"

"I want to talk to you!"

"I'm busy!"

"You are not!"

Seizing her roughly by the wrist, he pulled her back out onto the veranda.

His resorting to barbaric tactics made Patience struggle all the harder to remain civil. She knew if she let her temper rule—as she was sorely tempted to do—all would be lost.

"Let go! You're hurting me!" She tried discreetly to free herself from his steely grip while sending a weak smile in the direction of the bewildered guests watching from inside the house.

Moments later Cass backed her against a baluster in a secluded corner of the porch, and their eyes locked in a glacial stare.

"What in the hell are you doing here, Patience?" His face was inches from hers now, his voice ominously low.

Her pulse sped as the manly fragrance of his soap and shaving cream surrounded her. With a jolt, she realized that, despite his despicable lack of manners, he had become a devastatingly handsome man.

"Let go of my arm," she demanded.

"The hell I will!"

"The hell you won't!" In self-defense, she dipped her head and sank her teeth into the back of his hand, then twisted her wrist from his grip so swiftly that he could do nothing but let go.

"Damn!" He sucked in his breath, viewing the row of small, even teeth marks on the back of his hand. "You little witch, watch your language!" he hissed.

Her eyes met his. "Why? Are you afraid someone will hear your *wife* cursing?"

Cass glanced over his shoulder, obviously alarmed that her remark might be overheard and misunderstood. "What do you want, Patience?"

Satisfied that she'd discouraged him from further attempts to intimidate her, she lifted her chin regally, snapped her fan open, and moved deeper into the shadows. "Why, dear, dear Cass, whatever makes you think I want something?" she inquired in her sweetest tone.

"Why, dear, dear Patience," he mocked in a tone far from sweet, "because you always do."

"Perhaps if you had consented to see me when I came by your house earlier, you'd know what I want," she reminded.

"I had no idea it was you."

"And if you had known?"

His eyes narrowed. "I would have set the dogs loose."

Somehow his answer didn't surprise her, and it confirmed that he certainly hadn't mellowed over the years. He was going to be about as easy to reason with as a grizzly bear with a thorn in his paw.

"You should have made an effort to see who it was before you sent me away," she reproached.

"I was busy."

"Yes, I met her on the way in."

Cass flashed a smile, a lazy, arrogant curve to his mouth that she could barely detect. "Then you understand why I didn't want to be disturbed by you."

"Tsk, tsk. I see you haven't changed." Her voice lowered, and she knew what she was about to add would most certainly cook her goose, but she was powerless to let her opportunity pass: "You're the same little weasel you always were."

She realized after she'd bitten him that she'd ruined any chance of convincing him to let her use Josiah Thorton's house, so there seemed little need for the pretense of civility now.

"Weasel?" Cass fumbled in his pocket for another smoke, fighting the urge to strangle her. He knew it was useless to try and outwit her in a war of insults—he'd tried that six years earlier and had lost every time. The best thing he could do was stand his ground.

Patience watched warily as he calmly lit another cigar. "What are you still doing in St. Louis, Patience?"

"I live here, remember?"

"I remember." He blew out the match and tossed it aside. "But I thought you'd be gone by now."

"Ah, then you've thought of me over the years," she said.

He removed the cigar from his mouth and smiled indulgently. "Not even once."

She sighed. "A pity. And here I thought you were pining away for me all this time."

Cass chuckled mirthlessly. "What a dreamer!"

"A better question is what are *you* doing here in St. Louis?" she challenged. "I thought you'd be in River Run."

Cass drew on the cheroot absently as he casually set a booted foot onto the rail next to her. He stared into the darkness for so long Patience thought he intended to ignore her again.

"It's none of your business," he finally said simply, "but if you must know, I went back to River Run for a few months before an old friend wrote and asked me to join him in a business partnership here in St. Louis. That's why I came back."

"Josiah Thorton," she murmured absently.

His eyes snapped back to meet hers. "How did you know Josiah Thorton?"

"I didn't. I just know that he was your business partner . . . and that he died, leaving you the executor of his estate."

"Just how did you find out about that?" Cass was clearly unnerved that she knew even that much about his business dealings.

"Never mind how, I just did. It was Josiah's house that I came to see you about earlier."

"Josiah's house?" Cass studied her guardedly. "What about it?"

"I want you to rent the house to me."

"Rent the house to you?" Cass found the request odd, even for Patience McCord. "I wouldn't rent my horse's leavings to *you*."

"Nor would I accept them," she snapped.

"Then what makes you think I would rent Josiah Thorton's house to you?"

"I know you won't rent me the house for myself, but I'm hoping that when you hear that I have nine children who desperately need that house, you'll be willing to at least listen to what I have to say."

For a moment there was stunned silence as Cass slowly digested her words. She could see that her answer had taken him by surprise.

Suddenly he threw his head back and laughed uproariously, his white teeth flashing in the moonlight. His merriment continued to grow as Patience reviewed her remark to discover what was so amusing that it could send him into fits of mirth.

She could find nothing to warrant such an uncharacteristic show of hilarity.

"What's so funny?" she challenged.

Cass pointed at her, his eyes filling anew with unrestrained joviality. "You . . . and nine children!" He slapped his hand on his thigh and broke into another boisterous round of laughter as she watched with a jaundiced eye. She had a feeling that once she was able to discover the source of his amusement, she wasn't going to be half as lighthearted as he.

"What's so funny about the children and me?" she demanded.

As quickly as his gaiety had erupted, it came to a sudden halt. His eyes surveyed her dispassionately. "I can't imagine any man living with you long enough to father nine children. Is he addle-brained?"

Patience stared back at him the way she did whenever she was forced to deal with a simpleton, which at this point she was certain he was. "The nine children aren't mine."

"I didn't think so!" He roared again hilariously.

"If you can pull yourself together, I'll tell you why I have them," she said curtly. She was getting a little weary of his loutish behavior.

Cass gradually obliged, but with considerable difficulty. "Okay, humor me. Where did you get nine kids?"

"They're orphans. My Aunt Merriweather took them into her home to raise, and after she died I assumed the responsibility for their care."

"Of course you did! Grasping, conniving, spoiled Patience McCord giving unselfishly of herself to nine homeless children. Sounds exactly like you, my dear!"

He would believe that when it was announced that, through an unforeseen technicality, the South had won the war!

"You don't believe me?"

"I couldn't hope to *live* long enough to believe you, Patience!"

"Then I suppose it would do no good to plead with you to lease Josiah Thorton's house to me?"

"None whatsoever." Cass was not a heartless

man, and he regretted that innocent children would suffer from his refusal, but he wouldn't help Patience McCord cross the street, let alone rent Josiah Thorton's house to her.

"Mr. Claxton"—Patience's eyes locked with his stubbornly—"I know you and I haven't exactly been friends." She stoically ignored the choking sound he made in his throat and continued, "But I fail to see how you could let our personal differences stand in the way of providing a home for nine helpless children. I beg you to reconsider. I understand you have accumulated wealth beyond what most people can imagine, and you surely have no need for that large house. Please reconsider. I'm desperate. In another week the children will have no place to live."

It went against everything in Patience to resort to begging, but if it was for the children, then she would.

"Come now, Miss McCord, if what you claim is true, and you've turned into an unselfish saint"—which Cass couldn't believe for one moment—"then why are you making it sound as if I'm the one responsible for the children's misfortune?"

"You have the house," she said simply.

He lifted his brows wryly. "There are no other houses in St. Louis with twenty-four rooms?"

"I'm sure there are, but none so ideal and

none that I can afford. I'm afraid I can only offer a pittance to repay you for your kindness and generosity"—she nearly choked on the praise—"but the children and I will paint and clean and weed the gardens for a portion of our keep."

"What makes you think you could afford what I would ask?"

"I'm not sure that I can, for we have very little money. But when I saw the house, I knew it was exactly what I was looking for, even though it's old and run-down and needs lots of repair. Why, no one would think about purchasing it in the condition it's in now. Of course, I had no idea you owned it—"

"I don't. It belongs to Josiah Thorton."

"But he's dead, and you're the executor of his estate and the one most likely to inherit it, along with the rest of Mr. Thorton's vast holdings."

Cass's eyes narrowed again. "Who told you that?"

Daniel Odolf's face surfaced in Patience's memory as she quickly went on. "I can't say who told me, but wouldn't it be to your advantage to have people living in Josiah's house, people who would be able to care for it until the estate is settled?"

"And what happens once the estate is settled? Suppose I already have a potential buyer interested in purchasing Josiah's house. Would the kind-hearted, generous 'weasel' then dump you and your nine little orphans in the middle of the street?"

"Well . . . I'm not sure what would happen in that case." Patience had learned long ago to deal with life one day at a time. "It's possible that if I can't find another house at that time, I might be forced to take the children to my father in Cherry Grove, but I don't want to do that right now. With winter approaching, the long journey would be extremely difficult for the elderly couple who helps me run the home," she confessed.

"I hate to hear that, Miss McCord, because I'm not going to help you." Cass pitched his cheroot over the veranda and straightened to face her. "It looks like you're going to have to trick someone else into helping you out of your mess this time."

Her eyes narrowed. "You can't help me—or you won't help me?"

He grinned. "Both. I can't because Josiah's house is not mine to do with as I please—his estate won't be settled for months yet. And I won't because . . ." His eyes surveyed her insolently. "Well, I think we both know why I won't, don't we? Oh, by the way, I never received those annulment papers. Where are they?"

"You are heartless," she spat out. "So you'll just have to keep on wondering where those papers are."

He extended his index finger and tapped her under her chin warningly. "Watch it, sweetheart—your halo is wobbling." He grinned again. It felt good to turn the tables on her, for a change. After what she'd done to him, he was surprised she'd have the gall to come to him for a favor. But then he recalled that years ago she'd had the gall of ten women, and the way Cass figured it, refusing her tonight had just about evened the score.

Just about.

Patience felt her temper surfacing full force as he turned and started away from her.

Oh, she longed to shout at the top of her lungs where his precious annulment papers were, but she knew she didn't dare.

Squaring her shoulders, she called out to his retreating form pleadingly. "We don't have to have twenty-four rooms, you know. We can make do with far less!"

"Forget it."

"Don't you have *any* house you could rent to me for the children?"

"Nope, not even one. Good evening, Miss McCord. Real nice seeing you again." He threw his head back and laughed merrily.

Patience stamped her foot angrily. Good evening, indeed!

The man was an intolerable muttonhead who was going to pay for his highhandedness.

5

Twice in the following days Patience McCord went to Cass Claxton and begged him to reconsider. On both occasions he turned a deaf ear and told her in his most holier-than-thou tone that it would take an act of divine intervention for him to rent her a glass of water, to say nothing of Josiah Thorton's house.

She'd left enraged each time, to scour the town for another house, praying for that divine intervention he was so smugly sure she'd never find. And she didn't find it.

By Friday she realized she'd reached the end of the line. "I'm sorry," Patience told the children that night, "but we have no other choice.

We must start for Kansas at first light Monday morning."

She sat with her hands folded at the dinner table, trying to gauge the reaction on the bright young faces before her. The children—Aaron, sixteen; Payne, fourteen; Jesse, nine, Doog, eight; Margaret Ann, six; Lucy and Bryon, five; Joseph, four; and Phebia, three—stared back at her with solemn gazes.

They were aware of her diligent search to find a home large and inexpensive enough to house them. The worry lines etched on Patience's forehead tonight told them that the miracle they had hoped for had failed to materialize. In three short days they must vacate Aunt Merriweather's house, so they realized that there was little Patience could do but transport them all to Cherry Grove.

The challenge was overwhelming, even for a woman of her fortitude, but they were confident she could get the job done.

"Are we gonna ride in a wagon?" Jesse picked up an ear of corn and began to gnaw the tender kernels thoughtfully.

"I'll be able to gather enough money to buy a wagon and a team. Naturally we cannot hope for a wagon that will be large enough for all of us to sleep in, but the weather should remain mild enough so that we can sleep on pallets under the wagon at night. Corliss and Harlon will sleep inside."

Patience glanced over to assess Corliss's reaction to the news. She went about quietly dishing up potatoes onto the youngest child's plate.

Phebia was the baby of the household, a gurgling, brown-eyed, chubby-faced foundling who was left on the Merriweather doorstep three years ago by a mother who could no longer care for her. Estelle had been eager to welcome a ninth stray into the fold, and the other children had joined in to help with Phebia's upbringing.

"I know it's not the ideal time to embark on a journey," Patience admitted quietly, "but if all goes well we should reach Cherry Grove in six to seven weeks."

Patience knew they'd have to travel the length of Missouri, and then another hundred and twenty-five miles into Kansas; but it was only the end of August, and she figured they wouldn't have any trouble reaching their destination before the first snow.

She was relieved to see both Corliss and her husband nodding as she spoke, supportive as usual of any request she made of them.

"How are we going?" Harlon asked.

"I understand the most sensible way for us to go would be to take a boat to St. Joseph, then buy a wagon and supplies to transport us on to Cherry Grove, but because of our lack of funds, we won't be able to do it that way. We'll have to travel by wagon, keeping to the main route running across the state."

"All right. I'll see to getting the wagon and a team first thing in the morning," Harlon said.

"Thank you, Harlon. Wes Epperson over at the livery barn said he might have one he'd sell cheaply." Patience absently reached to cover Doog's fork in a mute reprimand as he prepared to launch a pea at an unsuspecting Bryon. "I think you'll like Cherry Grove," she told the children—although she herself had detested it.

Long ago, when she'd longed to return to the parties and gaiety of St. Louis, she'd begged Leviticus to let her go back to Aunt Merriweather's. Leviticus had ignored his daughter's pleading. He had moved his daughter to Cherry Grove to begin a new life, and he insisted she make new friends. The decision had forced Patience to take her own action. Cass Claxton was elected to take her back to St. Louis.

The marriage ploy had worked like a charm, though Patience realized now that using such underhanded tactics was unforgivable. She thought about her encounter with Cass two nights ago and felt sad. She was no longer the irresponsible, willful girl she had once been, and she had to admit her selfishness disturbed her deeply.

Now when she most desperately needed Cass's help—or more accurately, when she needed the house he controlled—she knew she could never convince him that she had changed.

Patience sighed wearily. Her father's words came back to haunt her: "You've made your bed; now you must lie in it."

"Will them Indians git us?" blond, gray-eyed Jesse asked solemnly as he wrapped a string bean around his forefinger.

The same concern had kept Patience awake long into the night. "I'm not sure we'll encounter Indians, Jesse, but if we do, we'll just keep our heads, and I'm sure the good Lord will see us through."

Aaron, the oldest of the boys, said quietly, "Ma'am, I hear tell it's not our heads they'd be after. It's our scalps."

Patience felt a shudder ripple down her spine.

Lucy's brown eyes grew as round as saucers. "Really?" A piece of corn dangled from her one remaining front tooth.

"Well, of course there's always that danger, Lucy, but I'm sure Patience will make sure that we keep our hair," Margaret Ann soothed as she dabbed the younger girl's mouth with a cloth napkin.

Patience had always contended—out of Margaret's earshot—that Margaret was a thirty-year-old imprisoned in a six-year-old's body.

"What may I do to help, Miss McCord?" Margaret inquired sweetly.

"I plan to make a list tonight of the duties that will be assigned to each of us. I'll try to have it completed by breakfast tomorrow morning." Patience sipped her coffee, trying to read the children's faces again. She was relieved to see that they seemed to take the turn of events in stride. Over the years, under Aunt Merriweather's tutelage, they had become exemplary children.

Margaret and Payne stood up and began to clear away the dishes, while Corliss wiped Phebia's hands and face and lifted her out of the wooden high chair. She handed the child her favorite doll, Marybelle, and swatted her lovingly on the bottom.

"Jesse, it's gettin' late. Time for Phebia and Marybelle to be off to bed."

"Yes, ma'am." Jesse pushed back from the table and led Phebia, who immediately popped her thumb into her mouth, out of the room.

"The wood box be gettin' low." Aaron reached into his pocket and slipped his cap onto his head. "I'll be filling it up for you, Miss McCord, before I turn in."

"Thank you, Aaron. I'll see you in the morning," Patience replied absently as she reached for the small slate and piece of chalk.

The rest of the children dispersed from the table in an orderly manner as Harlon went into the kitchen to retrieve the coffee pot. He carried it back to the table and lifted his bushy white brows expectantly at Patience.

"No, thank you," she refused. "I've had plenty."

Corliss bustled off to the kitchen to supervise the cleaning as Harlon sat back down at the table. The clock on the mantle chimed seven times while he scraped out the bowl of his pipe. Patience was deeply absorbed in making the list of supplies she would need to purchase for the journey. Money was tight, but she had been known to stretch a dollar until it cried for mercy. Now she would just have to stretch it until it expired!

She knew very little about such things as wagons and teams and the proper food to carry on such a long trip, but she had spent hours that morning at the general store, talking to a family who had traveled to Oregon by wagon two years ago.

Clifford Magers had explained to her that when she went to select a wagon, she must make sure that it was strong, light, and constructed out of well-seasoned timber—especially the wheels, since they would be traveling through an elevated region that was exceedingly dry this time of year. He warned Patience that unless the woodwork was thoroughly seasoned, constant repairs would be inevitable.

She'd have to travel light, he insisted, no matter how strong the urge was to take along furniture, potted plants, iron stoves, and grandfather clocks. He emphasized that should she succumb to temptation, the heavy items would only have to be discarded by the wayside later in order to conserve the animals' strength for their long journey.

In selecting her team, Clifford advised mules rather than oxen because they traveled faster and seemed to endure the summer heat better. But when she'd gone to the livery later that day, she discovered that mules were priced higher than oxen.

Wes Epperson told her he thought she'd be smarter to buy oxen over mules, assuring her that oxen stayed in better condition and were able to make the journey in the same amount of time. He contended that oxen would be less likely to stampede if they were spooked by Indians.

Patience would have preferred mules, but with her limited funds, she supposed oxen would have to be her choice.

She glanced up, aware that Harlon had been watching her for the past few minutes. She smiled encouragingly. "Is there something you'd like to suggest, Harlon?"

"Yes, ma'am."

Patience lay the chalk aside and folded her hands over the slate. "I'm listening."

"Have you given any thought to the dangers a

young woman and nine children will be facing once we're out on the trail?" he began quietly.

She sighed, sensing that all along Harlon had harbored misgivings about her decision. "I know there will be dangers, and I'm not happy about having to go, but taking the children to my father is our only hope of keeping them together."

"With all due respect, Miss McCord, I think we need a man—a good strong man who knows the wilderness to lead us on such a long journey."

Patience sighed. "I've thought about that, Harlon, but I have no such man, and it isn't as if we're traveling to some far away place like California or Oregon," she argued. "I'll have you to help me. You're a man."

"I'm an old man," Harlon reminded gently. "I can't do anything but hunt for fresh game and haul fresh water to the camp each night. You need a young man, a man strong enough to fight off Indians, wield a bullwhip, and drive a team of oxen."

Patience realized he was right, but what choice did she have? She didn't know such a man, and her scarcity of funds prevented her from hiring anyone.

"Maybe we can hire a bullwhacker to drive the team," Harlon mused.

"I don't know a bullwhacker, and even if I did, I wouldn't permit such a bully to travel with us."

Everyone knew a bullwhacker was the biggest show-off on a wagon train. His casual brutality to animals was deplorable, and he usually kept the women and children in constant fear. "Besides, I can use a bullwhip myself," she said. A former suitor had taught her how to handle a bullwhip almost as well as a man. She'd become accurate enough to swat a fly off the rump of an ox before the ox even knew a fly was there.

"Well, 'course, it's your decision," Harlon conceded. "I just wanted to make sure you'd thought about what we're gonna be up against."

"I have, Harlon, and I agree with everything you're saying, but I'm afraid we have no other choice. We will have to make the trip alone." She reached over and squeezed his hand encouragingly. "Aaron and Payne are developing into strong young men, and they will be able to drive the oxen. And though they haven't had much experience with a rifle, I'm sure they will learn quickly. The girls will pitch in to do all they can. You'll see, we'll be fine."

Harlon drew thoughtfully on his pipe as he listened to her rattle on about making a memorable adventure out of the journey.

It'd be memorable, all right! He'd traveled with a wagon train back in the fifties, and he could still remember the torrential rains, blazing sun, freezing winds, and the dust—miles and miles of swirling dust—that got into the eyes and clothes and food, tormenting the weary travelers until they thought they would lose their minds. He recalled the flies and the sickness . . .

"You'll see, we'll make it just fine," he heard her say again before she turned her attention back to her list.

"Well, I hope so," he muttered.

A few minutes later Harlon pushed away from the table and slowly got to his feet. "It sure would make it easier if you had a strong young husband to take us all to Cherry Grove," he said almost wistfully.

Patience glanced up from the slate. "Yes, it certainly would make it easier."

"Well, don't be frettin' none over what I've said." Harlon sighed as he stretched lazily. He stood and shuffled over to wind the clock. "Me and Corliss will do everything we can to help get those young 'uns to their new home. The good Lord will see us through. He always has."

"He always has." She nodded. "I've been praying about it, Harlon, and I don't think we have a thing to be concerned about."

Harlon nodded and announced he was going to turn in.

Patience bid him good night distractedly.

The lamp had burned low when she finally blew out the flame. She closed her eyes and clasped her hands around her waist, trying to ease the stiffness in the small of her back. Harlon's earlier comment drifted back to her: "It sure would make it easier if you had a husband."

Reaching for the candle, she rose to make her way to the darkened stairway, thinking about his observation.

Suddenly her hand paused on the railing.

It sure would make it easier if you had a strong young husband. Harlon's words echoed through her mind again, taunting, offering an almost prophetic challenge. *Someone who could take us to Cherry Grove . . .*

Her feet absently claimed a second stair, then hesitated again. It *would* make it considerably easier if she had a strong young husband to help out. He could escort them safely to Cherry Grove, and they could all stop worrying. She stood in the darkness, scowling thoughtfully.

Well, she *had* a husband. A good, strong, reasonably young husband who was more than capable of escorting them on such a journey. And why shouldn't he? Wasn't he partly to blame for her having to make the journey, since he'd refused to rent her Josiah's house?

Patience, there's no way on this earth that you could ever talk Cass Claxton into escorting you to your own lynching . . . well, maybe he would agree to take her to that, she amended grudgingly. But he would most assuredly refuse to lead her, two seventy-year-olds in failing health, plus nine homeless children safely across four hundred miles back to Cherry Grove, Kansas.

She took another step, then paused. No, he would *never* do it . . . unless . . .

Unless . . .

She smiled, and her feet began to move with purpose now as she hurried up the steep stairway, confident that if she put her mind to it, she might find a way he would.

Maybe it was time to show that smart-alecky Cass Claxton that Patience McCord *still* had the upper hand when she wanted it.

6

Monday morning arrived with a slow, steady rain falling from the eaves of the Claxton estate. In the distance occasional thunder rumbled unceremoniously, but all in all, the gray, cool morning was ideal for working. However, Cass found he had to struggle to keep his mind on the papers spread out before him.

He sat at his desk trying to concentrate while Laure draped herself over his shoulder, determined to offer him a tempting diversion.

"Oh, *mon chéri,* why must you always work?" she complained as she snuggled close against the broad expanse of his back. "Do you not think we could find more interesting ways to occupy ourselves?"

She nipped seductively at his left ear as her fingers began to nimbly work open the buttons on his shirt.

"Laure . . ." Cass warned, capturing both her hands in his. She giggled as he pulled her down onto his lap.

Her slender fingers threaded through the dark springy curls that grazed his collar as their lips met in a long, unhurried kiss.

Moments later he found himself gazing into her turquoise-blue eyes and admonishing her in what he hoped was his sternest voice. "What am I going to do with you?"

She pulled his ear toward her and whispered a suggestion that immediately brought an amused smile to his handsome features.

"Is not a morning more suited for making love than for working?" she whispered.

Cass's left brow lifted dubiously. "You left my bed not two hours ago, and now you're implying that I'm not paying enough attention to you?"

"Ah, but I am shameless when it comes to you, *mon chéri.*" Her tongue seduced the outline of his lips while she twined her fingers into the thick mat of hair exposed by his open shirt.

Cass's ensuing laugh was that of a man who knew his power over a woman and delighted in it. His mouth took hers again in a hungry, masterful kiss that obliterated all thoughts of completing his work. Laure would easily have had her way and returned to his bed to spend the rest of the morning if it had not been for the sudden rap that sounded at the study door.

She groaned in disappointment as Cass cut short the heated embrace and glanced toward the sound of the intrusion.

"Tell Mozes we do not want to be bothered," Laure urged with a throaty command.

Cass grinned and eased her from his lap. "Don't be so eager, love. There is time for both business and pleasure." She affected a pretty pout as he rose and walked toward the door, as a more persistent knock sounded.

He found Mozes waiting with an envelope in his hand.

"Yes?"

"I'm sorry to bother you, sir, but a telegraph message just arrived. I thought you would want to see it immediately."

"Oh?" Cass took the envelope. "Thank you, Mozes." He closed the door and crossed the room again.

"What is it, *mon chéri?*"

"I have no idea." Cass ripped open the envelope. A frown began to form on his forehead as his eyes quickly scanned the puzzling message:

NEED HELP STOP COME AS QUICKLY AS POSSIBLE STOP BEAU.

"Is it bad news?" Laure came to stand by his side, hoping to catch a glimpse over his shoulder.

"I'm not sure. It's from Beau."

"Your brother?"

"Yes, my brother in Cherry Grove. He must be in some sort of trouble." Cass absently pitched the message onto the desk and strode briskly toward the doorway.

"Where are you going?" Laure demanded.

"To Kansas." He flung the door open and shouted for Mozes.

"Kansas!" Laure wailed. "But you cannot! You will be gone for weeks! And there is a party Friday night."

"You'll have to struggle through it without me," he said.

"But this is most terrible!" Laure ran out of the study, trying to keep up with his rapidly retreating form. "When will you be back?"

"I'm not sure," he murmured distractedly. "I'll let you know." Bounding up the stairs two at a time, he shouted, "Mozes! Pack my bag! I'm leaving in five minutes."

"But, *mon chéri!*" Laure paused and slapped her hand against the railing angrily as Cass continued his ascent. *"Cherry Grove, Kansas?"*

Grand Dieu! She'd never even heard of the place!

The rain was coming down in heavy sheets by midmorning as Patience and her small entourage left St. Louis. The eight younger children struggling to keep up behind the covered wagon were forced to step lively as the wheels of the large prairie schooner sluiced through the deepening mud holes.

"Keep moving, children. The rain will surely let up before long!" Patience glanced anxiously over her shoulder as she gripped the reins more tightly and urged the oxen up a steep incline. The creak of harness and leather filled the air as the massive animals labored to pull their heavy burden.

Harlon rode ahead, his hat pulled low on his forehead in an effort to shield his face from the rain. Corliss rode in the back of the wagon, popping her head out every now and then to keep an eye on the younger children. Patience could hear her calling repeated warnings: "Stay together, girls. Jesse, take Lucy's hand—she's fallin' behind again."

Because the weather was warm, the children had been instructed to tie their shoes around their waists to prevent them from wearing out the leather on the long journey. They knew Patience couldn't afford to buy new shoes this winter, so not one complaint was heard.

Phebia rode next to Patience on the wagon seat, hugging her doll, Marybelle, to her chest to protect it from the pelting rain. "Me want to go hooooome," she had been sobbing almost from the moment they'd left the city limits. "Me getting all wet!"

Patience had tried to explain that they couldn't go home—they *had* no home—but to Phebia's three-year-old mind, the journey was tiresome already. She couldn't understand why Patience wasn't doing something to ease her discomfort.

The oxen topped the rise, and Patience pulled them to a halt to wait for the children to catch up. She sat looking out at the rain-soddened horizon, trying to shake the depression that had been with her since waking that morning.

They'd been traveling for more than four hours, and she was certain they had barely covered two miles. How would she ever see them all safely across four hundred miles?

No matter how hard she tried to convince herself that she could do it, the ordeal loomed bleak ahead of her.

When the rain lets up, we'll be able to move faster, she reasoned. *If it ever lets up*. The clouds hung even lower, shrouding the earth with a dark gray mist as another heavy cloudburst assaulted them.

Harlon rode up beside the wagon and had to shout to make himself heard above the torrential downpour. "I be thinkin' it might be a good time to stop for dinner!"

"I think you're right!" Patience called back, thankful for any reprieve.

"There's a grove of sycamores 'bout a quarter mile on up the road. Looks like as good a place as any to stop."

"I'll follow you!" Patience fought to keep the animals moving as lightning streaked wildly across the sky, followed by deafening claps of thunder. Phebia started to scream as Marybelle's straw-colored hair wilted in the rain.

"Phebia, darling, Marybelle will be fine." Patience chanced a quick pat on Phebia's knee before she was forced to grab tighter hold of the reins.

Her sympathy only served to remind Phebia of how thoroughly miserable she was, and she bawled more loudly.

Patience herself was close to bawling a few minutes later when she felt the wheel of the wagon lurch, then slip deeper and deeper into a quagmire she'd been unable to avoid.

Corliss poked her head through the canvas opening. "What's going on?"

"The wheel—I thinks it's stuck!"

Climbing down from the wagon, Patience stood in the midst of the cloudburst, hands on her hips, surveying the wheel that was hopelessly mired to the hub.

Phebia was screaming even harder. There wasn't a thread of dry clothing left on Patience, and if she could have gotten her hands on Cass Claxton at that moment, she gladly would have strangled him.

Cass was traveling fast and light. His horse covered the ground in smooth, even strides despite the worsening weather. Within fifteen minutes from the time he'd received Beau's message, he'd started on his way. His mind raced with the possibilities that might await him when he reached Cherry Grove. Was Beau ill? Had something happened to his wife, Charity? Surely it wasn't their little girl, Mary Kathleen . . . She had been a healthy, rosy-cheeked infant when Cass had last seen her, but that had been more than six years ago. Had something happened to her—or maybe to the twins, Jase and Jenny?

He flanked the stallion harder, and the lines of worry on his face grew deeper. Maybe something had happened to Ma . . . or Willa, the family housekeeper . . . or Cole and Wynne.

God, he should have kept in touch with his family. How long had it been since he'd seen any of them? Four, maybe five years . . .

The horse topped a rise, and Cass abruptly pulled it to a halt. The animal was becoming winded, and Cass realized he was pushing too hard. Running the horse to death was not only cruel and senseless, but it would only cost him another delay.

He rested against the pommel of the saddle for a moment, letting the horse catch its breath and cool a little as his eyes surveyed the valley below him.

His gaze stopped suddenly as it fell upon a covered wagon in the near distance, leaning contortedly to one side. Several people milled around in confusion, while a couple of young boys tried to unhitch a cow and a goat that were tied behind the wagon. A large chicken crate remained lashed to the wagon's side, the occupants flapping their wings and cackling loudly in the confusion.

A pioneer family in trouble, Cass thought absently as he pulled aside his rain poncho and extracted a smoke from his shirt pocket.

When the cheroot was lit, he sat watching what appeared to be an elderly man and woman along with a younger woman struggling to free the wheel from its muddy confinement. He could see now that there were children, a whole slew of them, surrounding the mud hole that had firmly trapped the wagon wheel.

After studying the situation for a few minutes, Cass decided the wheel was going to be impossible to free, the way they were going about it. He shifted uneasily in the saddle, grappling with his conscience. His first instinct was to swing around the wagon and be on his way.

After all, it wasn't his problem. If he stopped to help, he could be delayed for an hour or longer, and he could hardly afford the wasted time. However, he could plainly see that at the rate they were going, the family would be stuck there until the sun came out and the road dried out.

And some of those kids sounded real unhappy. He could hear a little girl sobbing her heart out.

He pulled his hat lower on his forehead, hoping to overcome his conscience. He'd never claimed he was a good Samaritan . . . but he was a decent sort, and he knew he couldn't just ride by and ignore the situation, much as he wanted to.

Ma would wring his tail if she ever found out he'd ignored someone in trouble.

Sighing, he tossed the cheroot aside and picked up the reins. There were times he wished he'd been raised a heathen. It would have made his choice easier right about now. He clucked to his horse, figuring he might as well ride down there and get it over with so he could be on his way.

After all, how long could it take to get one wheel out of a simple mud hole?

7

Six and a half weeks, Cass discovered. *That's* how long he would be paying for his act of benevolence.

Riding up to the wagon, he'd quickly recognized Patience McCord and his expression had gone from guileless to horrified. "What in the hell are *you* doing here?"

Rain poured from the brim of his hat in rivulets as he sat on his horse and stared down at her. It was uncanny how this woman turned up to haunt him. He didn't know why fate had ruthlessly thrown her in his path again, but here she was, her wagon bogged down in a muddy slough, while nine children stood helplessly beside the road, looking to him as if he had just come off a mountain with stone tablets in his arms.

"Well, hello!" Patience greeted him brightly as she stood ankle-deep in mud. "How fortunate we are that you've come along!" She smiled up at him.

Eyes narrowing, Cass stared back at her coldly. "I fail to see anything fortunate about it."

She brushed the strands of damp hair out of her face, ignoring his brusque manner. She'd fully expected rudeness. "Well, as you can see, we are in a good deal of trouble. Your assistance would be greatly appreciated."

"Ha!"

Patience blushed, casting an apprehensive glance toward Harlon and Corliss, but they were so engrossed with the problem that they didn't appear to have heard the exchange. "There's no need for sarcasm," she reproved him quietly. "We are in need of a good strong back, and yours should do nicely."

Cass was about to tell her what she could do with that idea when his head turned sharply at the sound of Harlon, groaning with misery. The old man was straining against the large pole he was maneuvering in an effort to pry the wheel from the mud.

"Harlon, your heart!" Corliss said fretfully; fear for her husband's health deepened the furrows of her weathered face.

Cass glanced back at Patience, and she could see that he was struggling with his conscience.

Phebia began crying again, setting up a wail that could be heard for miles. "Me sooo wet and hungrrry!"

Her doll's flaxen hair trailed through the mud as the three-year-old dragged Marybelle by the feet in her hurry to seek comfort from Patience. Woefully the child buried her face in Patience's sodden skirt and howled.

"Please, Cass, we need your help. There are other people involved here, not just me," Patience pleaded as Margaret Ann, Lucy, and Bryon joined Phebia to comfort her.

Climbing down from his horse, Cass shot Patience a pointed look that clearly said, *Just so you understand, I'm only doing this for them.* Briskly he motioned for Payne and Aaron to step forward.

For the next few hours differences were set aside as they worked as a team to free the trapped wheel.

Harlon wanted to help but couldn't, so he and Corliss were put in charge of feeding the younger children their noonday meal.

More than once Patience found herself a hindrance rather than a help. Cass would gruffly order her to step aside as he and the boys heaved and tugged on the stubborn wheel. In an effort to appease him, she would obediently step away, but moments later she would be back in the thick of the action, working as hard as she could.

At one point she found her arms locked tightly around Cass's waist as the oxen, Aaron, Payne, Doog, Cass, and she formed a human chain of brute strength. She had never thought of Cass as a man—at least, not in the way most women would think of him—but the unfamiliar feel of his steely muscles pressed intimately to her bosom as they strained against each other caused a feathery flutter in the pit of her stomach, a feeling she found hard to explain.

Around three, exhausted and knowing that the animals had to have a rest, they stopped for a few minutes. Wearily they sank down onto the saturated ground to eat the fatback and cold biscuits that Corliss pressed into their hands. Since the downpour from the leaden sky had never slackened, a more substantial meal was impossible to prepare.

Patience found herself longing for a cup of scalding coffee to ward off the growing chill that enveloped her.

The children milled around, making the best of the situation, but Cass and Patience chose to eat their food in a withdrawn and uncommunicative silence.

Handing him another biscuit, Patience finally decided to make a small attempt at civility. "I'm sorry there's no coffee."

Cass accepted the offering distractedly, his mind intent on freeing the wheel and getting on his way. "I've lost a good four hours," he muttered.

"Oh?" Patience bit into her second biscuit. "Are you going somewhere?"

Cass turned to look at her balefully as rain spilled from the brim of his hat in torrents. "Now why would you think that? Isn't this the sort of day any man in his right mind would go out riding for the pleasure of it?"

She shrugged.

"Then obviously I'm going somewhere."

"Well, what a coincidence that we should happen to run into each other this way," she said.

"Yeah, what a coincidence," he returned dryly.

"It was a stroke of good luck for us. I'm sure we'll be able to free the wheel soon and then be on our separate ways." She lifted her brow inquiringly. "Where was it you said you were going?"

Cass swallowed the last of his biscuit and stood up. "I didn't say."

"Oh." It was apparent that he didn't care to elaborate, and Patience didn't want to push her luck.

"Let's get at that wheel again."

Struggling to her feet, Patience smiled back at him brightly. "I'm ready."

It was late afternoon before they managed to pry the wheel free. The old wagon lurched forward as Harlon, Corliss, and the children sent up shouts of elation.

Payne and Aaron stood back, laughingly surveying each other, and their faces broke into big grins. Only the whites of their eyes and teeth showed through the thick layers of muck encrusted on their faces.

Confident the crisis was over, Doog leaned down and scooped up a handful of mud and flung it at Jesse. The tensions of the day eased as quickly as they had come, and soon the ensuing mud war caught up everyone in its spontaneity.

Patience glanced warily at Cass, who looked no better than she, and suddenly they both joined in the fun.

Patience thought the mud balls Cass repeatedly sent in her direction had entirely too much velocity behind them, but she stood her ground and returned fire in a full-hearted attempt to go him one better.

When a truce was finally called, they were all a pitiful sight to behold. Even Corliss and Harlon were covered in mud, having been innocently caught in the cross fire.

"You look funnnny," Phebia drawled as Patience, trying not to gag, spat out a clump of mud.

"Land sakes, I never saw such goings-on!" Corliss complained. She began shooing the children to the back of the wagon where a bar of lye soap and the water barrel were waiting.

Cass followed the crowd, and belated introductions were made. Patience didn't go into detail about how she knew Cass, saying only that they'd met before.

As soon as he'd washed up, Cass walked away from the boisterous group and headed in the direction of his horse. The rain had turned to a slow drizzle as he heaved himself into the saddle and turned to leave without a word of farewell.

Patience was helping Lucy wash the mud out of her hair when she caught sight of Cass from the corner of her eye. "Margaret, come help Lucy," she said quickly under her breath. "I have something I must tend to."

Cass glanced up and saw her striding purposefully toward him. Hurriedly he reined his horse in the opposite direction, but her hand snaked out and grabbed the horse's bridle, preventing his departure.

"I want to talk to you," she stated flatly.

"Sorry, I've already wasted a whole day."

Her eyes sparked with determination, a sign that Cass had come to realize meant trouble. "I seriously doubt you'll consider what I have to say a waste of your time," she promised.

"*Anything* you have to say I'd consider a

waste of my time, Miss McCord.'' He cut the reins to the left, and she was forced to step aside.

''Make that Mrs. Claxton,'' she corrected.

At first Cass thought he hadn't heard her right.

''Mrs. Cass Claxton,'' she repeated a little louder as he continued down his path of retreat.

The horse suddenly slowed again. Patience could see the muscles in Cass's back tightening, almost as if he knew what was coming. Without turning around, he spoke in a voice so ominous that it should have made her think twice about what she was about to do.

''*Mrs. Cass Claxton*—now what in the hell is *that* supposed to mean?'' He didn't know what she was trying to pull this time, but she wasn't going to rile him.

''If you'll stop being in such an all-fired hurry to get away from me, I'll tell you what *that* means.''

Cass turned his horse and walked it back to where she stood. He sat staring at her for a moment; then he slowly dismounted. His blue eyes fixed on hers with a silent warning; he prayed that her taunt didn't mean what he thought it did. ''All right, what are you up to this time?''

''I need your help.''

He made a disgusted sound in the back of his throat and turned to mount the horse again. ''Don't you ever let up?''

She stepped forward, and her voice held an underlying urgency. "I will, I promise, if you'll help me just one more time."

He eased into the saddle and tipped his hat politely. "Can't do it, lady. Sorry. I've got troubles of my own."

Her eyes narrowed spitefully. "You have more than you think."

Cass knew he should ignore her and leave before it went any further. She was spoiling for a confrontation, and he wasn't about to oblige her—but he couldn't ignore something she'd said.

"What did you mean by that 'Mrs. Cass Claxton' remark?" he asked, trying to remain unruffled.

She could see he was torn between tolerance and drawing his gun on her, so she decided to try a softer approach. She preferred not to antagonize him, but she wondered if that could be avoided. "You implied that you were traveling. Are you going to Cherry Grove?"

For one imperceptible instant she thought she saw his mouth slacken with disbelief. "No!"

"You're lying."

"I am not—but what if I were?" he snapped defensively. He swung out of the saddle again, deciding to stand his ground. If she wanted a fight, he'd give her one.

"You're lying. I know you are, and I want you

to take the children and me to Cherry Grove with you," she demanded before she lost her nerve.

"Over my dead body," he vowed.

"Mr. Claxton, if I could have arranged that," she said calmly, "I would have long ago. I think for your benefit—and for that of your French lady friend—you'd better listen to what I have to say."

Cass shifted his weight impatiently. "Laure? What in the hell does Laure have to do with me taking you, two elderly people, and nine children to Cherry Grove, Kansas?"

"Listen and listen well, Cass Claxton. If you escort us there safely, then I in return will present you with papers confirming that our marriage has been annulled."

Cass stiffened resentfully. "You'll give them to me regardless," he demanded.

"Maybe I will and maybe I won't. It all depends on you."

Cass was still astounded that she knew where he was going. Switching subjects, he snapped, "Just what makes you so cocksure I'm even *going* to Kansas!"

"I'm not sure you are . . . I just assume you might be, since I know you have kin out that way," she said simply.

"Well, forget it! There's no way I'm taking you or anyone else to Cherry Grove. I plan to travel hard and fast. I can't be dragging along twelve other people."

"We'll keep up," she promised. "Just help us drive the team and make sure we're not killed by Indians or wolves or the like."

"Now, how in the hell and I supposed to do that?"

"You can," she said, firmly believing that even though he was a miserable excuse for a man, his knowledge of the land would be invaluable. "The boys and Harlon will keep us in fresh meat and water, and I promise we won't ask anything of you if it isn't necessary."

"Just that I get all of you to Cherry Grove with your scalps still intact!"

Patience didn't like to think of it that way, but that's what she was asking. "Yes."

"Well, lady, the day you hand over those annulment papers will be the day we'll discuss my escorting you to Cherry Grove."

"Darn it, I can't give you the papers!"

Cass turned back to mount the horse. "Then consider the subject closed."

"I don't have the papers, Cass." She lowered her eyes sheepishly. "I know you're not going to like this, but I . . . I never got around to filing for the annulment."

There! She'd admitted it, and now all she had to do was live through his fury. Once that was over, she didn't care—she was going to use the annulment as a pawn to get her brood to their destination.

She waited apprehensively for his reaction. When it finally came, it was nothing close to what she had expected.

He simply groaned, laid his forehead against the side of the horse, and beat his balled-up fist on the seat of the saddle.

"Cass?" She edged forward, extending her hand to him sympathetically, aware that her news had come as a shock. "I promise, I *will* give you the annulment . . . Please don't think I enjoy using underhanded tactics . . . but you must see that my situation is impossible without your help—"

"You never got the annulment?" His voice sounded hollow, stunned, disbelieving.

"No . . . Actually, I forgot all about you once you'd gone," she admitted. "Oh, I thought about the annulment occasionally, but to be honest, a marriage to me means a church and a gown and pretty flowers and . . . we didn't have those. Although"—her face puckered worriedly—"I suppose the vows were just as binding."

She supposed! He lifted his head to gaze tormentedly into her eyes. "We've been married for *six* years?"

She nodded hesitantly. "I suppose."

He moaned and dropped his head against the saddle again.

"But that needn't upset you," she soothed. "If you're on your way to Cherry Grove, then what can it hurt if we ride along with you? I think we could make it fine on our own, but Harlon is concerned that we need a younger man to see us through the wilds. But I promise you, the very day we reach Cherry Grove I will have my father immediately file for our annulment. There shouldn't be the slightest bit of trouble in obtaining one." She smiled. "After that, why, you'll never have to see me again!"

His head lifted, and his eyes gazed over at the covered wagon swarming with children, then on to Corliss and Harlon, who were sitting in the wagon, looking as though they were about to draw their last breath.

Escort Patience McCord and eleven others over four *hundred* miles of rugged territory? The old couple didn't look as if they could hold up for another four.

Could she force him to do this, he wondered frantically. Maybe she was lying again and in her twisted way had come up with this ridiculous scheme to blackmail him into taking her to Cherry Grove. He knew she was devious enough to try anything, and yet he wasn't sure that she would lie about anything as serious as their annulment.

Since the marriage had never been consummated, it couldn't be valid, he reasoned, trying to grasp at any glimmer of hope. The haphazard ceremony had taken place in the middle of the road at the end of a shotgun. How legal could that be? He wished now he had taken the time to find out, but the whole incident six years ago had seemed so ludicrous, and once he'd dropped her off at her Aunt Merriweather's, he'd barely thought about her again.

Maybe the ceremony hadn't been legal, and maybe he wouldn't have to yield to her high-handed tactics, but an inner voice told him that she would lie and say the vows had been consummated and then Judge Leviticus McCord would have made doubly sure that the marriage was duly recorded in the proper place in order to protect his daughter's sterling reputation.

No, as hard as it was for him to swallow, Cass was afraid she had trapped him again.

"Well? Will you help us?" Patience waited for his answer, not sure what she would do if he refused her again. She'd just played her last hand.

Cass shook his head wordlessly, too heartsick to reply. The way he saw it, he had no choice if he wanted his freedom. She had gotten the better of him.

Shooting her a look that could have sent a strong man to his knees, he began to climb wearily back onto the saddle.

"Aren't you going to say anything?" she asked nervously.

Glaring at her silently, he turned the horse

toward the wagon and trotted off, his sagging shoulders clearly indicating how disillusioned he was with the world.

Patience sighed with relief. She assumed that meant he was going to help her.

8

"You think them Injuns will rip our stomachs open with a knife, whack our scalps off till the blood runs down in our eyes, then string our guts out on the ground for the buzzards to peck on?"

Cass slowly opened one eye to stare back into a pair of solemn gray ones. "I thought you were supposed to be fetching wood."

"I was." Jesse gestured toward a small pile of limbs and twigs lying at Cass's feet. "Now what about the Injuns?"

"What about 'em?" A fly buzzed in a lazy circle above Cass's head as he lowered the brim of his hat to shade his eyes from the glare of the midday sun.

"They gonna kill us?"

"I don't think so."

"How do you know?"

Cass glanced at Patience, who was standing in the stream. " 'Cause they're never around when you need them."

Patience's lips curved into a smile as she busied herself helping Corliss and the girls with the wash. It was Sunday, a day of rest—if washing, cooking, and standing guard over the camp while the men went hunting could be considered rest.

The night before, they had been fortunate enough to have found a grove of tall pines next to a clear-running stream, and they'd made camp. After Bible study, the children wandered off to fish and swim, enjoying their reprieve from the rigors of the trail. Actually they'd made good time, considering the obstacles a group of their size was confronted with daily.

Patience's smile grew as she recalled the wide berth she and Cass had given each other. The others knew something was wrong, but no one had any idea what it could be.

Corliss and Harlon noticed the animosity between Cass and her, but they were polite enough to ignore it. Patience knew Harlon was too relieved to hear that Cass had agreed to travel with them to ever question why.

At least one thing was going right. Patience

had been relieved to see the children take to Cass right away. Sometimes she worried that he might lose his temper with them, but she thought he'd shown a surprising amount of forbearance for their constant chatter and endless curiosity.

Aaron and Payne were clearly in awe of this man who seemed to know everything, and they were never far from Cass's side.

Phebia was the only one who still held herself at a distance. Although Cass had made several attempts to win her trust, she was still skeptical when it came to the tall, dark stranger who had come so suddenly into their lives.

But all in all, the days were beginning to settle into a routine, and Patience was thankful. She was beginning to think that her worries were groundless, that the trip might be made without incident.

She pretended to be unusually absorbed in her work as she listened to the conversation taking place a few feet from her.

"Bryon, leave my gun alone."

Bryon's inquisitive fingers had persistently crept over to explore the shiny Colt revolver Cass wore strapped to his right leg. The weapon was an enduring source of interest to the boys, who were familiar only with the old-fashioned muzzle-loading rifle Harlon kept in the wagon for protection.

Moments later Patience heard Cass warn

Bryon again as the child's curious fingers began to creep in the direction of the pistol.

Even Doog and Jesse were eyeing the weapon with a determined look in their eyes.

"Can't you see Cass is trying to sleep?" Payne admonished the smaller boys. He was leaning against the trunk of a tree whittling a new whistle for Joseph. "Why don't you go find something to do?"

"Don't want to," Bryon said disagreeably.

"Then let's take a nap," Aaron threatened. He wanted to sleep too, but the younger children were making it impossible.

"Don't want to!"

Four-year-old Joseph walked up and straddled Cass's chest. "Don't want to either!" he joined in adamantly.

Satisfied that no one was going to get any sleep, Cass sighed as he sat up and lifted Joseph from his chest.

Corliss raised her head and admonished sharply, "You children, git! Let Mr. Claxton rest!"

"It's all right, Corliss. I promised Harlon I'd help him fix the broken harness," Cass said.

"Now that you're awake, will you show us your gun?" Bryon persisted.

Patience had to turn her head to keep from laughing aloud.

Even Margaret and Lucy glanced up when

they saw that Cass was going to oblige. Dropping articles of clothing they'd been scrubbing, they scampered quickly from the stream as the shiny gun came out of its holster.

Cass squatted down on his haunches as the children gathered around him. Only Phebia, clutching her doll, chose to stand to one side and watch instead.

"A gun can either save your life or take it," Cass began. "You have to learn to respect whatever kind you decide to carry. This particular pistol is what they call a percussion revolver." He checked to make sure the cylinder was empty before he passed it to Aaron.

The young man's hands trembled with excitement as he examined the weapon closely.

"The fascinating thing about a percussion revolver is its fire power. Like a breech-loading weapon, a revolver can be loaded and fired rapidly. You can place six shots in the cylinder of a percussion firearm and fire it in a matter of seconds. That's quite an improvement over the time it take to fill the chamber of a muzzle loader with powder and ball and cap it," Cass explained.

Doog, Jesse, and Bryon pushed closer, eager for their turn to hold the gun.

Aaron reluctantly passed the pistol to Payne for his inspection.

"But Mr. Claxton," Margaret Ann said primly, "isn't that dangerous?"

Cass flashed a crooked grin at her. "Yes, but like anything else, you have to take the bad with the good. There's a possibility of the revolver discharging several chambers at once. The flashback of hot powder and gases from the gap of the barrel and cylinder could seriously injure a man."

Lucy flinched and moved closer to Cass, draping her arm protectively around his neck. "Throw it away," she insisted. "Me don't want you hurt! I wove you!"

Patience wasn't surprised to hear Lucy's flourishing declaration of love. Clearly she'd been enamored of Cass from the moment he'd joined them.

"*I* don't want you to be hurt. I *love* you," Patience said absently, correcting the child's diction as she wrung out a muslin petticoat.

At the sound of her voice all heads shot up, and the chatter ceased.

Patience glanced up, startled to see that they were all staring at her. She flushed a deep scarlet when she noticed Cass's eyes fixed on the front of her dress. Her color deepened as she wondered exactly how much the wet material revealed of her breasts.

Cass met her disconcerted gaze, and his eyes danced devilishly as he recognized her discomfiture. Then she realized the cad was amused by her innocent blunder! They'd mistaken her statement for a declaration, not a simple correction.

Even Corliss had misunderstood. She stood gaping at Patience, long johns dripping a wet path down the front of her dress as she wondered if her hearing was failing her. It was the first time she'd heard Patience say one decent word to the man!

"Land sakes! You all know what I meant," Patience snapped before she dropped her head sheepishly and returned to scrubbing the collar of Harlon's flannel shirt.

The children's attention returned to the pistol, but Patience's unsettled feeling lingered. She noticed that though Cass continued to talk to the children, his eyes repeatedly strayed to the front of her dress.

Other than the fact that he was a man, she could find no other reason to explain his sudden preoccupation with her bosom. He had certainly given no prior indication that he'd noticed her except as a major annoyance to be painfully endured, yet the way he was looking at her now . . .

She ignored the tingling sensation at the bottom of her stomach but grimly conceded that, try as she may, she was finding it increasingly hard to ignore the fact that he was an exceptionally attractive man.

Patience wasn't aware of just how serious the attraction had grown until she stepped out of the wagon a couple of mornings later and saw him stripped to the waist, shaving.

She stood in the shadow of the canvas, staring at him as he lifted his chin, eyed himself in the small mirror tacked to the tree, and drew the straight-edged razor across his cheekbone.

The sight of his bare chest covered with a mat of curly, light brown hair caused her mouth to turn dry.

Other than her father's, Patience had never seen a man's chest—and most assuredly Leviticus McCord's chest had been nothing like the one she now found herself staring at.

She shook away the disturbing comparison, ashamed of herself. She should be about her work, not ogling the man, but her eyes refused to budge from the tight ridge of muscles that rippled along his arms when he leaned closer to the mirror to carefully shave his upper lip and then around the long, dark sideburns.

How many women had been held against that chest, and how many had explored those ridges of steel-banded muscles at leisure? Patience found herself wondering. The lovely French girl, Laure Revuneau, popped unexpectedly into her mind, and Patience felt a stirring that was very close to jealousy as she wondered how many times Laure had been held in Cass's arms and been adored and caressed by him . . .

Patience was startled to find that the question both intrigued and annoyed her, and she hurriedly forced her feet into motion.

It didn't matter how many women had been in her husband's life. He'd made it clear to Patience that *she* would never be one of them, no matter how badly she was beginning to wish that she'd started out on a better footing with him.

Patience walked around the wagon, pretending not to notice him as she filled the coffee pot and swung it over the fire.

Corliss appeared, and they exchanged greetings. Corliss started flapping the skirt of her apron and making clucking noises as she gathered the six white chickens, five hens, and one rooster that she released from the chicken coop each night. The chickens seemed to sense when it was time to move on, and they flew up into the portable coop at the sound of her voice.

Giving both women a perfunctory glance, Cass said good morning as Phebia came around the corner, dragging Marybelle by her heels.

"Poor Marybelle's going to have a knot on her head," Cass observed as Phebia came to a halt beside him. She stood staring up at his imposing height silently.

Cass finished shaving and reached for a towel to wipe the stray remnants of shaving cream from his face. Reaching for his comb, he noticed Phebia still staring at him.

"Something I can do for you this morning, Miss Phebia?" Patience was amazed at the way he handled the child's continuing reticence, allowing her ample time to warm to him. He would make a wonderful father, she realized, and was surprised by her observation. A few months ago she wouldn't have wished him on her worst enemy, let alone an innocent child.

Phebia remained silent, but a few moments later Patience saw her tug at Cass's trouser leg.

He glanced down, and Phebia cautiously extended the rag doll up to him. After a brief examination, Cass discovered that Marybelle was missing an eye.

He reached for his shirt, slipped it on, and acknowledged soberly, "Well, this looks serious."

Motioning for Patience, who had been listening to the exchange while she'd dropped slabs of bacon into a large iron skillet, he ordered briskly, "Nurse, prepare to operate."

Playing along with his theatrical manner, Patience dramatically passed the fork to Corliss and went to the wagon to fetch her sewing box.

Moments later Marybelle lay on a large, flat rock, her one remaining eye staring sightlessly up at the three onlookers.

A new button that almost matched the old one was hastily located, and Nurse McCord set about her work. Phebia watched with round eyes as Patience's nimble fingers worked the thread in and out of Marybelle's tender cotton face, proving without a doubt to be a true angel of mercy as her skilled hands efficiently provided a new eye for Marybelle.

After the operation was completed, the patient was resting comfortably—though with one green and one blue eye.

But to Phebia she was as beautiful as ever. Even before Patience could pronounce the patient fit, Phebia had already scooped the doll into her arms and begun squeezing her tightly.

Cass reached for his hat and adjusted it on his head as he smiled down at the elfin three-year-old. "You know, Phebia, if you carry Marybelle in your arms instead of letting her face drag on the ground, she'll be likely to keep her eyes longer."

Phebia started to skip happily away when she suddenly paused and turned around. Slowly she walked back to where Cass was standing. Crooking one finger, she motioned for him to lean down.

Thinking she was about to reward him for saving Marybelle's eyesight, he obligingly crouched to her level, where the child's brown eyes somberly met his blue ones.

Suddenly her forefinger and thumb darted out and clamped onto his nose like a vise and twisted. Cass teetered backward as he felt a rush of scalding tears flood his vision.

"Phebia!" Patience dropped her sewing basket and bolted forward to break the child's hold.

Her fingers wrestled with the child's to break her steely grip as Cass wobbled back and forth, trying to retain his balance.

Finally Phebia gave his nose one final jerk, then calmly released it, stuck her thumb in her mouth, and skipped away to join the other children.

Cass fell backward onto the ground and lay prostrate for a moment. He had fought with men the size of giants and had come out in better shape. He looked up to find Patience standing over him, grinning.

"What in the hell is so funny? That kid nearly took my nose off!"

"I think that's Phebia's way of saying she accepts you," she offered.

"Accepts me!" His fingers moved to check his smarting nose for broken cartilage. "I'll have to blow my nose out of my ear from now on. She's maimed me for life!"

Patience extended her hand to Cass. He grasped it and she pulled him to his feet, trying to ignore the way her heart jumped when their hands touched.

"You know something?" he asked, irritably slapping the dust from his pants with his hat.

Patience had to work hard to keep a sober face. His nose was fairly glowing. "What?" she replied, wondering if his eyes had always been that blue. They were beautifully expressive, even though what they were expressing at the moment was an anger that could make him spit nails.

"That kid reminds me of you!"

The comparison hit her the wrong way. Patience whirled and started back to the fire to help Corliss with breakfast. She wasn't about to pursue that remark because no matter *what* she did, he managed to find fault with her. Even though she'd gone out of her way to be nice to him lately, he hadn't bothered to say one kind word to her. His attitude was beginning to hurt her feelings.

"Don't walk away from me while I'm talking!"

"When you say something worth hearing, I'll listen," she tossed back over her shoulder.

"Women!" Cass muttered to himself as he watched her stalk angrily toward the wagon. He rubbed his throbbing nose dourly. At least he was thankful that Phebia had picked a less sensitive spot to pound than Patience had those many years ago.

His eyes inadvertently focused on the gentle sway of Patience's hips, and he was shocked to feel a faint stirring in his loins. The image of her at the stream, and her small, firm breasts revealed through the bodice of her wet dress came rushing back to agonize him further.

Damn! That was all he needed! It wasn't enough that she'd thrust the responsibility of nine children and two old people on him. Now all of a sudden *she* was beginning to look good to him!

Resettling his hat on his head, he walked to his horse and began saddling it.

His eyes strayed back to camp where Patience was bending over the fire, stirring eggs. Had she always been that good-looking, or was he just getting desperate for a woman's company?

Giving the cinch a hard jerk, Cass decided that it had to be the latter. Or at least he prayed that it was. Surely the Lord knew he'd had enough troubles.

9

Unfortunately, trouble continued to plagued Cass the next morning. He had reluctantly agreed to keep an eye on the child while Patience, Corliss, and the other children went to gather the last of the wild berries.

While he shaved, Phebia played with Marybelle around his feet. He had to sidestep twice before he could convince her that she should go feed Marybelle a late breakfast and get out of his way.

To his relief, the child bought the idea and raced to get a biscuit from the supply box. She sat on a nearby rock, taking intermittent bites, then squashing crumbs into Marybelle's unyielding mouth as Cass finished his shaving in peace.

As he was wiping soap from his face, he heard Phebia let out a scream that raised the hairs on the back of his neck.

He whirled. "What's wrong?"

"Caw-doo. Me want caw-doo."

Cass stared back at her blankly. "Caw-doo?"

She nodded succinctly.

"Caw-doo, caw-doo," Cass murmured as he glanced around the camp, wondering what in the hell *caw-doo* meant.

"Caw-doo!" Phebia demanded, her tone becoming more belligerent.

"Caw-doo . . ." Cass was getting frantic. A thought came to him, and his heart nearly stopped. Kneeling beside the rock where Phebia sat perched, he whispered hesitantly, "Did you do something in your britches?"

Lord, he hoped that wasn't it. He'd never had to deal with something like that before, and he wasn't sure he could.

Her eyes narrowed, and her face puffed with indignation as she shook her head and cried again. "Caw-doo!"

"Okay. Caw-doo." Relieved, Cass starting grabbing anything in sight, trying to figure out what she wanted.

He held up her bonnet.

She shook her head no.

He held up the remainder of the biscuit she'd been eating.

"No!"

A bar of soap.

"No!"

A towel.

"No! Caw-doo!"

"Why don't you sit there and suck your thumb until Patience gets back?" he said, knowing that he shouldn't be encouraging her to continue a habit that they'd all been trying to help her break, but he was stumped.

Phebia stood up and stamped her foot authoritatively, clearly outraged by his stupidity. "Caw-doo!"

Cass could feel the sweat beginning to trickle down his back.

After several more futile attempts, he finally sat down on the rock beside her, admitting defeat. "Phebia, I'm sorry, but I just don't know what you want."

He glanced up, relieved to see Aaron returning with a bucket mounded with berries.

"Hi."

"Aaron, what in the hell does *caw-doo* mean?" Cass asked wearily.

"Water."

Cass looked up, startled. "Water?"

"That's what she calls water." Aaron grinned at Phebia. "You want a drink of water, squirt?"

Phebia nodded eagerly. "Me want caw-doo!"

Cass watched as Aaron led her to the bucket and reached for the dipper.

Caw-doo, he thought irritably. Damn! He could have sworn that it would be something a child would step in, not drink.

❁ ❁ ❁

A new, more disturbing kind of trouble arrived as four men came riding into camp around dusk the following evening.

It was a small party of buffalo hunters: one hunter, two skinners, and a cook. Their red wool shirts were dirty; their corduroy breeches stained; and the high Western boots they were wearing hadn't seen a coat of polish in years.

Corliss and Patience, happy to welcome company, cordially invited the men to stay for supper.

The hunters accepted their gracious offer and went about settling their stock for the night.

Had Cass been in camp, he would have sent the raw-boned buckskinners on their way. He felt nothing but contempt toward buffalo hunters.

The unscrupulous white hunters could present the first real threat to the group traveling by wagon. If there were Indians in the area, the sight of the hunters would be sure to provoke their fury, so when Cass, Aaron, and Payne rode in from hunting that night, Cass was none too happy to discover the four unwashed strangers in their midst.

"Patience, I want a word with you!" Cass ordered as he swung from his horse and handed the reins to Aaron.

He acknowledged the visitors' presence with a cool nod as he strode through the camp.

Patience rolled her eyes. Wiping her hands on her apron, she whispered to Corliss dryly, "The king has bellowed again."

Corliss chuckled. She was concerned and yet amused by the couple's open hostility toward each other. She and Harlon discussed the strange alliance nearly every night. Although they had no idea what was causing the couple to behave with such animosity toward each other, it was evident to them that Patience was attracted to Cass Claxton and that Cass was attracted to Patience. However, they had agreed that these young people were so mulish that they'd go to their graves before either of them would admit it.

Corliss knew that Harlon was beginning to fret about the growing stand-off between Patience and Cass. He'd taken an instant liking to the handsome young man who was deftly leading the group to its destination. More than once, he'd confessed that he hoped Cass might take a shine to Patience.

Corliss remembered Harlon's remark last night: "I just don't understand them, Corliss." He'd been brooding over the young couple while he was getting ready for bed. "Cass ought to be drawn to Patience like a magnet. She's pretty and smart, and I've never met a woman with a kinder heart. But instead of being attracted to each other, they both turn tail and run in opposite directions when one of them sees the other one coming."

"It's worrisome," Corliss had admitted. "They'd make a mighty fine couple. He's handsome, and she's as comely as a fairy-tale princess—and decent too. That little gal has worked hard to keep those children together. I tell you, Harlon, Cass Claxton could do worse than take Patience McCord as his wife."

A smile touched Corliss's lips as she remembered the way Harlon's faded eyes, for just the briefest of moments, had held a rejuvenated sparkle. "You know, Mama, her determination and zest for life puts me a whole lot in mind of you when you were her age."

Corliss found her face growing rosy at the way he'd looked at her. She hadn't seen that look in his eyes for a long time. "Oh, go on, now—I was never that pretty," she'd scoffed.

"You were," Harlon insisted. He gave her a jaunty wink that made her cheeks turn even brighter. "And you still are. Why, if it weren't for me being so bone-weary, I'd just prove it to you!"

Corliss knew that would be unlikely, but the thought was nice.

"My, my, aren't we feisty tonight?" Corliss said as she'd turned down the sheets and prepared to climb onto the feather mattress. His light-hearted banter had made her feel giddy—almost young again.

Harlon stood and stripped off his pants before climbing between the cool linens next to her.

"I hate to say it, but I've about come to the conclusion that it's Patience's age that's scaring Cass away." He'd removed his spectacles, folded them, and laid them on the floor of the wagon beside the bed. "She's in her twenties, you know, and the bloom has gone out of most women's cheeks by that age. Most are married by then and have children of their own. While Patience is still as pretty as a rose petal in the mornin' dew, I think her age is what's got Cass a little bit skittish."

"Could be," Corliss had acknowledged before yawning sleepily. "And her spunk might be worryin' him. I think it has him feelin' a mite cornered at times."

Harlon chuckled. "Yes, Patience's 'spunk' has had Cass more than cornered a couple of times."

They had lain quietly in the darkness, listening to nature's restful symphony outside the wagon. A smile tugged at the corners of Corliss's mouth as she recalled the days Harlon had courted her.

Those had been happy days, exciting days. 'Twas a real shame Patience couldn't experience that same joy, she mused. Lord knew, if anyone deserved happiness, Patience did. Corliss didn't know Cass well, but he seemed to her to be a decent sort of man. He was polite, always complimenting her after each meal, and doing more than his share of the work so that Harlon wouldn't have to overdo.

She concluded that it was just a shame that two such fine people were spitting at each other like two Tom cats sitting on each other's tail.

Corliss's attention returned to the present as she heard Cass impatiently shout for Patience again.

"Better go see what he wants," Corliss encouraged. "Margaret Ann and I will see to the biscuits."

"It better be important," Patience muttered under her breath as she handed the spoon to Margaret.

She found Cass preparing to wash for supper. He'd stripped his shirt off, causing her another flash of momentary distress.

Why his bare chest should fascinate her she wasn't sure. She just knew that it did so increasingly.

"Don't you ever keep your clothes on?" she snapped.

He glanced up. "Who stepped on your tail?"

"No one stepped on my tail . . . I'm just concerned that the girls may see you this way."

He lifted a brow inquisitively. "Is that the reason for your concern, or does it fluster *you* to see me without a shirt, Miss McCord?"

"The name is *Mrs.* Claxton," she reminded in a carefully controlled tone, just in case he'd forgotten that she still had the upper hand, "and of course it doesn't 'fluster' me to see you without your shirt. I've seen jackasses without saddles before."

For a moment she thought she saw a hint of a smile involuntarily tug at the corners of his mouth, but then he turned away and began pouring water into the enamel washbasin. "I see you're in another one of your aggravating moods."

"Did you want me?" she said curtly. He had no right to ride into camp and bellow out for her as if she were his handmaiden.

"Afraid not, but it looks like I have you anyway." He glanced up as he reached for the bar of soap, unperturbed by her waspish disposition.

Patience could see the tight play of muscles in his forearms as he began to work up a thick lather. "I don't have time to play games. What do you want?"

"I see we have company."

"Then apparently there's nothing wrong with your eyesight."

He leaned over and scrubbed his face and neck with the white lather as he continued. "Do you know who those men are?"

Patience wasn't sure if it was disapproval or mere curiosity she was hearing. Her eyes traveled the width of his broad shoulders and lingered there.

"No . . . I mean, I assume they are four weary travelers who'll appreciate a hot meal and a bit of pleasant conversation."

Cass rinsed off his face and neck and reached for the towel. He rubbed the cloth over his face, eyeing her dispassionately. "Well, you assume wrong."

She found her gaze unwilling to leave his bare torso. There were tiny droplets of water interspersed throughout the cloud of light brown hair splayed across his chest. A thin line of the same hair ran down toward his trousers and disappeared into—

Patience caught her shameless reflections as her gaze dropped sheepishly to study her clasped hands. "Then who are they?"

Without taking his eyes from her, Cass reached for a clean shirt and slipped it on. "They're buffalo hunters."

Her gaze lifted back to meet his. The revelation meant nothing to her. "So?"

He finished buttoning the shirt, and with his eyes still firmly fixed to hers, casually unbuckled his belt. He made no attempt either to divert her attention or attract it as he loosened his pants and begin to tuck his shirttail into the heavy denim.

She was appalled to discover that his actions not only brought a disquieting lurch at the bottom of her stomach but caused her to grow uncomfortably warm.

"So," he mimicked softly, "by inviting those particular men to supper, we're now likely to attract the attention of every redskin within a fifty-mile radius."

Why was her heart suddenly hammering in her throat, she thought wildly, barely hearing his answer. He would surely see her reaction to his blatant maleness, and wouldn't that give him a good laugh, she agonized. Patience McCord practically swooning over him!

She could feel the color flooding her cheeks. "I'm . . . sorry . . . I didn't know . . ."

It occurred to her that he might be deliberately amusing himself. He knew what she was thinking, and he was taking delight in her wantonness! Yet nothing in his gaze indicated such deliberate cruelty. On the contrary, if Patience hadn't known better, she would have sworn that he was looking at her with the same undeniable interest that she felt toward him.

For an electrifying moment blue eyes seared

deeply into violet ones, and Patience was aware of nothing more than his overpowering presence and the uneven cadence of her breathing.

Then, as if they simultaneously realized what was happening, their gazes split from each other. Cass reached for his hat as Patience eased to a safer distance on the far side of the makeshift washstand.

The incident left her puzzled and shaken. She found it hard to concentrate as Cass picked up the conversation in a tone that made her wonder if the events of the past few minutes had touched him at all.

"The harm is already done," he said. "We just have to hope there isn't a scouting party on these hunters' tails."

"Why would Indians follow them?" Patience was confused.

"Because they hate them. Unlike the Indian, who kills the buffalo for his own survival, the white man kills for business and pleasure." He picked up his gun belt and buckled it around his waist as he talked. "The Indians depend on the buffalo to supply medicine, cooking utensils, blankets, garments, boats, ropes, and even their tents. They use the sinews to make bowstrings and thread for sewing. Shoulder bones are used as hoes, and rib bones serve as sled runners. Even the animal's hooves are boiled down for glue. After the tribe has enjoyed the fresh meat of the kill, the women cut the meat into strips and hang them on racks to dry in the hot sun."

"To make jerky?"

"That's right, jerky. Later they pound it into powder and make pemmican, which will keep for years. Although there's still an abundance of buffalo roaming the plains, every buffalo killed is a direct threat to the Indians' existence. The white man's irresponsible slaughter continues to drive the herds farther afield, and I've heard some predict that the time isn't far off when the vast herds roaming the land will be only a memory."

"That seems impossible," Patience mused. "I've heard my father tell stories of seeing thousands of buffalo as they traveled across the plains."

Cass shrugged. "I'm sure that's true, but that will change. If the white man continues to kill buffalo for personal gain, how many will be left in ten, twenty years? Trust me, the Indian will do everything in his power to kill the men who threaten his survival."

"So if the Indians discover that we befriended the hunters, then our lives may be in danger?"

Absently he dusted his hat against the side of his legs. "No 'may be' about it. Our lives are in danger."

"Oh, Cass . . . I'm sorry. Corliss and I were just trying to be neighborly when we invited the hunters to stay for supper."

"Patience, I want you to listen to me." His tone was firmer than she'd ever heard it. "There's another danger I want you to be aware of. By their appearance, I figure these men have been on the trail for a while. My guess is they've been on a hunt somewhere in Kansas, Colorado, or Oklahoma, and they're on their way home. Now, I want you to heed what I'm about to say: A beautiful woman will be hard for them to ignore." His eyes locked with hers gravely. "I want you to go out of your way to avoid any personal contact with these men. Serve supper, then disappear and let Corliss and the girls clean up."

"All right." Her pulse fluttered at his admission that he found her attractive. Did he really think she was beautiful?

"With a little luck, those men will be on their way in the morning, and nothing will come of your misplaced hospitality. I've seen signs of a small wagon train ahead of us, four, maybe five, wagons traveling together. To be on the safe side, I think we'd be smart to catch up and travel with them for a few days."

"What about the Indians?"

"You let me worry about the Indians. You just do what I say and leave immediately after the meal. I don't want to have to save your hide if one of those men decides to haul your little fanny off for a romp in the woods."

Though he sensed that she was smart enough

to see the wisdom of his advice, Cass waited for her chin to lift with her usual show of rebellion.

He didn't have to wait long.

"You sound as if you care what happens to my 'little fanny.' "

"*Your* little fanny?" He threw his head back and laughed. Patience gritted her teeth in an attempt to control her temper. She was trying hard to show him that she was not the same irresponsible, headstrong girl she'd been six years ago, but at times this man simply pushed her too far.

"Honey, if I were interested in lookin' for a fanny, I'd find me a sweet-talking woman," he assured her.

"Like Laure Revuneau?"

His sly grin spoke louder than words. "Like Laure. Now, there's a fine woman."

"Are you going to marry this fine woman?"

To her gratification, the question momentarily stilled him. "You didn't answer my question."

He tipped his head subserviently. "How could I marry anyone, my lovely, when it seems I am already encumbered by a previous commitment?"

"Well, you don't have to worry about me," she snapped. "I can take care of myself."

"I'm not worried. Even if a man in a moment of lunacy took a wild fancy to you and dragged you away, you wouldn't be gone long. After he spent a few hours in your company he'd be hauling you back so fast it'd make your head swim."

"Is that so?" She could feel herself slipping, but Cass was infuriating her. Squaring her shoulders, she made sure his eyes could easily detect the ripe fullness of her breasts. While she wasn't as well endowed as some, the good Lord had provided ample ammunition to back up her next volley.

"Well, how would you know what a *man* would do with me, Mr. Claxton?"

Unperturbed, Cass's eyes traveled lazily over the bait she was offering. Not that he hadn't noticed her charms before—he had. And he had to admit she wasn't all that bad. But he wasn't about to let her know it.

"Well?" she demanded. She had waited long enough. She knew he couldn't deny that she was a full-grown woman, and she wanted the satisfaction of hearing him say it.

"Well"—his gaze moved over her dispassionately—"is there something in particular that I'm supposed to find impressive?"

Her eyes narrowed warningly.

"Oh . . . I'm supposed to notice that you've . . . developed?"

"That's right. You might notice that I've grown up in the past six years."

"Is that a fact?" He took a step backward as she took a step forward. Indeed she had blossomed from what he'd remembered. He grew uneasy as he felt the first stirrings of longing.

"That's a fact," she confirmed.

Patience knew her Aunt Merriweather was probably rolling over in her grave by now, but she was determined to prove her point. Cass was the only man who had ever dared to ignore her. Men had been known to fawn over her and shower her with extravagant compliments to snare her attention. They had begged for her hand in marriage, but she had blithely broken their hearts. She had never met a man who matched her in spirit, with maybe the exception of this man, and *he* wouldn't even concede that she was a woman!

"Tell me, Mr. Claxton," she said, arching her back and tilting her breasts higher to attract his gaze. "Exactly in what way do you find them lacking?"

"Since I hadn't noticed 'them' before, and I'm certainly not interested in 'them' now, why are we going to all this bother?" he asked mildly.

Their gazes met in a defiant deadlock. "Are you saying you're *flustered* by them, Mr. Claxton?" she challenged.

"Only by the fact that 'they' are in my way and 'they' are delaying my supper."

Determined to beat him at his game, she edged closer. "Most men would be curious to know how well their wives are endowed," she dared. "But, then, maybe you're not a man."

He eased back a step, but their bodies were touching, and the objects of contention were pressed firmly against the front of his shirt.

"I don't have a wife," he stated calmly.

"Legally you do. But even if you didn't, you're surely man enough to at least be curious."

"But, Miss McCord," he reminded softly, "only moments ago there seemed to be doubt in your mind that I am a man."

"Mr. Claxton, you haven't shown any proof to the contrary." Her heart was fluttering and her legs were threatening to buckle, but she wasn't going to back down from him.

He smelled of soap and water and leather, and he was heart-stoppingly male. Why was she provoking him this way, she asked herself. Why wasn't she trying discreetly to catch his eye instead of trying blatantly to knock it out?

"Well, now, is that what all this is about?" Calmly he removed his hat and laid it on the washstand.

Her eyes widened as he turned and captured her breasts in his hands, exploring the soft mounds with breathtakingly slow strokes.

"You needin' a man, Miss McCord?" he murmured. His arrogance seared her, but she was mesmerized by the cobalt blue of his eyes.

He drew her closer but warned himself to go

easy. This was only a game, one that he knew could quickly get out of hand. Though she rankled him, she was all woman—and he had been without the pleasures of one for weeks now.

"Let's just see how much woman you are, Patience McCord." His mouth lowered to graze hers softly. Her mouth tasted sweet and heady, and he had to remind himself that the purpose of this experiment was to teach her a lesson.

Patience's voice caught in her throat. The touch of his mouth sent fire racing through her veins. She could feel herself growing lightheaded and giddy. How long was she going to let this go on? And why had she taunted him, she thought frantically. He was not the sort of man who would permit such affronts to his manhood without turning the tables—she should have known that!

Cass felt her body go limp against his, and the sudden realization that she was not immune to his caress sent a feeling of masculine pride through him. He jerked her closer, surprised to discover how tiny she was. She felt exquisite and delicate pressed tightly against his large frame.

Willing to let her feel the unexpected effect she was having on him, he settled her closer between his legs, ignoring her murmur of protest. With a proficiency she found appalling, he slowly began to undo the buttons of her dress, one by one.

"If we're wantin' to consummate our vows,

honey, don't you think we should find a little privacy?"

Gasping, she jerked away, her eyes flashing angrily. "You brute! *What* do you think you're doing!"

He stared back at her guilelessly. "Why . . . isn't this what you wanted? I'm only tryin' to keep my little wife happy."

"You're disgusting!" She spat out the words contemptuously. Her fingers were trembling so badly that she could hardly work the tiny buttons back into place. "We were talking about those *hunters* abducting me!"

"Oh, yes." His gaze lightly caressed her breasts. "Well, rest assured, Miss McCord, I have no interest in anything you might have. If one of those hunters should threaten you, I'll just be keeping my end of the bargain if I'm forced to rescue you. You do recall the bargain? I'm to escort you to Cherry Grove safely, and you'll hand me those annulment papers." He reached out and tweaked her cheek mockingly as she turned her face away.

"Miserable polecat!" she flung back angrily, forgetting all about the attraction she'd felt toward him just moments earlier.

He flashed her an exasperating grin. "What happened? I thought I was a weasel."

"Polecat is just one name for your miserable species!"

She whirled and nearly stumbled into Margaret Ann, who had silently approached the warring couple.

"What is it, Margaret Ann?" she demanded in a shaky voice.

"Corliss said to tell you supper's ready."

Shooting Cass a nasty glance, Patience picked up her skirt and marched away.

Cass was not as unscathed by the encounter as he would have hoped. His eyes followed her shapely form as she walked back to camp. He could still taste her on his lips, and he had a feeling that sleep wasn't going to come easily tonight.

"You comin', Mr. Claxton?"

"I'll be along in a minute, Margaret Ann," he said absently, reaching into his pocket for a smoke. A frown deepened across his forehead as he cupped his trembling hand against the breeze and lit the cheroot.

Leaning against a tree, he waited for the unexpected reaction Patience had caused in him to subside before he joined the others for supper.

He tried to sort out the confusion of feelings she stirred in him and decided the idea of a man carrying Patience off might not be so far-fetched.

She wasn't so bad. Actually, she'd developed into a good-looking woman.

He took another drag off the cigar. Too damned good-looking.

❁ ❁ ❁

After supper the children gathered around the hunters' wagon, where gazing at .45 Sharps rifles, along with Winchesters, Remingtons, and Springfield trapdoor models held them spellbound.

Payne picked up one of the more than fifty Green River and Wilson skinning knives lying in the bed of the wagon and turned it over in his hands reverently. The wagon contained too many bull, calf, and cow hides to count.

"You say you've been in Colorado?" Harlon asked as he sat down next to the fire to light his pipe. He could hear the old cook begin to recite the tall, adventurous buffalo tales that were designed to make the children's eyes grow round with wonder.

"Yep, up near the border," Hoyt Willis replied as he stretched his long legs out before him and propped his head back on the seat of his saddle. His stomach was full, and he'd removed his boots for the first time in a week.

"I'd figure, with fall right around the corner, you'd be wanting to stay longer." Harlon assumed the hunters would follow the Indians' custom of hunting buffalo in September when the cows were fat and their wool the thickest.

"We'll be back once we've had time to visit our families and collect our money for the hides."

"You independent or working for someone?"

"Independent."

"Got a wife?" Harlon asked.

"A wife and ten young 'uns just waitin' for their papa to get home."

Harlon, who judged the hunter to be close to forty, thought the man stank something terrible. His shirt was saturated with animal blood and pieces of flesh where he'd wiped the skinning knife. His body was filthy, and his beard appeared to be matted to his face. Harlon hoped this man was thoughtful enough to take a bath and change his clothes before he saw his family again.

The night sounds closed in around them as the two men relaxed. The fire popped as a piece of wood burned through, sending a shower of sparks flying.

Hoyt's thoughts wandered to Patience McCord. He'd been disappointed that she'd upped and disappeared right after supper. His eyes hadn't left her all night as she'd moved around, ladling out stew and slicing corn bread.

Her waist was so tiny that Hoyt knew he could span it with both hands, and the thought of her in his bedroll brought a powerful surge to his groin.

The time he'd spent in a local thirst parlor in Hayes a few weeks ago suddenly seemed a long time ago. The measly couple of hours—and five dollars he'd paid for a crib woman in a curtained box in the back of the room—had barely slaked his hunger.

Images of the blond beauty with the violet eyes who'd darted curious looks at him during the evening meal rose to taunt him again. He could feel the tension in his body begin to build.

Damned if he wouldn't like to have her alone for a couple of hours.

"Where did the woman go?" he asked Harlon casually.

"Corliss? Why, I imagine she's getting ready for bed."

"Not your wife. The other one."

"Patience?"

"Yeah, Patience."

Harlon drew on his pipe and noticed it had gone out. "I'm not rightly sure . . . Why?"

"No reason." Hoyt tipped his hat over his eyes. "She and the Claxton man hitched?"

Harlon chuckled. "Nope."

"He seems right protective of her."

"Yes, that's his job."

A slow smile curved the corners of Hoyt's mouth. "She's not married, huh?" The thought sent a surge of anticipation through him. Was she still a virgin, he wondered. He reached to draw a horse blanket over the front of his breeches to cover the incriminating evidence of the path his thoughts had suddenly taken.

"Nope, she's not married."

Hoyt rolled to his side and settled his head more comfortably against the makeshift pillow. "Right nice-looking woman," he commented.

"That she is," Harlon conceded.

"Yessir." Hoyt's mouth curved into a satisfied smile as he settled deeper under the blanket. "Right nice."

10

The hunters cleared out right after breakfast the next morning. Cass was relieved to see their dust. He neither cared for nor trusted the one called Hoyt, for he had a feeling the man could be as mean as sin if he took a notion to be.

Patience was still clearly peeved about the encounter she'd had with Cass the night before. Her anger was simmering barely beneath the surface as she went about breaking camp.

Cass ignored her. He hadn't slept but a couple of hours, and his disposition wasn't the best this morning.

Beau's telegram still worried him, coupled with the fact that he'd had to make two trips to the stream last night just to cool off.

That rotten Patience McCord. He could wring her neck for starting her silly "see how I've bloomed—too bad you can't do anything about it" nonsense.

He vowed he wouldn't allow himself to be caught up in another situation like that, no matter how much she egged him on.

He crouched beside the wagon to check the left front axle as Patience came sailing around the corner carrying a pan of dirty dishwater.

The sight of him with his usual cheroot wedged at a cocky angle in the corner of his mouth set her off again. Determined to avoid another scene with him, she whirled and started off in the opposite direction, but suddenly her footsteps slowed.

Cass was preoccupied with the wheel, unaware that she was even in his vicinity. Pursing her lips, she struggled against the overpowering urge to fling the greasy water at him.

It would serve him right for treating her the way he had last night, she fumed, though she knew if she did, it would be tantamount to waving a red flag at a salivating bull. But he *deserved* every nasty, revolting, repulsive, obnoxious ounce of water in this pan.

Before she fully realized it, she was tiptoeing closer to the wagon. When she was within firing range, she straightened and reared back to take aim. Cass stood up and turned to face her just as the water came soaring out of the pan, headed straight in his direction.

His features went blank momentarily before what she was doing finally registered. His eyes widened in disbelief as he dodged to one side in a vain attempt to avoid the onslaught, but his defensive action came too late.

The dishwater hit its target squarely on the bull's-eye, leaving a trail of soggy bacon rinds dangling limply from the front of his drenched shirt.

Jerking herself upright, Patience could see that he was livid. His cigar sputtered, then sent up a limp trail of smoke from the solid dousing.

"Dammit, Patience!"

She looked at him with round-eyed innocence. "Oh, my, I'm so sorry. I didn't see you."

He spat the soggy cigar onto the ground, then squared his shoulders wryly. "Like hell, you didn't see me! You always throw dishwater on the axle!"

Out of the corner of his eye, he caught sight of a revolting chunk of garbage dangling from his shoulder. He angrily flicked it off.

She smiled smugly. "Well, sometimes I do." She shrugged, ignoring the blistering looks he was sending her way. "Guess we'd better be getting a move on."

She turned as he began peevishly fanning the front of his shirt, mumbling things under his breath she was sure a lady wasn't supposed to hear.

"Sure has started off a fine day so far," she observed offhandedly.

He was still eyeing her with hostile intent as she sauntered away, swinging the empty dishpan in one hand.

❁ ❁ ❁

Around midmorning the wind started to blow. Aaron was driving the team while Corliss rode on the seat next to him. Patience walked behind with the children.

Harlon wasn't feeling well this morning—summer complaint, he thought—so about an hour ago he'd climbed into the back of the wagon to catch a short nap.

Patience kept falling behind to oversee Lucy, Bryon, Joseph, Phebia, and Margaret Ann as they paused to gather armloads of wildflowers that grew wild along the pathway.

Cass rode his horse a good distance behind, keeping a close eye on the group. He'd seen nothing to indicate that Indians were in the area, but he knew that didn't mean they weren't there. Nor was he convinced he had seen the last of the hunters; he had a nagging suspicion that he hadn't. But for now, the small group was moving along smoothly. Any threat of trouble seemed remote for the time being.

As the wind picked up, he found his attention drawn more to Patience's skirt than to anything else. The heavy gusts would snatch up the flimsy cotton and toss it as high as her head, providing Cass with a glimpse of her shapely legs.

He tried, but found he couldn't ignore the recurring flash of bare skin that was as provocative—and as arousing—as any he'd ever seen. Although he hated to admit it, she was beginning to disturb him.

By the time her skirt soared a third time, his temper had risen along with other parts of his anatomy. It was plain he wasn't going to be able to cope with this misery all day.

He nudged his horse's flanks and quickly rode up beside her.

"Why aren't you wearing pantalets?" he asked.

Patience glanced up startled. "What?"

"Where are your pantalets?"

She drew back defensively. "I beg your pardon! What business is it of yours where my pantalets are?"

Truth was, she hadn't had the heart to put them on this morning. Her dress covered her decently, and it was just too hot for anything else. Besides, what she wore or didn't wear was certainly none of his business! The man had his nerve questioning her about her personal attire, she thought, but then, anything that scoundrel said shouldn't shock her anymore.

"Haven't you heard of sewing buckshot in your hem to keep your skirt from flying over your head?" he challenged in a tone that was almost belligerent.

She lifted her chin stubbornly. "No, I haven't heard of sewing buckshot in my skirt to keep it from flying over my head," she mimicked hotly.

"Woman, you're driving me over the edge."

"It wouldn't be a very long journey, now would it—"

Patience suddenly felt herself being scooped off her feet by a pair of incredibly strong arms and placed solidly in the saddle with him.

"*What* do you think you're doing? Put me down this instant!" she demanded as the children stopped walking and began watching the skirmish with wide-eyed fascination.

He had her wedged tightly between himself and the saddle horn. She was straddling the saddle, her skirt riding above her knees now. They were so close she could feel the solid imprint of his maleness pressing against her backbone.

She felt her stomach tighten as the reason for his outrageous actions suddenly dawned on her. The swine! He had been ogling her!

She twisted to confront him. Their faces were inches apart. The familiar smell of soap, leather, and maleness washed over her as she took a deep, self-righteous breath and said in a disgusted rebuke, "You should be *ashamed* of yourself!"

He grinned, aware that she'd guessed his motive, but not in the least disturbed by it. "That will be the day!"

"You . . . you heathen!" She struggled to free herself from the evidence of his blatant masculinity, angry to realize that she was actually thrilled by the effect she was having on him.

"You might as well pipe down," Cass warned. "If you don't have the good sense to keep yourself covered, then I suppose I'll be forced to see that you do."

"What do you mean *covered*! I was covered! I can't help it if your perverted mind—"

"Payne, you'd better see to Jesse and Doog. They're wandering too far ahead," Cass reminded, interrupting her heated tirade as he calmly reined the horse back in the direction he'd come. He gave the horse a little kick, and it trotted off, with Patience still protesting loudly.

"This is an outrage, and I demand you put me down this instant!" she railed.

To her dismay, Cass threw back his head and gave a wicked laugh, nudging the horse to an even faster gait. She gasped indignantly as she felt his hands slip beneath her breasts to steady her, then grow more daring as the soft mounds fell in and out of his palms with the horse's jarring gait.

"How *dare* you!" She struggled to salvage

what little pride he'd left her as he laughed again and pulled her roughly against the front of his protruding breeches.

"Talk about an outrage—just look what you're doing to *me*, Miss McCord!"

"You . . . you barbarian!"

Undaunted, Cass pulled her closer to nuzzle her neck, calmly pointing out, in case she hadn't noticed, who had the upper hand this time.

Her hand shot out to slap his face, but he quickly thwarted the move.

"My, my!" he taunted with a crooked little grin. "I think the lady protests too much!" He drew her even more tightly against his maleness, his tongue beginning to explore the outline of her ear.

To Patience's horror, she felt herself growing limp in his arms. She *hated* what he was doing—or did she love it? The rogue was making her feel giddy and light-headed, and . . . and . . . unusually warm . . .

"You're disgusting!" she spat out, but Cass noticed she was struggling less now. His hands masterfully began roaming all over her body, delighted with her reaction.

"You're not going to pretend you don't enjoy my company," he murmured.

Patience kept her eyes fixed stoically ahead of her. "I don't enjoy it—I hate it!"

"Of course you do," he cooed sympathetically. His fingers lightly brushed the tightening tips of her breasts. "It's your little ol' body that's screaming for mercy," he whispered suggestively.

"Cad!"

"Liar!"

"You're perfectly disgusting, and while you may think you're bothering me, you couldn't be farther from the truth," she maintained loftily.

Lord, she wished he'd keep his hands to himself!

"Ah, my lovely, if you only knew how disgusting I can be!" he murmured, letting his tongue slide exquisitely over the delicate lobe of her ear. Chills ran up her spine, and she vowed she would get even with him for this outrage. His hand traveled lazily down the length of her rib cage as he whispered in low, soothing tones, "I can assure you, you would love every appalling moment in *my* bed!" He heard her soft intake of breath, and he chuckled.

"I want you to put me down!" she gritted through clenched teeth. She was appalled he could get to her this easily.

"Well, anything you say, darling."

Before she knew what was happening, she went sailing off the horse, hitting the ground with a solid thud.

"Cass Claxton!" she wailed.

Cass sat on the horse, grinning. At her!

All of the unexpected commotion caused Corliss to stick her head out of the back of the wagon. "Everything all right back here?"

"Everything's fine, Corliss. Miss McCord just insisted on walking again." Cass tipped his hat at Patience. "Don't tire yourself, darlin'."

Corliss looked blank for a moment, then shrugged and dropped the curtain back in place. She failed to understand what was going on.

Lucy grasped on to Margaret Ann's hand, looking as if she might burst into tears at any moment, as Patience picked herself up out of the dirt and stalked toward the wagon.

"Don't worry, Lucy," Margaret Ann said primly, but she looked a little concerned herself. She draped her arm around the smaller girl maternally. "I'm sure the weasel knows exactly what he's doing."

✿ ✿ ✿

Late that afternoon the wagon topped a rise, and they spotted a small caravan traveling about a mile ahead. Cass was relieved to count five wagons and fifteen to twenty head of cattle in the train.

"I'm going to ride ahead and see if they'd mind if we joined them," Cass told Harlon.

"Seems like the smart thing to do," Harlon agreed. "We'll wait here until we get a proper invite."

Thirty minutes later Cass returned bearing the news that they'd been awaiting: They were welcome to join the wagon train.

That night, six wagons formed the customary pear-shaped corral, the pole of each wagon pointing outward, and the hub of the fore wheel of the next wagon set close to the hind wheel of the wagon just ahead of it. The exact placement of the wagons formed an enclosure large enough to pen the animals belonging to the train. It also provided defense: Indians rarely attacked a train when in corral.

The women of the train quickly formed a comfortable relationship. When the children had been safely tucked in that night, they sat around the fire, stitching handwork and exchanging small talk. The men enjoyed their pipes and cigars while they discussed the weather and how many hostile Indians they were likely to encounter.

It was decided that they probably wouldn't encounter any Indians until they reached Oklahoma. That bit of news relieved Patience because they would be leaving the wagon train when it reached St. Joseph, to veer north to Kansas.

She glanced up from the quilt she was piecing as she heard Cass excuse himself, saying that he was going to turn in early.

Ernest Parker's teenage daughter sprang to her feet to say good night. It was evident from the look in the young beauty's eyes that she'd developed an immediate case of puppy love for the dark, blue-eyed, curly-headed stranger, who promptly rewarded her with a smile guaranteed to melt any woman's heart.

Patience watched Cass's departure with mixed feelings. The events of that afternoon still lingered with her. It made her heartsick to admit that she'd actually enjoyed riding with the brute! The feel of his body pressed tightly against hers, the sensation of muscled thighs holding her firmly in place, masculine hands gripping hers solidly to prevent her from scratching his eyes out—all this had left her feeling unsettled. She had to admit no other man had ever touched her life in quite the same way, making her feel so aware, so vibrantly alive . . . so in need of . . . something.

She'd had to remind herself twice just this evening that she would be three times a fool if she were to let herself fall in love with Cass Claxton. He was a rogue and a rakehell who'd treated her as badly as she'd treated him.

When they reached Cherry Grove and she provided him with the annulment papers, she was certain that that would be the last thing he'd ever want from her, and she was confident she would never see him again.

She recognized he had every reason to want her out of his life, but the realization didn't make her growing feelings for him any easier to bear.

Why did I do the things I did, she silently

agonized. *Why couldn't I have been the perfect lady, one who would have captured his heart instead of his ire*? Now it was too late to hope he would ever see her as anything but the rotten, despicable, strong-willed girl he thought her to be, and in her heart she couldn't blame him.

By an act of defiance and deceit, she still shared his name, but it was a woman like Laure Revuneau who would share his bed and eventually win his heart.

Ernestine Parker's lovesick gaze was not the only one that followed Cass's tall form as he strode toward the wagon tonight.

Patience was ready to admit, at least to herself, that she was falling in love with the very man she'd so foolishly forced to marry her.

And there was nothing she could do to hold it back.

❁ ❁ ❁

The following morning Lucius Waterman's voice rang out a warning: "Steep hill comin' up!" And it ricocheted down the line of wagons.

Patience eased the team to a halt as Cass rode up beside their wagon.

"Better let Aaron take the reins. Looks like there could be trouble," he said.

Patience shaded her eyes from the hot sun with her hand and squinted back at him. "Do you think he can handle the team?"

Aaron was wiry and slight of build, although he insisted he was as strong as two grown men put together.

"He can handle it," Cass affirmed before he rode ahead to assess the hill. It was a bad one, steep, with little room for error. A frown creased his forehead as he tried to determine the safest angle of descent. There didn't seem to be one. Having the wagon fall and smash beyond repair while being windlassed down the steep grade wasn't something he cared to think about.

He returned as Patience climbed down from the wagon. Dismounting, he removed his hat and ran his sleeve over his forehead. "Get the children together and keep them at a safe distance," he said quietly. "Tell Harlon and Corliss they'll have to walk down the hill. I don't want anyone near this wagon except Aaron and me."

Patience's eyes lifted to meet his expectantly. "Is it that bad?"

"It isn't good," he admitted as he adjusted his hat back on his head.

"Then I'll drive."

"I want you to do as I say. Aaron and I will take care of the wagon. You and the children stay back."

Realizing it wouldn't do any good to argue, Patience went in search of the children while Cass took Aaron aside.

She could see the two talking, and her heart

filled with pride. It was almost as if he *were* her husband, instructing their son in a lesson of manhood. A terrible sense of dread began to fill her. If either one of them should be hurt, she didn't think she could bear it.

The train was alive with activity as the women called out to children and men started unloading some of the heavier pieces from the wagons and setting them beside the road.

When two of the women realized they were parting with their family heirlooms, they began crying and begging their husbands for compassion. The men managed to continue though they kept apologizing and assuring their wives that they were only doing what had to be done.

Since Patience and Corliss had brought nothing but the bare necessities, the McCord wagon was ordered to the head of the line.

"Payne, you and Jesse scout around for a full-sized pine tree," Cass instructed as he knelt to check the left front axle. There was even less lubricant in the hub than when he'd checked earlier that morning. "Doog, go tell Patience I need the bottom side of a bacon slab."

"Yessir!" Doog scampered off as Harlon hurried over to help. By the time Doog returned with the requested bacon rind, Harlon and Cass had removed the white oak wheel. Cass took the bacon fat and carefully wrapped it around the hub axle. Moments later the wheel was slipped back into place.

"Think that'll work?" Harlon asked.

"It should."

"Mr. Claxton?" Ernestine Parker stood at Cass's heels, her eyes wide with worry. "You do be careful, you hear?"

Cass winked, sending the poor girl's pulse thumping wildly. "I plan to do just that, Ernestine."

Payne and Jesse returned with the news that they'd found the full-sized pine.

Reaching for the ax, Cass told Payne to grab the long hemp rope lashed to the back of the wagon and follow him. The tree was quickly felled, then fastened to the back of the wagon to serve as a brake.

When he was confident that everything was in order, Cass swung up onto the seat of the wagon beside Aaron. He removed his hat and wiped his forehead on his shirt sleeve. "Well, I can think of things I'd rather be doing."

Aaron swallowed nervously. "Yeah, me too."

Cass turned to face him with a slow grin. He'd formed a real affection for the boy. "I suppose you know all about the birds and the bees?"

Aaron frowned and then grinned sheepishly. It seemed a strange question for a time like this, but he supposed Cass was just trying to make things seem normal. "Well . . . uh . . . there's a couple of things I've been meaning to have you clear up for me."

Cass chuckled ironically. "Son, there's a couple of things I still don't know."

Aaron's grin widened. "Yessir!"

"You've noticed that pretty little Ernestine Parker, haven't you?"

Aaron's Adam's apple bobbed as he flushed a deep red. "Yessir . . . a little."

"A little, huh?"

"Yessir . . . a little."

Cass grinned, deciding the boy was relaxed enough to start. "You about ready to get this wagon down the hill?"

"Yessir!" There was a slight tremble in the young man's voice, but Cass saw that his hands were steady as he picked up the reins.

His eyes locked on Cass with silent admiration. Aaron had never known his father, but if he had, he thought he'd have wanted him to have been exactly like Cass.

"Then let's get this over with so the women can stop their fidgeting."

"Yessir."

"I want you to take it real easy. Keep the reins good and tight, and ease the animals down real slow. The tree will act as a drag, but it's up to you to see that the animals don't get away."

"I can do that, sir."

Cass clasped one of Aaron's thin shoulders confidently. "I know you can."

Cass stepped off the wagon and turned to give a sharp whistle, indicating that they were ready to take the first wagon down. The other members of the train stopped what they were doing and came to watch.

"I'll need a couple of volunteers," Cass called out as he pulled on a pair of leather gloves.

Matt Johnson and Lewis Brown stepped forward. They were young men with strong, sturdy backs.

Glancing around to see where Patience and the children were, Cass found them standing off to the side, looking worried. Patience tried to smile as her eyes sought to convey confidence to Aaron. He was young to have so much responsibility thrust upon his shoulders, she thought sadly.

Aaron could feel sweat trickling down the back of his shirt as he gripped the reins so tightly that his knuckles began to turn white.

"Okay, son, let's—"

"Cass!" Patience suddenly shouted.

Cass glanced up. "What?"

"Please . . . be careful!"

He nodded curtly, surprised that, for a change, she wasn't cheering for him to fall down the hill and be trampled by a herd of longhorn.

"Let 'em roll!" he shouted.

The wheels on the wagon began to turn as Cass, Matt, and Lewis latched onto the rope tied to the tree, letting their weight act as an additional drag.

The crowd of onlookers held its breath as the wagon began to laboriously descend, rattling loudly down the incline. The hill wasn't long, just incredibly steep.

Aaron gripped the reins, keeping his eyes fixed straight ahead. Sweat poured down the sides of his dust-streaked face as he urged the animals in low, soothing tones to take it easy.

The harness creaked and the wagon tongue clanked as the team strained to control the heavy load. Overhead, clouds began to block the sun as a threat of rain sprang up.

Cass watched the clouds, praying that a thunderstorm wouldn't develop before they'd gotten all of the wagons safely down the hill.

Patience held her breath, trying to ignore the tight band of fear suddenly gripping her middle. Her heart was in her throat, and her eyes were riveted on Cass. She could see the muscles in his arms bunching tightly as he strained against the rope, while the weight of the wagon dragged him and the others helplessly down the hillside.

Patience wished she could take his place, that the dangers he was facing could be hers. It wasn't fair that he might be injured . . . or perhaps killed trying to help her.

Suddenly the wagon began to pick up speed, moving faster and faster. The anxious shouts of the men echoed through the countryside as Aaron threw all of his weight against the reins, trying to force the animals to slow down. A fierce gust of wind nearly pulled the canvas off the wagon as the first clap of thunder sounded.

Patience closed her eyes and began to pray aloud in a frenzied litany. "Don't let them be hurt, don't let them be hurt, don't let them be hurt . . ."

The minutes seemed like hours, and the heat closed in around her. She felt light-headed and faint, and the children's excited voices seemed to come to her from far away.

Suddenly a whoop went up, and Patience felt her knees buckle with fear.

"They made it!"

Her eyes flew open. Tears of relief began to stream down her cheeks when she saw that the wagon was safely at the bottom of the hill. She could see Cass, his clothes filthy now, but blessedly safe and sound, calmly untying the rope in preparation for the next wagon.

A flurry of clamoring feet swept her along in their wake as the children rushed down the hill to meet him.

Margaret Ann and Lucy descended like a whirlwind, throwing their arms around his waist, nearly dragging him to the ground in their exuberance.

Aaron hopped from the wagon, his flush of victory and his wide grin assuring the others that he was going to be hard to live with for a while.

Ernestine, who'd been headed for Cass, stopped and blushed prettily when Aaron turned his smile in her direction. He winked, a gesture he'd picked up from watching Cass, and her face turned a deep crimson.

"Was that fun?" Doog prodded Cass eagerly, his eyes conveying his deep longing to be old enough to do such an exciting thing.

"Never had so much fun," Cass teased as he tried to control the girls who jumped around his feet like grasshoppers.

Margaret Ann demanded a hug, then Lucy, then Phebia, and of course, Marybelle. Cass knelt down to good-naturedly oblige the ladies, though he was wary of Phebia's intentions. She still had an unnerving way of latching onto his nose when he least expected it.

Patience breathlessly arrived as Cass finished the hugs and stood up. With a cry of relief, she threw herself into his arms. "Oh, Cass . . . I thought you were going to be killed!"

His arm tightened around her as naturally as if he'd held her a hundred times before. "Why would you think that—"

She prevented him from finishing his sentence

as she grasped the back of his head and hugged him with all her might. For a moment he froze. Then he pulled back as his startled eyes met hers.

Patience hadn't realized what she was going to do. She hadn't planned to reveal the depth of her feelings, but now she realized she was glad she'd done it. And she would die if he cast her aside in front of the children.

Cass's eyes filled with amusement, and a grin started at the corners of his mouth as he recognized the alarm growing in her eyes. "Why, Miss McCord," he challenged softly, "I didn't know you cared."

"I . . . I didn't know either," she confessed.

His amusement disappeared, and the blue of his eyes darkened as he contemplated the meaning of her admission. "Well, well, what do you know about that!"

She held her breath as he looked at her. It was as if he were seeing her for the first time.

Their gazes continued to do silent battle, and she prayed that he would be kind. Her eyes unashamedly issued a plea, one Cass found himself strangely powerless to refuse.

He glanced down at the children and winked; then, gathering her in his arms, he hugged her warmly. "Thank you, Miss McCord. Sure do appreciate your concern," he bantered.

For a moment she was caught by surprise, but then she enjoyed the unexpected. He felt exactly as she thought he would: splendidly male, superbly masculine, exciting, stimulating—wonderful.

She sighed as she stood on tiptoe, her arms encircling his neck more tightly.

"Thank *you,*" she whispered into his ear.

If it hadn't been for the children, Patience would have stayed in his arms forever. But the sound of their embarrassed giggles broke the spell. Cass heard the children's snickers and suddenly broke the embrace as quickly as it had begun.

Clearing his throat, he tried to ignore the tittering still coming from the children. "Storm's about to break. I've got other wagons to see to," he said gruffly.

A new, headier thrill shot through Patience as she realized that he was as shaken by the encounter as she was. "Yes, of course," she murmured.

He turned to the children, who were still chortling. "If you children don't have anything better to do than stand around giggling at the old folks, I'll find something to occupy your time," he warned.

They squealed and scampered in all directions.

Patience watched him walk up the hill with her heart shining in her eyes. *The storm's already broken, Mr. Claxton,* she thought with a grin. *You just don't know it yet.*

11

Sunday was a cool, overcast day with the wind blowing from the west.

Around noon Harlon was fording a creek when his horse lost its footing and fell. The sudden impact threw him, and in its struggle to regain its footing, the horse rolled on Harlon's leg and broke it. Cass had set the leg that evening.

It was just one of those accidents that can happen on the trail. Apart from Cass's concern for the old fellow's recovery, he realized that the accident meant there would be one hand fewer to help with the work.

At seventy-five, Harlon's bones were brittle and slow to heal. It could take months—or longer—before he'd be on his feet again. But everyone agreed that he was lucky to have come out of it with his life.

They had been on the trail for five weeks, and Cherry Grove was a little more than a hundred miles away. Cass was confident that he could get by without Harlon's help. Aaron and Payne were old enough to accept extra responsibilities.

The October mornings had a nip to them now. Cass knew it wouldn't be long before Indian summer would give way to the howling winter winds. But they should reach their destination long before that, so he wasn't concerned.

After supper that evening he walked to the back of the wagon to visit with Harlon, who lay on a mattress looking peaked, with his foot propped up on a pillow.

Patience had brought along a little bluemass for emergencies, but Cass could see that Harlon was still suffering.

"Can I do anything for you, Harlon?"

"Thanks, son, but I can't think of a thing I need."

Cass perched atop a bundle in the wagon and lit a smoke.

"I'm much obliged to you for settin' the leg," Harlon said. "I told Corliss I don't know what we'd have done if you hadn't been here to help us."

"You don't need to thank me. I was glad to help."

"You've been a real godsend to Patience—well, to all of us. I hope you know that."

Cass appreciated the praise but found he was uncomfortable with it. "Patience is a strong woman. She'd have made it with or without my help."

Harlon's old eyes twinkled. "She's not as strong as you might think, boy."

Cass was discreetly silent, and Harlon could sense he would prefer to drop the subject. Deciding to oblige, he glanced at the splinted leg resentfully. "I could just kick myself for breakin' this dad-burned thing! I won't be no use to anyone now," he complained.

Cass smiled. "Don't worry about it. It'll heal."

"Well, I shore hope so. I don't want to be no trouble to anyone."

"You're no trouble."

Harlon reached for his pipe and smoked in silence for a while, enjoying the distant sounds of someone strumming on a guitar.

"Gettin' colder," Harlon observed.

"Yeah."

"Seen any signs of Indians?"

"I saw a scouting party a few days ago."

"Think they'll be givin' us any trouble?"

"They watched us for a while, but they lost interest pretty quickly."

They listened to the voices of Patience and Margaret Ann as they approached the wagon.

"Margaret Ann," Patience was saying, "before you go to bed I want you to run over and ask how old Mrs. Medsker is this evening." The elderly woman had been ailing during the noon hour, and Patience was concerned that she might need something.

"Yes, ma'am," Margaret Ann replied and skipped off to do as she was told. She was back within minutes. "Mrs. Medsker said she didn't think it was any of your doin's how old she is," Margaret relayed.

Cass grinned as he heard Patience's sharp intake of breath before she hurriedly skirted Margaret off to Winoka Medsker's wagon to explain the misunderstanding.

"How come a nice-looking chap like you never took a wife?" Harlon asked. It seemed to him that a man Cass's age ought to have his own children's mistakes to chuckle about.

"Guess I just haven't found the right woman yet."

Harlon thought of Patience again and wondered if Cass wasn't missing a good opportunity to start a family.

"Harlon, I'd like to talk to you about something."

"Certainly."

"I guess I'm asking your advice."

"All right."

"Hoyt Willis has been following us for days."

Harlon glanced up, a frown furrowing his forehead.

"Is that right?"

"What do you think he wants?"

Harlon drew on his pipe thoughtfully. "Hard to say."

"I've been wondering whether I should let it pass or pay a visit to Mr. Willis one of these evenings."

"I don't know, son. The man 'pears as ornery as a freshly castrated bull to me."

"I don't want him disturbing the women," Cass warned.

"No, we couldn't put up with that."

"What do you think I should do?"

"Well, I think I'd wait him out. If he shows any sign of wanting to cause trouble, you can deal with him then. There's no use raisin' a stink if the man's merely travelin' the trail with us."

"Yeah, guess you're right."

"Just keep a close eye on him."

"I plan to."

Harlon drew on his pipe again, sending a plume of smoke rolling out of the wagon. "You don't suppose the women have noticed him?"

"I don't think so. Patience would have mentioned it if she had."

As much as Patience irritated him, Cass didn't want her subjected to a man like Hoyt Willis.

Harlon sighed. "Well, maybe we're just borrowin' trouble."

Cass's gaze followed Patience as she and Margaret Ann emerged from the Medskers' wagon. He didn't know why he found Hoyt Willis's presence so disturbing, but he did.

"Yeah, maybe we are."

But even Aaron mentioned Hoyt Willis's continuing presence a few days later as he watched Cass saddling his horse.

"Have you noticed that skinner's been following us for days now?"

"I've noticed him."

"What do you think he wants?"

Cass shrugged.

"You think he has his eye on Miss McCord?"

Jerking the cinch tighter, Cass frowned. "I think if he's fond of wildcats, he's on the right trail." He swung in the saddle and adjusted his hat low on his forehead.

"You're not worried about him?"

"Not in the least."

Aaron grinned. He knew that it wasn't indifference toward Miss McCord that made Cass so sure of himself. It was plain old know-how that gave him the confidence to face up to any situation that came his way.

"Mind if I ride behind your saddle this morning?" Aaron asked.

"You're not driving the wagon?"

"No, sir. Miss McCord said she was going to."

"Then climb aboard."

As the horse trotted through camp, Cass spotted Patience rolling up the night's bedding and storing it in gutta-percha sacks.

Their gazes met, and he tipped his hat mockingly.

She stuck her tongue out at him.

"Miss McCord's a right fine-looking woman, isn't she?" Aaron remarked as Cass spurred the horse into a gallop.

"I suppose she'd do in a pinch," Cass allowed in a disgruntled tone.

Aaron's grin widened. He figured that Cass meant it'd depend on just who was doing the pinching.

❁ ❁ ❁

Toward late afternoon the train of wagons stopped to water the stock in a wide brook they'd happened to find. The cool, clear water felt heavenly as the people splashed it onto their sunburned arms and faces. The children's delighted squeals were heard for more than an hour as they laughed and played in the bubbling water. Just as they were loading to leave, a new wagon came rolling in.

"Oh, brother!" muttered Patience irritably as she saw that the old buckboard was decked with an outrageously gaudy yellow-fringed awning.

It was a wagonload of fallen angels.

The women of the train hurriedly gathered the children and herded them into the wagons in an effort to shield their young eyes from the unsavory sight of *those women.*

A few of the husbands grudgingly followed suit, but not without one or two curious glances at the new arrivals.

However, the less-than-cordial welcome didn't dampen the spirits of these soiled doves. They piled out of their buckboard and headed straight for the water.

Within minutes they were cooling their ample assets in the stream, oblivious to the resentful looks fired in their direction. There wasn't actually a beauty in the lot, but that didn't seem to discourage the men's rapt attention.

Patience kept a close eye on Cass as he and Aaron sat on the horse with their eyes glued to the spectacle going on before them.

Even Payne's and Jesse's eyes were rounder than usual as they peeked around the corner of the wagon. Corliss hollered for them to *git*, and their heads quickly disappeared.

A buxom redhead seemed determined to capture Cass's attention. She gave the handsome stranger her come-hither smile, displaying her dazzling white teeth and full cherry-red lips as she dipped her lace handkerchief into the stream and let the cool water slowly trickle down into the deep, deep, deep—Patience wasn't sure it was ever going to reach bottom—crevice of her blouse.

Cass's mouth curved into a lazy smile as his eyes trailed the path of the water enviously. He leaned closer to the pommel, taking a slow drag on his cheroot.

It was clear to Patience that the redhead had snagged his undivided attention.

"Afternoon, ma'am. Mighty hot today."

"Yes, it is," she agreed in a sultry Texas drawl.

"You ladies traveling far?"

"Far 'nuff." She lowered her lids demurely. "Where you-all goin'?"

"Kansas."

"Sure 'nuff? Why I have a dear old grandma who lives in Wichita."

"That so?"

"Sure 'nuff. Are you by any chance going to Wichita?"

Cass shook his head, his eyes still traveling leisurely over her provocative display of swelling flesh. "No, ma'am, afraid not."

"Well, that's too bad . . . Listen, sugar, we'll be stopping not far down the road tonight. Maybe you'd like to drop by, so I could give you a letter to mail to my dear, sweet grandma once you reach Kansas." Her smile suggested that a letter was the last thing she planned to give him.

Patience had heard enough. Her hand reached for the bullwhip under the wagon seat. She stood up, whirled it around her head a couple of times, and let it fly.

Cass heard the deafening crack of the whip about the same time his cigar splintered into oblivion.

Stunned, he lifted his blank gaze to encounter Patience's snapping eyes as bits of tobacco fragments swirled to the ground.

"It's time to be on our way," she spat out.

The butt of his cigar dropped from his lips and rolled down the front of his shirt before it dawned on him what had happened. His face turned crimson, and for the first time in his life he was speechless.

Patience wielded the whip a second time, and the wagon lurched forward. The other drivers followed suit, and the train started moving again.

Once they were out on the trail Patience glanced back to see if Cass and Aaron were following. She was relieved to see that they were, but they were trailing at a distance.

"Guess I showed that cow-bagged Jezebel

that she best not mess with my husband and expect to get away with it," she muttered tightly under her breath as she swung the whip again and sent it blazing over the oxen's heads.

She realized that her temper had gotten the better of her, that she'd gone too far this time. Cass would be mad as a hornet and probably yell at her for embarrassing him in front of the whole wagon train that way, but he'd deserved it.

A grin finally escaped its bounds as Patience recalled the horrified look on his face when he'd realized what she'd done.

But he *sure 'nuff* had it coming.

❁ ❁ ❁

Camp was quieter than usual that night. Since Mort Harrison had the first watch, he was preparing to take up his post.

Meanwhile, Buck Brewster sat beneath a tree, playing his violin, a sweet, lilting refrain that floated pleasantly through the wagons.

Cass lay on his bedroll, looking up at the stars. It was a clear night, and the heavens were ablaze with God's handiwork.

Aaron and Payne had rolled up beside Cass tonight. He sensed that the two boys had something on their minds, but he could wait until they were ready to reveal whatever it was that was bothering them.

"You got a pa?" Aaron asked.

"My pa died just after I was born," Cass replied. "He was huntin' one day, and his gun went off accidentally. The bullet hit him in his left eye. The men he was with said they didn't think the wound killed him but that he died of a heart attack from the shock."

"I think mine's dead too," Payne admitted, though he couldn't be sure. He had been alone for as long as he could remember.

"Sure would be nice to have a pa to talk to or maybe a ma," Aaron mused.

"Mothers are special," Cass admitted, remembering his own mother and how long it had been since he'd last seen her.

A few minutes passed before Aaron finally broached the subject uppermost in his mind.

"Cass . . . those women we saw today . . ." As he sat up his voice trailed off hesitantly.

Cass felt himself start to grin and quickly squelched the urge. These boys were on the verge of manhood, eager to taste the fruits of life. They didn't have a pa to confide in, so Cass guessed he'd been chosen to answer their questions. "What about them?"

"Well . . ." Aaron cleared his throat, "they were prostitutes, weren't they?"

"Yes, they were."

Aaron was quiet for a moment, and Payne sat up. "A man's not supposed to be with that kind of woman . . . is he?"

"Well, I guess it depends on the man. Some men take their pleasure where they find it, while others prefer to find a good woman and settle down and raise a family."

"The Good Book says prostitutes are evil," Payne reminded them.

Cass nodded and added quietly, "The Good Book also says 'Judge not, lest ye be judged.' "

"Have you ever been with one of those women?" Aaron asked.

Cass sat up and reached into his pocket for a smoke, wishing the conversation were a little easier to handle. "Rule number one: A gentleman never says who he's been with."

"Even if he's been with one of them harlots?"

Cass eyed Payne dryly as he lit the cheroot. "You seem to be well versed on this subject."

Payne flushed. "Well . . . I saw this book one time . . ." He stopped and grinned sheepishly.

"Well"—Cass fanned the match out—"a man don't go spreadin' it around, especially not if he's been with one of those harlots. But the kind of woman you'll want to tie up with will smell like wildflowers after a rain; she'll have skin as soft as cotton; and her hair will feel like French silk when you run your fingers through it. She'll be gentle by nature, and she'll have a way of making a man feel eager to come home to her at night."

"What about the other ones?" Payne asked. He already knew what he was *supposed* to want.

"The other ones aren't that bad either," Cass admitted.

"Then you've been with the bad ones?" Aaron asked quietly.

"Boys, there are few 'bad' ones. Some are misguided, and some do what they have to to survive. Women have different natures. One will have needs as powerful as a man's, and the next one might shy away from the bed until she's properly wed."

"Which kind do you prefer?" Payne prompted.

Cass preferred not to answer that one. "I treat all women with respect, and I'd suggest you do the same. When you bed a woman, you treat her like a lady, no matter what other people think of her. And if you should accidentally father a child, then you must be man enough to accept your obligation. My brother Cole always taught me and my other brother that a man's a son of a bitch if he does any less."

The three lay back in unison to stare at the stars for a while, mulling over what had been said.

"What kind of woman do you think Miss McCord is?" Payne asked.

"Payne, she's a good woman!" Aaron gasped. "Isn't that so, Cass?"

"I would imagine."

"Don't you know?"

"Not really." Cass realized he didn't know anything about Patience, other than she was like a burr under his saddle most of the time. What sort of woman was she, he wondered. Beautiful, yes, he couldn't deny that. Over the last six years, she'd become a lovely, desirable woman, charming when she wanted to be, and a blessed saint when it came to dealing with children.

She showed no signs of being the spoiled-rotten, self-willed girl he'd been forced to marry, except when she had to deal with him.

However, the kiss they had unexpectedly shared had been warm and full of promise, revealing another side of Patience McCord that he'd never considered before. Would she please a man in bed? Cass feared she would—only too well. Had he enjoyed her kiss? He couldn't deny that it had stirred him. He couldn't deny that he'd liked it—was even beginning to like her. And that was worrying him.

"I think I'll just try out a few of those prostitutes before I look for a nice woman," Payne decided.

To him, it seemed like the only sensible way to handle the dilemma.

"Well, you better not let Miss McCord in on your plans," Cass warned.

He made a mental note to take Payne aside for a more detailed discussion of the subject. He had a feeling that the boy had missed a point somewhere.

"You think she'd be real upset, don't you?"

"Boys," Cass said, rolling to his feet and resigning himself to the fact that, between this conversation and his encounter with the redhead that afternoon, he might have to sleep in the creek tonight, "I try not to think of Patience McCord one way or the other."

Aaron looked up and winked. "But she's pretty hard to overlook, ain't she?"

That was another question Cass chose to ignore. "Go to sleep, boys. I think I'll take a ride."

Cass strolled off as Aaron, rolling up inside his blanket, closed his eyes and tried to conjure up an image of Ernestine Parker.

He wondered if she'd be a family-raisin' woman or one of them girls mentioned who had needs as powerful as a man's . . .

Well, it didn't really matter. Like Cass, there weren't *no* woman gonna hog-tie and brand him—not if he could help it!

12

Patience had just pulled the pins from her hair and was about to give it a thorough brushing when she saw Cass come walking back through camp. She was surprised to see that he was still awake.

The fires had burned low, and Buck Brewster was slipping his fiddle into its case, preparing to retire for the night.

Cass paused to speak to a young woman who sat in a large rocking chair just outside one of the wagons. She was trying to soothe her fretful infant who'd been ill for days.

"How's the baby tonight?" he asked.

"I think she feels a mite hotter than she did."

MarDean Gibson's wan smile was mute testimony to the strain she was under.

Cass felt the baby's forehead, and his brow furrowed with concern. "Do you need another bucket of cool water?"

"No, thank you. Boyd said he'd fetch me one when he got up." Boyd and Mardean had been taking turns sitting up nights with the infant. Cass felt sorry for the young couple. At sixteen, they were barely more than children themselves.

"I'll hold your baby if you'd like to rest a spell with your husband," Cass offered.

Mardean gazed tenderly at the sleeping child on her lap. "I'm beholden to you, Mr. Claxton, but I want to stay with her," she said softly.

Giving Mardean's shoulder a friendly squeeze, Cass smiled. "If you need anything, you let me know."

Her face brightened momentarily. "Thank you. I surely do appreciate your kindness."

Patience watched the exchange out of the corner of her eye, and a feeling of envy engulfed her.

What she would give to have Cass speak to *her* with such compassion, such concern, such caring . . . Her thoughts wavered as she watched him walk to where his horse was grazing.

Now where did he think he was going at this hour, she fretted. She watched him pick up his saddle and sling it over his shoulder. Suddenly

Patience was sure she could guess. He had to be going to visit the wagon of prostitutes.

He was going to see that redhead, she thought frantically. And the two of them were not going to spend their time composing a letter to dear old grandma in Wichita!

Scalding tears sprang to her eyes, and she swiped them away angrily as she tried to tell herself that she didn't care. *Of course* he was going to visit that redhead. He was a man, wasn't he, and hadn't the woman issued him a blatant invitation that afternoon in front of the entire train?

Somewhere there existed a legal document verifying that Cass Claxton was her legal husband. However, Patience wouldn't even try to fool herself into believing that any document could prevent him from indulging in sins of the flesh. He was a young, virile man who'd been on the trail for weeks, and who by now—borrowing from one of her Aunt Merriweather's more colorful expressions—was probably hotter than a two-dollar pistol. The mere thought of this outrageous act of perfidy made her flush with renewed anger.

Well, she wasn't about to permit it. She would not allow him to disgrace her by running off in the middle of the night to cavort with one of those women of easy virtue.

As she began moving toward the wagon, she conceded to herself that her logic might be flawed. After all, no one on the train knew that she and Cass were married, so he could hardly disgrace her in their eyes.

But *she* knew they were married. And the thought of his being intimate with another woman, when he'd avoided her—his own wife—like the plague, set her blood boiling.

Sometime during the past weeks, she had unconsciously begun to think of Cass as her property—her man. Now she asked herself if a woman didn't have a right to protect what was hers, even though what was hers had never wanted to become hers in the first place!

She reached the wagon, and her hand fumbled under the seat for the bullwhip while she kept her eyes trained on Cass. He was acting just as if he were simply about the business of saddling his horse for an innocent moonlight ride!

He had one foot in the stirrup when he paused momentarily. Cocking his head to one side, he thought he could detect the sound of a whip oscillating in midair.

The meaning of the ominous whir suddenly sank in. He swore under his breath, and he braced himself mentally for what he knew was coming.

The soft *wisp, wisp, wisp* grew louder.

"Patience, you'd better think twice," he warned.

She wondered if he'd seen her coming or if

he'd grown eyes in the back of his head. She stood behind him in her nightgown, whirling the whip above her head.

"Where are you going?"

"That's none of your business."

"Oh, yes, it is."

Wisp, wisp, wisp, wisp.

"Patience—"

"You bean-headed jackass! You're not going to that woman!" A menacing crack rent the air, and Cass clamped his eyes shut and gripped the pommel tightly as he felt the back of his shirt split in half. He sucked in his breath, waiting to feel his blood gushing in streams, but he gradually realized that she hadn't touched his flesh, a fact, he decided, which had most likely saved her blasted life!

"Don't push me, Cass. I can draw blood," she warned in a tight voice.

"What's this all about?" he demanded. She was glad to hear that, for once, his voice sounded thready instead of cocksure.

"You are not going to that woman."

"What woman?"

"*That* woman!"

"What woman? I wasn't going to meet a woman—I was going for a ride!"

He didn't know why he was bothering to inform her of where he was or was not going. She didn't own him. He started to turn around and tell her so when the whip cracked again.

This time it sliced through his sleeve and separated the fabric cleanly from his shoulder.

"Don't lie to me! You were going to see that woman!"

Cass had had enough. He whirled and lunged at her, and a struggle developed as Patience fought to retain control of her weapon. But his strength easily overpowered hers. They fell to the ground, and he landed on top of her.

"Get off me, you big oaf!"

Angry as she'd ever seen him, he sat up and snapped the whip in two.

"I have another one!" she said defiantly.

Casting the remains of the broken whip aside, he glared at her. "Miss McCord," he said in a voice so ominous that she felt the hair on her arms prickle, "you are sorely testing me."

"You were going to that . . . that woman," she accused. The little girl inside her wanted to cry, but the woman inside her refused to give him the satisfaction.

"I was not—and what if I was? You have no right to be telling me what I can do! I'm doing what I said I'd do. I said I would get you, the children, Harlon, and Corliss to Cherry Grove safely, and I'm trying my level best to do that. Now, woman, you've browbeaten me, badgered me, bullwhipped me, and badmouthed me about all I'm going to stand for. You're going to stop!" He was so angry that he began shaking her until she felt her teeth rattling. "Do you hear me?"

"If you want a . . . a . . . woman," she scoffed, "why don't you come to your wife?" Patience couldn't believe it was her voice offering him such liberties, but his resulting look of sheer horror confirmed that it was.

"My wife!"

"Your wife . . . I am, you know—no matter how hard you try to deny it!"

"I don't want you to be my wife! I've told you that a hundred times."

"But that doesn't change the fact that we are husband and wife," she argued.

"Let me get this straight. You're suggesting that just because of some idiotic, meaningless ceremony that took place in the middle of a road six years ago, I should want to bed you?" he echoed incredulously.

"Well . . . yes." Their eyes were still locked. "I . . . I wouldn't object to your demanding your husbandly rights," she said meekly. It would be a far better choice than letting him go to that woman.

"Bed you?" he repeated as if she had just volunteered him to be the prime target of a firing squad.

"Don't sound so shocked. Husbands and wives do it all the time."

She knew she was living dangerously. He would likely turn her over his knee and give her a sound paddling for even suggesting such a thing, but she didn't care. She would gladly follow through with her madness and pay the piper later.

"Oh, good Lord!" He slumped over, resting his face in the hollow of her neck, fighting to ignore her audacity. But he found he couldn't.

By some cruel act of fate Patience was offering herself to him; and when he weighed her proposal he was faced with the alarming fact that her timing couldn't have been better. Seeing those women today, talking with Aaron and Payne tonight—it wasn't fair. It just wasn't fair.

For a moment Patience thought he was going to break down and cry like a baby.

She lay immobile, reveling in his nearness as she felt his chest, then his shoulders, then his whole body begin to tremble.

His weight, though heavy, felt wonderously exciting pressed against her. She found she liked the feel of him, and she hoped he wouldn't be in any hurry to move away—at least, that's what she was hoping until she discovered that he was not overcome by sadness but by mirth. His body began to heave with barely suppressed hilarity.

"What is so funny?" she demanded when she realized that he was laughing at her.

"You!"

"I fail to see how my suggesting that you take

me to bed should bring about such hysterics." She struggled to sit up, her pride mortally wounded by his rejection.

His hand snaked out. "Now wait a minute." Slowly he eased her back to the ground. "I didn't say I wouldn't accept your offer."

He managed to keep a straight face, knowing that to consider her offer seriously would be the act of a desperate man. Nevertheless he was not a fool: He had to admit that he was desperate for a woman's company.

This woman was a spitfire, a hellcat, and the biggest obstacle he'd ever tried to overcome, but she was also a beautiful, desirable woman—and she was his wife, albeit in name only.

He was fully aware that if he bedded her, he would surely consummate their union. However, once they reached Cherry Grove he could make it clear that he wanted a divorce instead of an annulment. So why shouldn't he bed her? Lord knew he'd earned the right.

"All right. I'll bed you."

She seemed pleased yet startled by his uncomplicated surrender. "Just like that?"

His eyes narrowed. "Yes. *Now* what do you want? Pretty words? Because if you do . . ."

Drawing a deep breath, she warned herself not to overreact—she was finally making some progress. "I don't expect pretty words."

The moment wasn't how she'd imagined it

would be, but she conceded that it would have to do.

"All right." He released her from his hold and glanced around, seeking a private spot.

"We'll need privacy." He stifled the urge to throw her down on the ground and jump on her like a half-starved animal.

"I know the perfect place."

Cass followed her down a moon-drenched trail, still wondering if he had completely lost his mind.

There was a part of him that needed—*ached*—to be with a woman. Yet another part of him warned that he would be committing the worst mistake of his life. This could throw a kink in their agreement, but he hoped that it wouldn't. She seemed as eager to shed herself of him as he was her.

He was going to bed Patience McCord. *Bed Patience McCord!* The thought still astounded him. Yet concern over what he was about to do was overshadowed by just plain lust as his gaze focused on her feminine backside.

She hurriedly led him through the thickets and brambles until they reached a small clearing. As they turned, their eyes met, then glanced away discreetly. "Is this all right?"

Cass glanced around. "Yes."

They stood facing each other as moonbeams

played on her hair. It turned the flaxen mass to spun gold. Cass found himself eager to touch it.

"Well?" she said.

"Well."

"I . . . I guess we'll have all the privacy we need right here."

"Yeah . . . I suppose we will." He didn't know why he suddenly felt as awkward as a schoolboy. He stepped closer to her. The fragrance of her lilac-scented skin gently teased his senses into painful awareness.

She looked at him, waiting.

Claxton, you can't take her without touching her, he thought. Reaching out hesitantly, he drew her into his arms.

Her small body fit against his surprisingly well, and the instantaneous tightening in his loins assured him that he had nothing to worry about. The act would be completed before he could think about the insanity of what he was doing.

Patience was seized by momentary panic as she felt a rush of heat. It was as if by this gentle but intimate gesture he had already begun to make love to her. *This is what you wanted,* she reminded herself. *He's a man, and you longed to be desired and enjoyed, to be fulfilled as a woman.*

Her arms slipped around his waist shyly as he hesitantly brought his mouth down to brush hers.

"Cass," she complained, "we are going to

make love . . . Must you go about this so unemotionally?"

"All right." His mouth took hers roughly as he jerked her closer against him.

Her body suddenly went fluid as all her fantasies, all her needs, all her darker desires suddenly centered on him.

His first instinct was to take her quickly, reminding himself that there was no need for the usual niceties; he could just complete the act and be on his way.

She moaned softly as their kiss deepened, and her stomach knotted tightly as she began to experience the raw hunger of the man. It took her breath away, to feel his need—but she had hungers of her own that were begging to be explored. Her passion easily matched his, and she heard his sharp intake of breath as his hands began to skim across her breasts.

Cass could feel her heart racing against his hands. He was both pleased and alarmed by her swift response. He wasn't sure what he'd expected, but it wasn't this loving; this striving to please; this warm, giving woman he had in his arms.

She pressed closer, startled to feel the urgent pulsing of his need for her. Momentarily she was shocked—but the knowledge that she was the cause of this heated response excited her more than it frightened her. Closing her eyes, she allowed him—no, actively encouraged him—to begin taking liberties she had let no other man even dream of, savoring every delicious new feeling he was bringing alive.

Almost afraid of what was happening, Cass suddenly aborted the kiss, burying his face in her hair as he drew in a ragged breath.

This was not going as he'd planned. All of a sudden he had this crazy urge to take all the time in the world to make love to her, to savor the moment, to linger as he explored the lush curves and gentle swells of her young body. *Just get it over with, Claxton. Don't encourage her,* he berated himself.

"Do you want me to take off your gown?" he murmured raggedly.

"Yes."

Their gazes locked in the moonlight, and she felt complete abandonment as she saw his eyes grow dark with passion.

Not sure that it was the right thing to do, but wanting to do it anyway, she hesitantly reached out and guided his hands to the row of tiny buttons on her gown.

Touched by her honest simplicity, Cass gazed down at her, knowing he couldn't go through with it. He wasn't that much of a heel—yet. His hands dropped away guiltily. "Patience, this is no good . . ."

Recognizing the doubt in his eyes, Patience

quickly grabbed his hands and brought them back to the row of buttons. "Please, Cass . . . If I were Laure Revuneau, you wouldn't hesitate," she baited.

Damn! Why did she have to mention Laure? He groaned silently. Just the thought of the hot-blooded French temptress automatically set his hands into motion again.

Slowly he worked the buttons loose, and Patience felt goosebumps rise on her skin. In a moment the gown fell away and dropped to the ground. For the briefest of moments she had to quell the urge to run, to hide her nakedness from him. She could feel the heat rising to her cheeks as she turned her head away, but quickly she straightened her stance, determined to prove to him that, with only a little coaxing, she could be every bit the woman he needed her to be.

Cass stood staring at her, the expression in his eyes telling her more eloquently than words that she didn't need to worry. He found her desirable.

Her young, ripe curves made him want to throw caution to the wind. His eyes lingered on the small, firm breasts, and his breathing grew more shallow as he slowly drew her back against the width of his broad chest. Gazing deep into her eyes, he asked again softly. "Are you sure this is what you want, Patience?"

His tone had changed. It was more gentle now, more forgiving.

She gazed up at him, finding it impossible to speak. She was overwhelmed with wanting him, needing him, but she didn't know how to tell him so.

But miraculously he knew.

His hands were unsteady as he began to unbuckle his belt.

"You're sure you're not having second thoughts?" He could see that she was trembling.

"No." She was trembling only because he couldn't seem to take his eyes off her, but she was happy she pleased him.

He smiled at her this time. Just at her. "Well, you can't ever accuse me of not trying to talk you out of it!"

She returned his smile faintly, feeling as if she were drowning in the blue of his eyes. "No, I certainly can't ever accuse you of that."

His belt fell away, and she saw him unbutton his pants, then step out of them.

Her heart lurched as she got her first real look at a half-naked man. Though he still wore underwear she could see he was all muscle and strength. The imprint of his maleness bulging against the front of his long johns suddenly seemed to jump out at her. She swallowed, unable to keep her eyes off the intimidating sight.

Her hands crept up to cover her mouth. "Cass?"

"Yes?"

She wet her lips nervously. "Exactly . . . exactly how does this work?" she whispered.

His hands paused. "Exactly how does *what* work?"

"Exactly how does . . . a man make love to a woman?"

His face went totally blank. "You don't know?"

"No . . . I don't." She thought she knew, but she couldn't be certain. Oh, she knew what parts of the body were involved—she just wasn't sure how they were all supposed to work together.

She felt foolish having to ask such a question, but after seeing his ample endowment . . . well, she simply had to know. Her parents had seen to it that she was well-educated in everything but life itself. Naturally, she'd heard whispers among her schoolmates. If what she had seen the animals doing in the barnyard was also the way *people* went about it—well, she just hoped it wasn't.

"You've never been with a man?"

"No."

"Your mother never spoke to you on the subject?"

"No." Shyness suddenly overcame her, and she snatched up her gown and held it against her breasts protectively. "I asked Mother about it many times, but instead of answers there was only this strained silence," she confessed.

If her scanty information about the act was accurate, she couldn't—not in her wildest dreams—picture her father and her mother participating in such a spectacle.

"What about your aunt? Surely she told you something."

"Aunt Merriweather?" Her eyes widened. "Dear me, no. She would never have spoken of such a thing."

Cass didn't want to believe what he was hearing. First Aaron and Payne; now her. Was there something in the air tonight that brought out the innocents of the world? And why should they all be thrown in his lap, he agonized.

He wasn't able, given his present condition, to give another lecture about intimacy between a man and a woman. For one thing, his own frustrations wouldn't permit it. Secondly, he wasn't her father. If she wanted to know about such matters, she'd have to ask someone else.

But she was looking at him with curious eyes as if she fully expected him to answer.

He sighed. "Look, Patience, you'd better let your husband explain this to you."

"But you *are* my husband."

"On paper only, dammit!"

For the moment she conceded the point. "All

right, but you can't tell me you haven't been with many women, and you weren't *their* husband."

"Those women were different," Cass snapped. "I am not going to be the one to educate you."

Sensing his imminent retreat, she stepped forward. "Oh, please, Cass. I . . . I have to know. If you won't tell me, who else can I go to?"

"Talk to Corliss."

"Oh, I couldn't! I'd be embarrassed to tears."

"Then go to one of the other women on the wagon train."

"I can't do that. Please, Cass . . . you tell me."

"Surely you can find someone more qualified than I am to explain Mother Nature to you."

He swore tightly under his breath. If this wasn't just like her, he thought, getting him all stirred up, offering herself to him, then calmly dropping the news that she didn't know how. He should have expected as much, but he hadn't.

"There isn't anyone else I can go to." Patience knew he was angry with her again, and she didn't want him to be. Just once, she wished she could do something right where he was concerned.

"I'm sorry. I'm perfectly willing to go through with this," she pleaded, "but I have to know how!"

"Patience—"

She straightened, her eyes flashing with determination. "Tell me how, Cass—man-to-man, so to speak." She was not some empty-headed twit who ran from the truth. All he had to do was explain the procedure, and she was quite sure she could carry it out. She glanced at the front of his long johns again and frowned. Well, almost sure.

Cass sighed, realizing that she wasn't going to let up until he told her. "All right," he said calmly, pulling her down on a rock beside him. "You want it man-to-man, I'll give it to you—man-to-man. But remember, you asked for this!"

In the simplest, most basic terms—verging on the extremely blunt, at times—he proceeded to describe the act to her graphically and entirely from a man's point of view.

He didn't even try to soften the blow.

As he talked her eyes began to grow round. He could see her wide-eyed gaze darting wildly from the center of his underwear back to the front of her gown. She was clearly appalled by what he was telling her.

At first she was sure that he was making the whole thing up. She might be innocent, but she wasn't dumb. There was no way *that* could fit into *that*.

But he calmly insisted that there would be no difficulty.

When he was through, she looked at him for a long moment. "Well, I never!" she said.

He returned her look dryly. "*Now* you tell me."

"Why, it sounds perfectly revolting!"

"It isn't. It's enjoyable."

She knew he was lying this time.

Her ardor severely dampened, she hurriedly pulled her gown over her head. "It's late . . . I should be getting back to camp."

"Why, I thought you wanted to go through with this," he countered with mock surprise.

"Well, I'll have to give it some thought," she murmured distractedly.

Cass watched as she turned and beat a noisy retreat through the bushes.

Grinning, he reached into his pocket for a cheroot. *Claxton, you should be ashamed of yourself for scaring her that way,* he thought. But he wasn't. He was just miserable as hell now. He shifted about on the rock uncomfortably. He supposed he'd take that swim.

A devilish grin broke across his face as he thought about the look she'd had on her face when he'd explained how everything worked.

It *did* sound a mite hard to accept.

13

The next morning when Patience walked around the wagon, she found Mardean sitting in the rocker cradling her infant to her bosom.

Tears were rolling silently down the girl's cheeks as Patience knelt beside her. She reached out to smooth a stray lock that had fallen across Mardean's forehead. The girl looked exhausted. "Mardean . . . is the baby worse this morning?"

Mardean lifted her red-rimmed eyes, and Patience saw in them the depth of human misery: Mardean's child was gone. She rocked back and forth, quietly holding her infant's lifeless body.

Sometime during the night, her baby had died.

Patience didn't know how things could get

much worse. Last night with Cass and now this tragedy. Why did the world have to be so complicated?

There was a bright sun overhead, birds chirped, and the squirrels chattered noisily in the trees. It didn't seem a proper day for a burial.

The small group stood around the shallow grave as Lucius Waterman spoke the words of interment. His voice was solemn as he opened his worn Bible and read from Matthew 19:14: "But Jesus said, Suffer little children, and forbid them not to come unto me; for of such is the kingdom of heaven."

Patience stood between Cass and the children, wondering if she would be able to cope with such loss. The children that stood quietly beside her were not her own, yet she loved them all as dearly as if she'd carried them in her womb. Her heart went out to young Boyd. He stood tall with his arm around Mardean, who was sobbing openly. Patience could see that he was trying to be brave, even as his own grief streamed from the corners of his eyes.

Lucius spoke words of comfort and encouragement as Boyd and Mardean's family and friends listened in silent sympathy.

Patience could feel a kindness in all of them, a deep understanding. The grim reaper often lurked on the trail, and they were all aware of the dangers that could befall them.

Lucius closed his Bible and surveyed the small group. "Let us pray." Lifting his gaze upward, he began in a reassuring voice, "Father, we know not why You have called Susanann Gibson home today, nor do we question Thy will. Grant her parents the strength they will need to see them through their loss. Lend us the strength to give comfort and sustain Boyd and Mardean through the dark days ahead. God, we pray that You grant mercy upon us all. Amen."

Four men stepped forward, and as the mourners began to drift away from the gravesite, Patience could hear the scraping of the shovels. She knew each thrust of dirt would lay bare Mardean's heart.

After the service, the others broke camp, allowing the grieving parents the last remaining moments with their child.

Patience could see the young couple standing next to the mound of fresh dirt, holding onto each other tightly.

She wondered if she would ever receive the kind of love Boyd felt for Mardean. If a tragedy befell her, whom would she go to for comfort?

Her eyes searched for Cass. She found him busy hitching the team to the Gibsons' wagon. She suddenly needed the assurance that he was near.

Gathering the last of their supplies, she

stowed them in their wagon, them ambled over to where he was working.

She perched on the tongue of the wagon and watched as he adjusted a piece of harness.

Phebia ran up, crying. She'd smashed her thumb—the sucking one. With solemn eyes, she silently extended her injury to Cass.

"I don't think it's serious, but I'll put a bandage on it," he reassured her.

Minutes later Phebia skipped happily away, dragging Marybelle by the hair. Her injured thumb was encased in a huge, snowy-white bandage.

"Maybe now she'll stop sucking the thing," Cass remarked as he turned his attention to the harness.

"She seems to rely on you more and more in all her crises," Patience teased.

Cass shrugged. "She's a good kid."

Patience sighed and clasped her hands together in her lap. "Real sad about the Gibson baby, isn't it?"

Cass glanced her way, but he kept working. "It is."

"I'll never get used to the thought of death." Her eyes grew misty as they wandered back to Boyd and Mardean. "I know we shouldn't question God's will, but you wonder why He would want to take a baby . . ."

"Losing someone is never easy, but when a child is involved, it makes it harder."

She looked at him. "You sound as if you've had firsthand experience."

"I guess I have. A few years back my brother lost both his wife and the child she was carrying." Cass jerked the leather straps together tightly. "The loss almost killed him."

"I'm sorry."

"Guess it was meant to be. After a year or so he remarried a little gal named Charity, and from what I hear, he couldn't be happier."

"Would that be Beau?" she asked softly. She'd met Beau Claxton years ago when she'd gone to Charity Burkhouser's soddy to ask Cass to escort her back to St. Louis.

"It was Beau."

"Do you have other family?"

"An older brother, Cole, and my mother. They live in Missouri."

"No sisters?"

"No sisters."

She was pleased to find that they could carry on a normal conversation without fussing. It felt good for a change. Maybe they were making progress, she thought wistfully, realizing that it would probably last only long enough for her to finish her next statement.

"Cass?"

He glanced up. "Yes."

"There's something I want to confess to you."

"All right." He wasn't overly curious. Nothing she could say would surprise him.

"I sent you the telegram from Beau."

Cass never even glanced up. The suspicion that she'd tricked him into taking her to Cherry Grove had entered his mind once or twice, but now the knowledge that she had actually done it was tempered more by a feeling of relief than of anger. "I see," he said quietly, relieved to learn that Beau wasn't in any trouble.

She blinked, stunned by his benign acceptance. "You're not angry?"

He looked at her this time, long and hard. "Would it do any good if I were?"

"No." She lowered her gaze to study her hands. "I realize that it wasn't a nice thing to do."

"You seldom do anything that's nice where I'm concerned."

She looked away again. "I know."

"Exactly why do you do these things, Patience?" he asked, wishing, for once, that she could explain what drove her.

"I don't know . . . I suppose because nobody ever cared enough to stop me."

"Your folks never taught you the wisdom of asking for favors instead of bullying your way through life?"

"I guess maybe they tried. But after Mama died, Daddy was so wrapped up in his grief that he just went off into his own little world. Seemed to me the only way I could get his attention was to throw fits, make demands, and act perfectly outrageous. When I found out that he wasn't going to come out of his shell long enough to do anything about it, then I suppose I just got worse."

She lifted her eyes, and Cass could see that they were bright with unshed tears. "What my father didn't realize was that I was hurting too. When I lost Mama, I didn't know where to turn or what to do. It isn't right to make a fourteen-year-old face death all alone. I needed him, Cass . . . but he wasn't there for me. Then he upped and moved us to Cherry Grove, Kansas, to begin a new life, and I didn't know anyone at all. I was sure that my world had come to an end."

"Did you ever let your father know you felt this way?"

"No." She sighed. "He wouldn't have understood. He's a good man, but he hasn't the faintest idea of how to deal with a child."

"So you were lonely and miserable, and you decided to trick me into marrying you and taking you back to St. Louis."

"I see how horrible that was now, but at the time I thought it was my only salvation. I knew if I could just return to Aunt Merriweather, then everything in my life would be all right again." She sighed, glad to have her weighty admission finally out in the open. "I always felt loved and wanted by Aunt Merriweather, but I guess she had a way of making everyone feel that way."

Cass stopped what he was doing and stepped over to tilt her chin up to meet his gaze. Her eyes were lovely, he realized with a start, violet-blue with long, soot-colored lashes. "Patience, I'm going to tell you something, so listen to me. You don't intimidate people into loving you. You earn people's love by being honest and decent, by being a woman of your word. That gets their attention every time."

"Maybe it isn't attention I want," she whispered. "Maybe I want to be loved the way Boyd loves Mardean."

"I know of nine children who think you've hung the moon," he reminded.

"I know . . . but sometimes I despair that no man will ever love me," she added softly.

"That's foolish."

She smiled, her eyes bright with tears as she gained courage. "Maybe I want to be loved by a man like you."

Their eyes met, and she wasn't sure of what she was reading in his gaze . . . pity . . . sympathy . . . maybe something entirely new. Could it be a grudging realization that she wasn't as bad as he'd thought she was, she wondered.

"Then I suggest you give a man like me a reason to love you," he said simply.

They studied each other, unprepared for the swift response they were triggering in each other. He recalled the way she'd looked the night before, standing before him in the moonlight, naked, innocent, vulnerable. He wished now that he'd been gentler with her.

"Cass! Cass!"

Cass and Patience glanced up to see Jesse dashing headlong in their direction.

Cass frowned. "What is it, Jesse?"

"Doog . . ." Jesse was panting so hard he could barely get his breath. "Doog . . . fell . . . down a big hole."

"A hole?" Startled, Patience sprang up from the tongue of the wagon. "Where? When?"

"Just . . . now . . . Come on . . ."

Cass paused long enough to grab a rope; then the three raced through camp, shouting for extra hands to help with the rescue.

Corliss poked her head out of the canvas flap. "What's going on now?"

"Doog . . . he's fallen into a hole!" Patience shouted.

"Land o' mighty!" The flap fell back into place as Corliss began to search frantically for her shoes.

The growing assembly fought their way through dense briars and thickets, tearing off the prickly vines that angrily snatched at their clothing. A stitch formed in Patience's side, but she ran on, her shorter legs barely able to keep up with Cass's long-legged strides.

They ran for more than a half mile before Jesse skidded to a halt. With wide eyes, he pointed to the ground expectantly. Noting the thin beam of light shining down through the opening, Cass determined that Doog had fallen into the shaft of a deserted well.

Dropping to his stomach, Cass narrowed his eyes and peered down the hole. "Doog?"

"Yessir?"

"What are you doing down there?"

"Just sittin' here."

"Is he all right?" Patience crowded closer, trying to hear the exchange.

"Are you all right?"

"I'm not sure . . . I—I want out of here!"

Patience glanced up to see Ernest Parker and Boyd Gibson already tying a loop on the end of a rope. She was stunned to see Boyd, but here he was, temporarily casting aside his grief to help another.

She felt a gentle hand on her shoulder, and she turned to find that even Mardean was there, lending her silent support.

"Doog, I'm going to lower a rope. I want you to grab it and loop it around your waist," Cass ordered.

"I can't . . . My arm is all funny-looking, and it hurts real bad!"

"Is it broken?"

"I don't know . . . Maybe."

Cass hoisted himself to his feet, his eyes gauging the size of the shaft's opening. It would be tight, but he could fit through it. He turned back to Patience. "I'm going to have to go down there."

"Oh, Cass . . ." Patience edged forward, concern for his safety etched on her face. "Be careful . . ."

A loop was quickly tied in a second rope and dropped around Cass's waist. Ernest, Lucius, Boyd, and Laurence Medley, Mardean's father, took hold of the other end.

"We're ready anytime you are." Ernest handed Cass a rifle. "You better take this."

Cass accepted the rifle, then removed his hat and handed it to Patience. "Here, make yourself useful and hold this for me."

"Please"—Patience's eyes locked helplessly with his—"please . . . I'm so worried . . ."

He grinned. "You worry too much."

Seeing her lower lip begin to tremble, his smile faded. "I'll be all right . . . okay?"

She nodded wordlessly.

In a completely uncharacteristic gesture—at least toward her—he reached out and tugged her nose playfully, then turned to face the four waiting men. "Gentlemen, I hope you have strong grips."

Moments later the men began to carefully lower Cass down into the dark shaft.

Patience couldn't bear to watch. She turned and buried her face against Martha Waterman's shoulder.

The hole was close to fifty feet straight down. Loose rocks bounced and skidded off the walls as Cass began to maneuver his way slowly down the sides of the shaft.

"You still down there, Doog?"

"Yessir."

"Any particular reason you picked this day to fall into a hole?" Cass asked, trying to keep the boy's mind off the problem.

He was about a fourth of the way down when he felt the rope give. A fine sweat broke out across his forehead as he braced his feet against the wall, tightened his grip, and waited. Seconds later, the rope went taut again.

"No, sir . . . I was just a chasin' a rabbit, and I was runnin' real hard . . ."

As Cass eased down another few feet, a barrage of loose rocks clattered noisily down the sides of the walls. When the dust finally settled, Doog called out expectantly, "Cass? You still there?"

"I was the last time I looked. How about you?"

"I'm still here."

"Good."

"You scarit?"

"A little . . . What about you?"

"A little."

"Your arm hurting you?"

"Yessir."

Cass was halfway down the shaft.

"Is Miss McCord up there?"

"Yes, she is."

"I'll bet she's scarit, huh?"

"She looked a mite peaked . . . Doog, can you see me yet?" It was the longest damned shaft he'd ever seen, Cass thought.

"Yessir."

"Well, hold on. I'll be there in a minute."

"Okay."

"How much water's down there?"

"Not much . . . just a little."

Cass could hear the faint trickle of running water. The well being almost dry would make the rescue easier.

"Cass?"

"Yeah?"

"Better hurry. Them snakes are making me kinda nervous," Doog admitted.

"Snakes?" Cass paused, his heart sinking.

"There's three great big ol' ones just kinda layin' here lookin' at me."

Cass muttered an obscenity under his breath.

He wasn't afraid of snakes, but he didn't necessarily cherish the thought of having a tea party with three of them at the bottom of a well.

"What'd ya say, Cass?"

"Nothin'."

After a few minutes Cass could see the bottom. Doog was sitting with his feet drawn up on a ledge, staring up at him. "Where are the snakes?" Cass asked, trying to adjust his eyes to the dim light.

Doog pointed in front of him. "Right there."

They were there, all right. Cottonmouths. Coiled up and waiting for company.

"Listen, Doog, I'm going to brace myself, and I want you to swing yourself out to me."

Cass deliberately kept his tone neutral, hoping to keep the boy from knowing what they were up against. Apparently the child couldn't determine from the snakes' thicker, shorter bodies, from their darker coloration, from the cotton lining in their mouths that they were any different from other water snakes. But they were very different.

"My arm hurts."

For a moment Cass had forgotten about the child's injured arm.

"All right . . . Let me think for a minute." He could feel the sweat trickling down his back as his eyes went back to the snakes. This was not going to be his day—he could feel it.

"Cass, are you all right?" Patience's anxious voice came to him from far up the shaft.

"We're doing fine!" he called back.

One of the snakes opened its mouth, displaying the white markings on its upper lip as if to warn the intruders that they were asking for trouble. Cass felt his skin crawl.

"Just fine," Cass repeated softly, hoping to make himself believe it.

"Them snakes dangerous?" Doog asked when he noticed Cass's preoccupation with them.

"They're cottonmouths, son."

Doog's eyes widened, and he jerked his feet back closer to his body. "They're poisonous?"

"Now, listen. It looks like I'm not going to be able to come all the way down to get you. I know your arm hurts, but I'd like for you to try and jump to me," Cass said calmly.

Doog stood up slowly, his gaze still fixed solidly on the snakes. "Well . . . all right . . . I'll try . . ."

The boy was light, maybe sixty pounds, Cass estimated. His weight would be easy to handle if the men above could control the unexpected jerk on the rope.

"Patience!"

"Yes!"

"Tell Lucius I'm going to have Doog jump to me. I figure he weighs around sixty pounds, so tell the men to brace themselves!"

Seconds later she returned. "They say they're ready!"

Cass looked at the snakes, then back to Doog. "It's important for you to be real accurate. I'll try to get as close as I can. All you have to do is latch onto my hand."

"Yessir."

Cass got a good grip on the rope with one hand, and stretched the other one down to the boy.

Doog glanced back at the snakes.

"Don't look down," Cass cautioned softly.

Doog obediently lifted his eyes. "I'm scarit," he whispered, "real scarit, Cass."

"I know." He motioned with his hand. "All you have to do is grab onto my hand."

Doog swallowed.

Cass waited. The sound of a snake's hissing echoed through the dark chamber.

"Okay, I'm gonna jump," Doog decided. He edged closer to the ledge as one of the snakes began to uncoil.

It slithered across the body of the smaller one and paused.

Taking a deep breath, Doog shut his eyes.

"Doog, take your time." Cass could see the boy was nervous, and they couldn't afford a mistake.

Doog suddenly leapt, his hand grappling wildly for Cass's. Their fingers brushed in midair moments before Doog plummeted to the floor of the shaft.

Screaming, the child flailed wildly in the stagnant water before springing to his feet and backing fearfully away from the snakes that were beginning to move in for the strike.

"*Casssss!*" Doog's voice was bordering on hysteria.

Cass swore under his breath as he slid the rest of the way down the wall, dropping the rifle in his hasty descent. His boots hit bottom, and in a running dash he caught Doog up by the seat of his pants as two of the snakes struck out.

Jerking the boy aside, he swore as the snakes struck again.

Cass jerked frantically on the rope. "Pull!" he shouted.

Sweat ran down the sides of his face as Doog screamed again. Cass glanced down and saw one of the snakes slithering across the toe of his boot.

The rope jerked once and went slack.

"Doog, can you reach the rifle?" Cass shouted as he kicked out at one of the snakes, catching it with the toe of his boot and sending it through the air.

Doog was terrified. He clamped his eyes shut and shook his head. "Noooo . . . I'm scarit!"

The second snake lunged again as Cass jerked backward, unable to hold on to the rope this time.

He could hear voices coming from above as

his feet slipped out from under him. He fell into the water, still trying to hold onto Doog.

Cass thrashed about in the water, his hand groping for the rough hemp as the snakes came swimming toward them. His hand froze as it closed over something alive. Swearing, he flung the snake against the wall and searched for the rope again.

Doog screamed as all three snakes struck again, one catching the edge of Cass's boot this time.

"Tell us when you're ready to come up!" Patience shouted down the shaft, unaware of the drama taking place below.

Cass swore as one hand finally located the rope and his other hand grabbed the rifle that was tilting precariously on the ledge. "We're ready!" he shouted.

"You ready?"

"*Pull, dammit!*"

Suddenly the rope went taut, and Cass with his arm around Doog went sailing up the side of the wall. Doog clutched on to Cass and the rifle with his good arm, his injured one dangling at his side. His eyes were riveted to the snakes that were still determined to punish the trespassers.

About halfway up, the rope slipped down again, leaving them dangling helplessly in midair.

Cass held tightly to Doog as the boy buried

his face against his neck and shook like a leaf in a high wind.

"Don't let us fall," the child moaned.

Cass hazarded a cautious glance down the long, narrow shaft where the snakes lay waiting. "Lucius will see to it that we don't."

Moments later the rope began to move again.

"Listen, Doog, I don't see any need to let Miss McCord know about our little friends down there," Cass said as they neared the top of the opening. "It would only upset her—women are real funny about snakes, you know—so why don't we just keep this between us men?"

Doog nodded without raising his head, confiding in a muffled voice, "I think from now on I'm gonna be real funny about snakes too."

Seconds later Lucius lifted Doog out of the shaft and pried the rifle from his fingers.

A cheer went up as Cass emerged into the bright sunlight. He gave a sigh of relief. He couldn't remember when daylight had ever looked so good to him before.

It was all Patience could do to keep from rushing over and throwing herself into his arms. Instead she hurriedly embraced a sopping-wet, much-relieved Doog.

Corliss ran her hands over the boy's upper body and diagnosed his injuries as a sprained shoulder and a bruised arm. As she prescribed a sling and a period of rest, Doog, who was openly distressed by all the fuss that the womenfolk were making, tried to wriggle from her grasp and edge toward the other boys.

Assured that the child was none the worse for wear, Patience released Doog to Corliss's care and hurried to Cass's side. At least she would be able to see for herself that he wasn't injured.

Ernestine Parker was fawning over Cass again. Had the child been one year older, Patience swore that she'd have told the girl to find her own man.

"Are you all right?" Patience asked, placing her hand on Cass's wet sleeve possessively.

"I'm fine." Cass and Doog exchanged a conspiratorial glance, and they both grinned.

"Well, I appreciate your going down there in that awful, dark hole to get Doog." Patience surveyed Cass's wet clothing expectantly. "I'll bet it was just terrible down there."

Cass shrugged.

Phebia marched over and immediately demanded that Cass remove the bandage from her thumb. Since it had only been for show anyway, he complied.

"Good! Now I can suck it again." She popped the thumb back into her mouth contentedly.

"Folks, we best be gettin' on the trail," Lucius warned. "We've lost nigh on to four hours today."

The group began to trail off toward their

camp, talking among themselves about all the strange happenings the morning had brought.

The children clustered around Cass and Patience as they started walking. Cass casually placed his arm around Patience's waist as Corliss fell into step, carrying Phebia and Marybelle.

Doog was busy extolling his adventure to the other boys, obediently omitting the part about the snakes, though Cass could tell it pained him to have to leave it out. Without that exciting part, it sounded as if he'd simply fallen into a hole and Cass had come down to fetch him.

Patience smiled contentedly as they walked along enjoying the lovely fall day. She thought they looked like a real family as the twelve of them sauntered down the road together.

A real family.

14

The next day, Hoyt Willis made his move. He crouched behind a tree, watching Patience as she went about her work. One hour—twenty minutes at the least—and he'd show Patience McCord what a real man could do for her. He wiped the back of his hand across his stubbled chin, trying to control his eagerness.

It was Sunday, and the men were off hunting. The women had gone to the river shortly after their church services to do the week's wash. It was about the only time they had to catch up on the week's gossip without the men being around to scowl at them. They were chattering like magpies as they went about their work.

It wouldn't take Hoyt long to do what he was

here for. All he had to do was get the little missy alone.

Patience helped Corliss most of the morning, but shortly before noon she announced that she and Phebia were returning to camp to begin the baking.

Corliss absently waved her off, never missing a lick in telling her story about how Jesse had put a frog in Bryon's bedroll two nights ago. She was describing the howl the five-year-old had sent up.

After feeding Phebia a biscuit and a cup of milk, Patience put her down for a nap. Almost everyone had drifted out of camp by the time she turned her attention to making bread. She had just dumped several cups of flour into a large wooden bowl when she heard footsteps approaching. She glanced up and was startled to see the buffalo skinner she'd befriended several weeks earlier.

Hoyt Willis stood looking at her, a grin spreading across his dirty features. He tipped his hat politely. "Afternoon, ma'am."

Patience stepped back as his foul smell washed over her.

"Mr. Willis . . . what are you doing here?"

Hoyt's eyes traveled hungrily over the bodice of her dress. "I thought you might be sparin' me a cup of coffee, ma'am."

"Well . . . I suppose I can." Patience didn't

like the idea of the man being around while Cass was gone, but she didn't want to be rude.

She walked to the large pot hanging above the fire and poured coffee into a tin cup. Hesitantly she handed it to him.

His fingers brushed hers intimately as he took the cup. "Thank you, ma'am. I'm right beholden to you."

Patience nodded and moved away quickly. She was dismayed to see him amble over and settle himself comfortably upon a rock a few feet away from where she'd planned to work.

Deciding she could do little about it, she returned her attention to mixing the bread.

"Right purty weather we're havin'," Hoyt remarked as he took a sip from the cup.

She nodded, not looking up.

"Sure was sorry 'bout the old man a breakin' his leg. At his age it'll take a spell to heal."

Reaching for the salt, Patience felt a tightening in the pit of her stomach. How would he know Harlon had broken his leg—unless, of course, he'd been following them?

"Where is the rest of your party, Mr. Willis?"

"Jest call me Hoyt, honey."

A warning light entered her eyes as she turned and met his gaze evenly. "My name is Miss McCord."

"Yes," Hoyt's eyes focused on the gentle rise

and fall of her breasts. "I know what your name is." His gaze never wavered.

"Then use it when you speak to me."

Hoyt grinned. He liked a woman with spunk—made his effort more worthwhile. "The other fellers are camped down the road a ways."

"I'm surprised. It was my understanding that you were eager to get back to your families. I would think you could travel much faster than we can."

"Oh, we ain't in no hurry," Hoyt said. "I just kinda like to take my time and enjoy the scenery—you know what I mean?"

Patience knew.

"Where's your man today, Miss McCord?" His tone remained friendly, but Cass's earlier warning about the man was making Patience feel uneasy. She wondered how far away Cass was.

"Are you referring to Mr. Claxton?" she returned coolly.

"Yeah, Mr. Claxton. Where he be off to on such a fine day?"

"He's hunting nearby."

"That so?" Hoyt peered at her over the rim of his cup as he took another swallow of coffee. "You know, if I had me a fine-lookin' woman sech as you, I'd be sending them young bucks off to do my huntin'."

The implication in his voice hung heavily between them.

Patience continued her work, ignoring the innuendo about how he'd spend that time.

"I suppose the old man is around?"

"Harlon's . . . resting in the wagon." Patience didn't want this man to think she was alone without protection, so she quickly added, "He's here in case there's any trouble."

Hoyt glanced toward the wagon about thirty feet away. "Is that a fact! 'Course there ain't much an old feller with a broken leg can do, now is there?"

"Not much," Harlon's voice suddenly agreed as the barrel of his gun slid out of the back of the wagon and leveled at the center of Hoyt's chest. "But ol' Myrt here can sure get her point across!"

The tin cup clattered to the ground as Hoyt sprang to his feet. He jumped back as the hot coffee seared through the material of his shirt. "Here now, I was just makin' conversation. T'ain't no call to be gettin' all riled up!"

"You git on out of here, Mr. Willis. We don't take to the likes of you comin' around botherin' our womenfolks," Harlon said calmly, keeping the gun firmly on its target.

By now Jesse, Doog, and Joseph had returned to camp for dinner. They stood watching the tense exchange with wide-eyed curiosity.

Hoyt cast an uncertain look in Patience's direction.

"He means what he says, Mr. Willis. You'd best be moving on."

A look of sheer hatred flared unchecked in the skinner's eyes. "All right, but you'll be regrettin' this, missy!" He yielded in a voice so tight that Patience barely caught the message. Then he whirled and walked away.

The boys came running to Patience, their eyes aglow with excitement. "What'd he want, Miss McCord?" Doog asked.

Patience drew the boy close, distractedly giving him an assuring squeeze. "Nothing, Doog . . . Just a cup of hot coffee."

But Patience knew what he had wanted, and the realization sent a cold chill down her spine.

❀ ❀ ❀

The men had a good day of hunting. Laurence Medley had even killed a small doe.

That night there was fresh venison steak for all.

After supper Cass took Aaron and Payne down to the river to wash. The three whooped and yelled as they plunged headlong into the icy water, the shock nearly stealing their breath away. Hurriedly they waded to the bank to lather themselves with the bar of soap Patience had supplied.

Jesse and Doog sat nearby, skipping rocks on the water. They didn't see any sense in washing again. They'd just bathed last night, so they had a whole week to go before they had to subject themselves to such misery again.

The sun was sitting behind a row of towering trees, casting its mellow glow on the red and gold leaves shimmering with vivid splashes of color. The air already had a sharp bite to it, and being wet didn't help matters, Cass thought as he washed faster.

"How many rabbits did ya kill today, Payne?" Doog wanted to know.

" 'Bout six, I guess."

"How 'bout you, Cass?"

"Twelve rabbits and four squirrels."

"Gosh!" Doog would be glad when he was old enough to go hunting with the men. Fact was, he'd be glad when he was old enough to do anything.

"What did you boys find to do to keep out of trouble?" Cass asked.

"Nothin'. We just sat down here and threw rocks in the river, whilst we listened to them women cacklin' like a bunch of ole settin' hens." Doug and Jesse giggled.

"Hear anything interesting?"

The two boys looked at each other sourly. "Not a thing."

Satisfied that they were socially acceptable again, Cass, Aaron, and Payne waded out of the water. They shivered as they dried off and put on clean clothes.

"That skinner came to camp today," Doog announced.

Cass's hands suddenly paused in buttoning his shirt. "Hoyt Willis?"

"Boy, is he nasty dirty!" Jesse observed as he made a disgusted face.

"What'd he want?"

"Miss McCord said he just wanted a cup of coffee," Jesse relayed.

"But Harlon had to turn the gun on him," Doog said.

Cass finished dressing and sat down to pull on his boots, trying to digest the news. He hadn't talked to Harlon tonight. The older man was asleep during supper. Since his leg was keeping him up nights, Corliss hadn't wanted to disturb him.

"Why did Harlon turn the gun on him?" Cass finally asked.

Doog was about to skip another rock when he let his arm slip back to his side. "Don't know . . . 'cept I think the skinner wasn't bein' real mannerly to Miss McCord."

Cass stood up, his eyes suddenly flashing with anger.

Aaron, sensing trouble, reached out to put his hand on Cass's arm warningly. "Best check with

Harlon afore you get all riled. Doog's stories aren't too reliable at times."

"They are so!" Doog turned to Jesse. "Didn't that ole skinner come to camp today?" Jesse lifted his eyes to Cass. "He did, Cass. Honest!"

"Aaron, look after things here," Cass said. "I have business to tend to."

"I'm coming with you." Aaron stepped forward, meeting Cass's eyes solemnly.

"I appreciate your offer, but I can take care of this matter myself," Cass refused quietly.

"I know you can, but there be four of them. I figure that's two apiece."

Cass grinned. "You think you can handle two?"

Aaron drew his unimpressive stature to its full height. "Yessir."

"Then I guess you and I better go teach a certain skinner a few manners."

"Can I go too?" Payne was on his feet, eager to do his part.

"I'd rather you stayed here," Cass said as the five began to walk back to camp. "With Harlon down, we need to leave a man here to help the women."

"Oh . . . all right." Payne didn't think the job he'd been delegated sounded half as exciting as going out to knock that skinner's brains out, but he supposed it was just as important. Someone should be here to look after the women, and, like

Cass had said, it needed to be a man. Payne's chest puffed with pride.

"Gentlemen, I think we'd better keep this under our hats," Cass advised as they drew closer to the camp. "The women will get all fussy if they know where we're going."

The four boys nodded, giving their unspoken promise to keep the mission quiet.

"Gosh, I don't like girls!" Doog complained. "They're always taking the fun out of everything."

Cass clamped his hand on the boy's shoulder sympathetically. "Try to hold that thought, son."

Patience glanced up as her men came walking back into camp. She felt such a warmth when she thought how the boys idolized Cass. It was apparent that Aaron respected and loved Cass deeply, and she wondered what the boy would do once they reached Cherry Grove and Cass left.

She watched as Cass and Aaron broke away and paused to converse with Harlon for a moment. Seconds later, the two emerged from the wagon and matched strides as they went to saddle the horses.

Realizing they were about to leave again, Patience abandoned her dishwashing to run to catch up with them.

"Cass!"

He turned and saw her hurrying toward him. Pausing, he waited until she had caught up.

"Where are you going?" she asked, fighting to catch her breath.

"Aaron and I have a little business that needs tending," he said easily, his tone never giving away their true intent.

She frowned. "Business—tonight?"

"We shouldn't be gone long."

"Well . . ." She looked from Cass to Aaron doubtfully. "You be careful . . ."

Cass nodded. "We plan to."

She turned and started away, then paused. She reached out and put her hand on his arm.

Cass looked at Aaron and grinned as he pulled her close for a reassuring hug. "You're worrying again."

"I just can't help it. It seems to me you're storying about where you're going." Patience had an uneasy feeling that Cass was keeping something from her.

Cass drew back and grinned at her innocently. "Me? Story to you?"

"Don't you look so innocent, Cass Claxton!" She placed her hands on her hips. "You'd story to me in a minute." She turned to Aaron. "Is he storying to me?"

Aaron shrugged and grinned sheepishly.

Cass chuckled and reached out to draw her back into his arms. He gave her another hug, then turned her in the direction of camp and smacked her fanny. "Go wash your dishes, woman."

Patience still had a niggling feeling in the pit of her stomach that something wasn't right as she watched him walk away.

Exactly *what* it was she wasn't sure, but she had a feeling it wouldn't take her long to find out.

15

It was getting close to midnight before Cass and Aaron returned to camp. Patience thought she'd never seen two more disreputable-looking characters in all her life.

Their clothes were filthy; their shirts were torn at the shoulders; and both were sporting what would turn out to be the biggest, blackest shiners Patience had ever seen.

They got off their horses and turned to face her guiltily. She saw that each had a pumpkin tucked under his arm.

"You've been fighting!" she accused, drawing her wrapper closer against the night chill. She'd lain awake for hours, listening for their return.

"Fighting?" Cass shot a knowing glance at

Aaron, and they both grinned. "We have not. We've been picking pumpkins." He gallantly extended his bounty to her.

Corliss emerged from the back of the wagon. Seeing Aaron's sorry condition, she squired him off to patch him up. That left Cass in Patience's care.

"I have never seen such going-ons!" Patience usually borrowed one of Corliss's standard sayings when she didn't know what else to say. Quietly she set the pumpkin aside and stepped over to help him to the washstand.

He good-naturedly shrugged her away, insisting that he didn't need any help.

Patience decided that whatever he'd been doing, it had left him in a good mood. He was buoyant and elated, completely unconcerned that she'd been up most of the night, worrying herself half to death.

Pouring water into the enamel basin, she reached for a bar of soap.

"If you've been out all this time consorting with that woman . . ." she began, remembering the redhead who'd just been itching to get her hands on Cass. If that woman continued to fool with her man, she'd break her in two! "Why . . . why I can't believe you'd subject Aaron to such—"

"Redhead, redhead! Is that all you can think about?" Cass complained. "Do you honestly think I'd let a woman do *this* to me?" It was a low blow to Cass's pride.

Patience wrung out the cloth and began scrubbing his face just as she would have scrubbed Phebia's. "I don't know what to think of you! And I didn't say anything about a redhead—you did!"

"Ouch! That hurts!" His voice was muffled by the flying cloth.

"You'd better not have taken Aaron out to teach him things he shouldn't know yet!"

"Aaron is sixteen years old. What he doesn't know, he should be learning." Cass sucked in his breath painfully as the soap seeped into one of his open wounds. "Will you stop it! I can wash my own face, woman!"

"What *have* you been doing, Cass?"

"I told you. I had business to take care of." He wasn't about to tell her where he'd been, because if she found out that he'd gone out to take care of Hoyt Willis, then she'd assume he'd done it as a favor to her—which he hadn't. Anyway, he didn't think he had. He was pretty sure that he'd just wanted the skinner out of his own hair.

"And you involved Aaron in your rowdy mission?"

"You bet! He's a great kid." Cass had a new respect for the boy. He'd witnessed grown men tumbling tonight under the hands of a youth filled with sheer grit and determination.

Patience didn't know what the two had been up to, and it didn't seem likely she was going to find out. But there was no way on earth she believed they'd been out picking pumpkins.

"You should be ashamed of yourself!"

Cass sighed, realizing that she wasn't going to let up until he appeased her. "All right, I'm ashamed of myself."

"You are not!"

"I know it, but I figure you're not going to pipe down until I say that I am."

Patience irritably dabbed white salve on his cuts, silently admitting that she'd been more scared than angry. From every appearance they had been fighting. She found a smile threatening as she wondered what their opponents must look like now.

"It's a wonder you weren't shot."

"Not a chance. I'm smarter than that."

She helped Cass out of his soiled shirt, handed him the washcloth, and went to get a clean shirt from his pack. By the time she returned he was looking more presentable. Handing him the clean shirt, she walked to the dying fire to pour a cup of coffee.

Frost was settling on the ground, and a bright harvest moon was hanging overhead. The midnight hour gleamed as brightly as day.

She turned and finally smiled. He accepted the unspoken truce with a feeling of relief. She handed the tin cup to him. "Drink this. It'll help to warm you."

He slipped into his coat, his gaze locking with hers gratefully. "Thanks. Why not stay and share a cup with me?"

She was surprised by his invitation. It was the first time he'd ever asked her to join him, and she fought the urge to read more into his unexpected request than he might mean.

"Thank you. That would be nice." She busied herself pouring a second cup of coffee as he walked over to pick up his bedroll. Moments later they left camp so that they wouldn't disturb the children who were sleeping beneath the wagon.

They walked side by side until they came to a grassy knoll where Cass paused. Patience helped him unfold the bedroll.

"It's getting chilly," she remarked as they sat down and settled their coffee cups on the ground beside them.

"Another month and the snow will be flying." He glanced at her, suddenly aware that she was wearing only her nightgown and a flannel wrapper. "Would you like my coat?"

"I'm warm enough, thank you."

They sat for a moment in an easy, compatible silence as they sipped the coffee.

"Hoyt Willis paid a visit to camp this afternoon."

"That right? What'd he want?"

Patience frowned as she thought about the vile buffalo skinner and his crude intentions. "He asked for a cup of coffee, but I think he was up to no good. Harlon had to ask him to leave."

"Oh?"

"Aren't you a little surprised he's still around?"

"No."

"You don't think he might be intending to cause some kind of trouble?"

She thought about mentioning the insinuations Hoyt had leveled at her, but she knew if she did it would only add to his troubles, so she left out some details about the incident. She was confident that Harlon had properly discouraged the vulgar man from coming around again.

Cass tipped his hat forward and lay back on the bedroll. "I'm not worried about Hoyt Willis, and there's no need for you to be either."

"Well"—Patience was confident that Cass could handle whatever trouble Hoyt Willis could cause—"I'd sure be happier to know that he was a hundred miles on down the road."

They shared the silence again.

When Patience finally turned to say something, she had to cover her mouth to stifle her giggles.

Cass raised himself halfway up, his brows drawing into an affronted frown. "What's so funny?"

"You . . . you look like you tangled with a wildcat!" *And lost,* she added mentally.

A muscle quivered in his jaw, and she could tell that he was trying to restrain his amusement. "You think it's funny, huh?"

Her eyes gleamed with merriment. "Yes . . . I never knew a jack-o'-lantern could be so ferocious!"

He shrugged and lay down again. "Go ahead and laugh."

"Thank you, I believe I will!" She broke into another round of mirth, and by the time she was near tears he'd decided to join her. He knew that he looked a sight, but it had been worth it. He and Aaron had taught Hoyt Willis a lesson tonight that the man would never forget.

"You remind me of the time Jimmy Lonigan pushed me into a mud hole," she teased. "I declare, I was a mess. My face was caked with mud; my dress was ruined; and the lovely yellow ribbon Mother had tied in my hair that morning looked like a soggy noodle. I was never so humiliated! I pitched a temper tantrum of such magnitude that my teacher was forced to send one of the younger boys rushing out the door to get my mother to come take me home." She laughed merrily. "I didn't return to class for a week, and I'm sure the teacher thought that was too soon."

Cass grinned as he pictured her fit. "What made Jimmy Lonigan want to push you into a mud hole?"

Patience looked down at him, managing to keep her features deceptively composed. "Why, I just can't imagine! I was such an angel!"

They laughed together, and Patience thought it had the nicest sound.

"I remember being embarrassed in front of the whole schoolroom once." Cass gazed across the moonlit meadow as the corners of his mouth lifted with amusement. "My brother Beau had brought a frog to school one day and stuck it in Elsbeth Wilson's lunch pail. Elsbeth was a real pain. Her folks were rich, so she always had more than the rest of us, but she was miserable. She always looked like she'd been eating persimmons. When she opened up her pail, that bullfrog jumped out onto her desk and swelled up with a loud *barrroopt!* You could have heard Elsbeth screaming for miles."

"What did the teacher do?"

"Because I'd laughed the hardest, the teacher thought I'd put the frog in her lunch pail, so she made me sit in the front of the room all afternoon, holding that frog on my lap, apologizing to Elsbeth every few minutes for being 'unsociable and crude.' "

Patience giggled. "And your brother didn't say a word in your defense?"

"Are you serious? Beau sprang out of his seat, pointed a self-righteous finger in my direction, and hollered that I shouldn't have been so mean, and that he was gonna tell Ma on me when we got home!"

They had another good laugh together. Patience couldn't remember when she'd had so much fun. When their merriment had died away, Cass swiveled to look at her.

"I'll bet you were one of those prissy little girls, in your frilly dress, with your hair in big blond curls that hung down to your fanny."

She nodded. "Mother insisted on my wearing my hair that way. Butch Michaels was forever dipping one of my ringlets into his inkwell," she admitted.

"He was probably sweet on you and just wanted to get your attention."

"Oh, he got my attention, all right! I gave him a black eye every Monday morning. It got to where he'd run when he saw me coming out the door."

Cass grinned. "I bet!"

She cast her eyes down shyly, knowing that he was teasing her this time. "I was pretty terrible most of the time."

"You haven't improved a whole lot since."

Patience glanced up, and he winked at her.

"Oh, you . . . how would you know what I'm like?" she accused. "You've never taken the time to get to know the real me. You're always blustering around, shouting at me, acting as if I'm about to give *you* a black eye every Monday morning."

"Butch Michaels has my complete sympathy," he said dourly. "I've experienced a couple of your black eyes."

Patience knew that he was speaking figuratively, of course.

"I'll admit that in the past I gave you reason to feel that way about me, but I wish I could convince you that I've changed, Cass . . . Even if I do backslide a teeny bit occasionally."

"A teeny bit? I'd say your lapses are more like rock slides!"

"Nevertheless, I am better."

Than what, he wondered to himself. "Well, if that's what you think . . ." he said indulgently.

"It's what I know. I'm really not a bad person."

He shrugged. "Who am I to argue? You were the perfect lady the day we met," he conceded dryly. "You remember? I just happened to step into your path while we were in Miller's Mercantile—"

"You didn't just happen to step into my way," she corrected. "You deliberately blocked my way."

"But you do recall the incident? You had just

bounced fifteen or twenty spools of thread off Edgar Miller's bald head because he didn't have a certain color you wanted."

Patience blushed. "That was a long time ago."

He eyed her evenly. "I sang tenor for months after that!"

"I said I was sorry."

"Since then you've tricked me into marrying you at the point of a shotgun, maneuvered me into taking you to Cherry Grove, deliberately thrown that nasty dishwater all over me, and with the aid of a bullwhip, thoroughly humiliated me in front of the whole wagon train and seven prostitutes. Then that same night, you turned the whip on me again, nearly peeling the hide off my back because you'd gotten it into your head that I was riding off to meet a redhead—"

"That whip never touched your back!"

His eyes narrowed. "A fact, I might add, that saved your life!"

Her eyes dropped sheepishly as he continued, "In the time I've known you, you've browbeaten me, cussed me, spat on me, threatened and coerced me more times than I can count on both hands—now tell me again how you've turned into such a nice person! I'm having a hell of a time believing that!"

She knew he was right. She had treated him

terribly. "I wish we could just start over," she confessed as a heartfelt sigh escaped her.

He was silent for a moment, and she wondered if he was angry with her again. Then he said quite calmly, "Well, I guess there's no law that says we can't."

Her eyes flew to his face, and his steady gaze assured her that she hadn't heard wrong. "Do you mean it?"

"I mean it. I don't enjoy this bickering any more than you do, and for the sake of everyone else, I think we should try to get along with each other. I can't say I'm ever going to forget what you've done, Patience, because I'm not sure I ever could. I'm the kind of man who likes to control my own destiny—and I damn sure plan on having the *only* say about whom I marry. No woman's ever gonna hog-tie and brand *me*. But I'll concede that people can change, if they want to."

Patience's heart tripped and thudded at his words. "Thank you," she said softly. "Does that mean you do believe I've changed?"

"That means I'm going to work on it a little harder."

"Thank you . . . because I'm beginning to care for you quite deeply."

"Well, just don't let it get out of hand," he warned.

"What would you say if I told you I needed

you?'' She knew the question was wanton, shameful, but it popped out anyway.

He slowly lifted the brim of his hat to look at her.

''I do, you know,'' she said.

''You mean emotionally?''

''I mean physically too.''

He lowered his hat again. ''I thought we'd been all through this. We're not going to bed with each other. A man doesn't take a woman—at least not a woman like you—unless he plans to make her his wife. I don't plan to make you my wife, Patience.''

She reached out, tipped his hat up. ''Right now, for this moment, I'm going to forget you said that, Cass Claxton! Once we reach Cherry Grove, you'll be a free man—no matter what you choose to let happen here . . . tonight.''

Love shone brightly in her eyes, and she prayed that, for once, he would recognize it. They gazed at each other as they had done many times before. His eyes were shadowed by the moonlight, making them seem darker. Still, she could see in their depths that he wanted her, perhaps more desperately than he would allow himself to admit.

''Patience . . . nothing is going to happen here tonight. It would be senseless . . . I'll admit I'm beginning to like you, but it isn't love.'' The very word scared the devil out of him.

"Cass, right now I don't care how you feel about me. I'm lonely . . . very, very lonely, and I'm beginning to wonder if I'll ever be able to make a man happy. I need you to hold me, to love me. I need someone to care just for me, even if it is only for tonight."

In a vague way Cass understood how she was feeling. The children and the trail made demands on their energy every day, and there were times when he, too, wished he could go to someone to ease his troubles.

"Surely I'm not so unlovable that you couldn't want to be with me," she argued. "You're a man, I'm a woman."

"Patience . . ." He *did* want to hold her, make love to her. He knew it wasn't right. In fact, it was wrong—but she was making it impossible for him to say no.

Sensing his growing weakness, she leaned over and her mouth brushed his persuasively. "Cass, please . . . just for one night . . . teach me how to be a woman."

Her lips continued to brush back and forth with lazy seduction.

"I thought after our talk the other night—" Cass objected weakly.

"I thought it over," she murmured. And she *had*, many, many times. "What a man and woman do when they make love doesn't sound all that bad. Besides, if Corliss lets Harlon and my mother let my father . . . it can't be that bad!"

They exchanged a slow, tantalizing kiss, and desire began to override common sense. "It isn't bad," he relented as their lips parted briefly. "It's pleasurable, and I'm sorry I misled you about it—"

He hand came up to cover his mouth. "Then love me, Cass, now . . . tonight . . ."

He groaned, and she suddenly found herself lying on the ground beneath him. She caught her breath, whispering his name.

She was innocent and he was worldly. He knew it wasn't a fair match, but he was blinded by the feel of her warm and willing body as she lay beneath him. Her urgent, whispered pleas were more than any man could ignore.

Her lips parted, and her eyes glowed with desire as her breasts rose and fell with each breath.

His eyes flashed a gentle but firm warning as he gazed into her eyes. "All right, but *I* make love to *you*."

"Meaning?"

"Meaning I consent because I want you, Patience . . . maybe I have for a long time—I don't know. But we're going to make love for no other reason than that I care for you, desire you, want you—but *not* because you've asked me to." His brow furrowed sternly. "That's a habit you're going to have to break. Other men are not going to have to be asked twice."

A satisfied light entered her eyes. "Maybe I won't be asking other men."

A muscle quivered in his jaw. "I'll whip your fanny if you do." His lips recaptured hers, more demanding this time.

When they parted many long moments later she whispered, "I promise you, Cass. I will never, ever deceive you again." And she meant it. Never again would she manipulate him. Never again would she impose her selfishness on him. From this moment on she would love him as deeply and wholly as she knew how.

He said nothing because he knew nothing to say, but she saw that the look in his eyes was one of understanding. "I hope you know what you're doing."

"I don't," she admitted with a cheeky grin. "But I figure you know enough for both of us."

A slow grin replaced his frown of worry. "Oh, you think so!"

She sighed. "I'm afraid I know so."

He pulled the pins from her hair, allowing the fragrant mass to tumble around her shoulders in a glorious cloud. His fingers slipped through the silken mass, and he drew her face slowly back to meet his.

The kiss ignited an ember that had been smoldering for weeks, and Patience knew that what she was about to do was right.

Their lips parted, and he brushed a kiss across her forehead as he began slipping her gown slowly—ever so slowly—over her head.

"You want to learn to please a man, huh?"

She nodded.

He drew her to her feet. Their eyes met and held as his large hands began a leisurely exploration of her body. He brushed his fingertips across the tips of her breasts, causing her to catch her breath with expectation. The crisp night air made her even more sensitive to his gentle ministrations.

"Are you afraid?"

"No . . . well, maybe a little."

His eyes darkened even more as his hand ran over her flat stomach, her tiny waist, along her arms.

"You can't hazard a guess what a man might like?"

"Well, if I were a man I would probably like to be touched here . . . and here . . . and maybe here . . ."

Cass's soft intake of breath told her she was probably right. His hands drifted over her bare bottom, squeezing her, then moved up her spine to send tingles racing through her.

"Yeah," his voice dropped to a husky timbre

as his eyes lowered to caress her nakedness. "You're getting close."

"And maybe here . . . and here . . ." He caught her hand and steadied it momentarily. "Most men are kinda partial to right here."

Her body seemed weightless, light, wanting him to seize control as their mouths came together again.

He was like a rich, heady wine drugging her with pleasure. His hands, gentle before, now began to tease, to excite, to take. Though Patience didn't have the slightest knowledge of this form of love, she trusted that he would be gentle with her.

"I don't want you to think about what I told you the other night . . . Making love can be beautiful."

"Oh, Cass, I knew you would make it so," she whispered as her own hands became bolder. He was all sinewy muscle and warm, pulsating flesh.

Cass wasn't sure he deserved the trust he saw in her eyes, but he was moved by it. "I won't hurt you. I want you to remember this night and know what it means to be a woman."

She smiled up at him, her heart overflowing with love. He knew her better than anyone. He knew all her weaknesses, and yet he still wanted her. The realization made her want to cry.

Their lips met again, all restraints abandoned

this time. Though he knew he had to move slowly, his body was hungry to take, to possess, to control. Taking her hand, he brought it back to him, murmuring softly, "You realize this may hurt."

Nodding, she closed her eyes. The feel of him pressing against her bare stomach suggested that pain might be inescapable.

Their mouths suddenly became inseparable, hungry, searching. There was so much for her to absorb: his scent, his taste, the unfamiliar feel of his manhood throbbing to claim her.

His hands explored, probed, paid homage to what had before been only a mystery. Her breathing was faster, more pronounced. Cass realized it was the first time in a long time that he was doing the leading with a woman. The teaching and the knowledge of her innocence made him heady with desire.

"Patience . . . I'm sorry . . . There are times when a man can't take it as slow as he would like to . . ."

Whimpering, she anchored her fingers in his hair and cradled herself more deeply into his arms. Desire, hot and urgent, raced unchecked through her. "I never thought . . . I never imagined it would be like this . . ."

Their kisses deepened, their tongues tempting, tantalizing, teasing, making them grow bolder, more daring with each passing moment.

They joined slowly, he keeping the rhythm easy and gentle. He had never had a woman be so giving, respond so completely and with so much love—but then nothing about her surprised him any longer.

She squeezed her eyes shut. The pain was there, as he'd said it would be, and suddenly his gentle motion took on a urgency that could no longer be contained. Her eyes suddenly opened, and above her she saw the velvety black sky and a million twinkling stars. And Cass was looking down at her with a look she couldn't quite make out—of tenderness, of hunger, of pride. Then he cried out her name, his arms imprisoning her trembling body as the pain dissolved and turned to ecstasy.

Her eyes closed again as she felt herself tumbling over and over into the inky blackness, willing the delicious sensations bursting throughout her body to go on forever.

❁ ❁ ❁

The tenderness lingered long afterward. Patience lay beneath Cass, trying to make sense out of what had just happened. She didn't regret one moment, but she wondered what must he think of her now.

She took small consolation in the fact that he seemed in no hurry for her to move, and she herself was in no hurry to break away.

"Well, what do you think now?"

She sighed. "I think you were trying to scare me the other night."

He chuckled as his hand caressed her bare bottom. "I'm sorry."

"You should be. I think I'm going to take to this quite well."

They rolled onto their backs on the blanket and gazed at the stars. As they exchanged kisses, he drew her closer to whisper into her ear. He told her things any woman would long to hear.

The magic of the night slowly slipped away; and long before she welcomed it, dawn signaled the coming of a new day.

"I have to be getting back. I don't want Corliss to know I've been gone." She slipped into her gown, aching to hear him say that the night had meant as much to him as it had to her, but he didn't.

They stood and he gathered her into his arms for one final long kiss.

"I'll be along shortly," he said when the kiss ended.

"Yes, breakfast will be ready soon," she said, disappointed. As she turned she was suddenly overcome by emotion. For one brief moment she thought she might fling herself back into his arms and beg him to tell her that she meant something—anything—to him. For him she felt a most incredible love, and she knew that what they had shared was the most wonderful thing that had ever happened to her. But she also knew that, as kind and gentle as he had been, what they had shared had not touched him.

"Patience?"

She turned. "Yes?"

"You can stop worrying," he said softly. "You're going to make some man very happy one of these days."

A smile, tiny though it was, came forth. "Thank you."

Squaring her shoulders, she lifted her head and walked back to camp, determined, painful as it would be, to try and put the events of this night behind her.

16

By the end of the week, the wagon train reached St. Joseph, Missouri, wherc Patience, Harlon, Corliss, the children, and Cass were preparing to say good-bye to their new friends before veering east toward Kansas.

Patience was going to miss Mardean, Winoka Medsker, Lucius Waterman, and Buck Brewster's sweet fiddle music. The group had formed close bonds, and Patience knew she would miss the ones who had become like family to her.

But they were all determined to substitute happy faces for tearful good-byes. After they cleared supper away that Friday night, the women brought out the pies and cakes that they'd managed to bake during the week. Meanwhile, Buck tuned up his fiddle for dancing.

The camp took on a festive air as the weary travelers set their troubles aside and, as Corliss put it, 'just let their hair down for a spell.'

Patience became breathless and rosy-cheeked by midevening. Though they'd traveled more than fifteen miles that day, the men had kept the women dancing nearly every jig. Patience thought Cass had forgotten her by the time he got around to claiming her for a dance.

"Miss McCord, may I say you look right fetchin' tonight," he complimented as he whirled her beneath an ebony sky full of twinkling stars.

"Oh, I do thank you, kind sir," she returned, matching his airy tone. "Your silver tongue just makes me feel ever so giddy, but I *was* beginning to fear that you were never going to come over and 'fetch' me."

"Been waiting for me, huh?" He threw his head back and laughed, whirling her around merrily, and she thought she would burst with happiness.

She gazed into his eyes and grinned. A change had taken place in their relationship since the night they'd made love. He was more at ease with her, less prone to being provoked, more willing to cooperate. "I thought I was going to have to whip Ernestine Parker and take you away from her," she said.

He winced. "I thought I was going to have to ask you to."

The music suddenly slowed to a waltz, and Matt Johnson stepped over to claim Patience. Cass motioned the other man away as he drew her possessively back into his arms, settling her closer this time.

Smiling, Patience laid her head against his shoulder and closed her eyes contentedly as he moved her away from the fire, into the deepening shadows.

"Sorry I didn't have time to eat dinner with you and the children," he apologized as the darkness wrapped its silky arms around them.

"We missed you, but I'm sure Laurence appreciated your helping him repair his axle."

"Lucy still cranky?"

Patience nodded, mechanically carrying on the conversation, but her thoughts were wandering. She loved his scent, his smell, the feel of his broad chest pressed tightly against her breasts.

"Maybe she's just tired of traveling," Cass said.

"Maybe, but it won't be long now before we're home."

They became lost in the sweet strains of the violin as he drew her even closer, drinking deeply of the intoxicating fragrance of her hair. Through her skirt she could feel the imprint of his maleness, barely restrained, exciting.

"Cass?"

"Hmmm?"

"Do you ever think about the other night?"

He appeared to be weighing his answer, and she wondered if she had overstepped her bounds. Finally he said, "If I were to be completely honest, Miss McCord, it would only make your head swell."

She savored a flood of satisfaction as she drew back to gaze into his eyes. "Then you do."

"I never said that."

"But you do." She felt her stomach tie in knots as he gazed back at her.

"All right," he confessed. "I do."

Her breath quickened as she reached out to trail her fingers tenderly down the side of his face. He moved back as if her touch had unnerved him.

"Then meet me again tonight."

"No."

She wasn't discouraged, wouldn't allow herself to be. "Please."

"Patience, no." She recognized the familiar stubbornness in his voice and steeled herself for a fight.

"Why not?" She knew it was madness, but she wondered how she'd lived so long without love.

"I don't want you to be hurt," he told her, his tone becoming more gentle.

"You would never hurt me." Her fingers lightly stroked his shoulder blades. "Don't you know how I ache to be with you, to lie in your arms once more?"

"I want you to stop talking like that." He bent close, his lips perilously near hers. "We'll reach Cherry Grove in a few days. No matter what has passed between us"—his voice lowered—"I'll expect you to hold to your promise concerning the divorce."

"I intend to."

"The minute I get you and the children settled, I'll be on my way."

"I understand that."

Their mouths moved nearer.

"I don't want you going all hurt and weepy when I leave," he warned. He paused and gazed deeply into her troubled eyes. "It's going to be hard enough to leave the children. I've lain awake the past few nights, trying to sort through my feelings, and I realize I've grown more attached to all of you than I should have. Aaron and Payne look up to me as the father they've never had. And I'm sorry, really sorry, that I can't be here for all of them . . . Jesse, Doog, Joseph, Bryon, Lucy, Margaret Ann—God, Margaret Ann!" A look of respect came into his eyes. "What a match she'll make for a man someday—Lucy, Phebia . . . you."

In many ways Cass knew that Patience had

come to depend upon him as much as or more than the others. "But I *will* be leaving, and should I take you to my bed again, though I can't deny that it would be my pleasure, it would only make our parting harder when the time comes for me to go."

"Then don't go!" she urged in a broken whisper, suddenly wishing she had more control over her emotions. She had been struggling so long to find herself, to know the real Patience McCord, but it had taken this man to show her that she could be the woman she'd always longed to be. She didn't know how she could bear losing him now, so soon after he'd taught her the real meaning of love.

"I have to leave, Patience. I'm not ready to settle down to one woman . . . I may never be."

"Not even Laure Revuneau?" Patience knew she was out of line, but she had to know what he felt for Laure.

"Laure?" Cass realized that he hadn't thought of the French beauty in weeks.

"I believe she was hoping for a Christmas wedding, with you."

She felt him grow tense. "I guess she's free to hope all she wants. No woman's gonna hog-tie and brand me."

Her pulse leapt expectantly. "Then you aren't planning to marry Laure?"

He sighed. "My only plans are to return to

St. Louis and attend to my business, which has been sorely neglected of late."

Her eyes met his unashamedly. "I'm going to say something you're not going to like."

"Then don't say it."

"I'm in love with you, Cass, deeply in love."

His face changed and became hard. "Patience . . . don't do this—"

"I am, Cass. I'm sorry, but I am." She stopped dancing and caught his face in both her hands, not caring that others were watching them now. "I love you and I will never, ever give up hope that someday, no matter what I've done in the past, you will return my love."

"Patience," he warned, pulling her hands away and drawing her face to his chest. "You're making me nervous as hell!"

"I know you always have been a mite skittish," she acknowledged with a broken sob, "but you can't stop me from loving you. You're the best thing that has ever happened to me."

"No, Patience. It'll do no good for either one of us to think that way. I can't return your love. We're no good for each other," he said sternly, and she wondered if he wasn't trying to convince himself more than her.

She thought of all the times she had rejected other men—easily, cruelly, and without much thought for their feelings. She guessed the good

Lord had had His fill of her nonsense and had sent Cass Claxton for her penance.

But if He had, she would gladly accept her punishment and pray that the Lord would see fit to extend it.

❁ ❁ ❁

"We could meet tonight."

"No."

"We have only three days left. We could slip away for just a little while and . . . and I would have something to remember you by." Patience knew she was sounding like a shameless hussy lately, but she didn't care. She loved Cass so fiercely, so completely, that she was willing to endure any name anyone wanted to call her if he would spend one night with her again. "Please, Cass, what could it hurt? If you're worrying about my virtue, the damage has already been done."

"Patience, how many times do I have to tell you no—I won't be asking you to my bed!"

"I'm asking you to *mine*!"

Cass was not sure how long he could keep refusing. He wanted her. He ached for her, but he knew that if they made love again, it wouldn't satisfy the hunger in him but only nourish it.

His need for her was becoming a raw craving, one he had to fight daily. He cared for her—maybe he did even love her at times—but there was still a part of him that wouldn't accept the verdict. She had tricked him more times than he could count, and he wasn't sure he could ever really trust her. And when it came down to it, what good was love without trust?

She sighed. "You might as well give in to me. I'll ask again."

"And I'll just keep refusing."

And she did. And he did. And she did. And he did. Every night, until Cass thought he would lose his mind. But he took hope in the knowledge that if he could make it through one more night, then the battle would be over.

It was the last day out, and Cass deliberately rode well ahead of the wagon. At noon, he took his meal and ate with Aaron and Payne under a distant tree.

Surprisingly Patience left him alone.

Later that night, when everyone was safely tucked in bed, Cass took his bedroll and went in search of a place to sleep. All during supper he had watched Patience move about camp. His passion demanded that he ask her for a moonlight walk, then passionately fulfill her every need, yet his common sense told him that he only had to make it through one more long torturous night, and he would once again have his freedom.

Spreading the blanket on the ground, he went to the creek to wash up. When he returned five minutes later, Patience was already lying on the blanket.

"Oh, hell!" He stared down at her, shifting on one foot impatiently. He just didn't have the strength to go through this again!

"Hello." Her smile was beguiling and meant nothing but trouble. "Isn't it a lovely night?"

"What are you doing here?"

Her lower lip formed a teasing pout. "Why are you always so cranky?"

He looked down on her dourly. "I guess a man wouldn't need one of those crystal balls to see what you're up to."

Her smile turned wicked as she rose and presented her back to him. She began to remove her shirt, then her blouse.

"Patience," he warned.

A camisole sailed against his chest, and he groaned.

Deciding he was simply going to ignore her, he dropped to the bedroll and jerked his hat determinedly down over his face. If she wanted to catch her death, he wasn't going to waste his breath trying to stop her.

He suddenly tensed as he felt her hand on his belt.

"Patience, don't make me get mean with you," he growled.

"Now, now, darling," she purred throatily. The belt suddenly loosened, and he felt the top button of his breeches give way. "I know you must be exhausted from trying so hard to ignore me. I'm just going to help you relax a little."

He was aroused instantly, and the sight was encouraging to Patience.

"I don't need any help, and it wasn't a bit tiring to ignore you."

Her hands began to ease his breeches down. "Well, you just did a wonderful job," she praised, sliding her body up his long length, her mouth coming to rest against his with a long, unhurried kiss.

Cass's lips parted for one blissful moment as he moaned, his hand slipping up to capture a bare, satiny globe.

"You're naked," he accused resentfully against her lips.

"My, my, so I am! How do you suppose that happened?" Her fingers loosened the buttons on his shirt. "You know, you almost had me believing your little act until I saw the way you were looking at me during supper tonight."

"I wasn't looking at *you*. I was watching the dog."

"No, you weren't watching the dog. You were looking at *me*. You couldn't take your eyes off me, not once." She placed her hands on his hard flat belly, caressing, taunting.

"You're really asking for trouble, lady."

She smiled and leaned down to kiss him. "So humor me."

Moments later his flannel shirt came off, and her hands made quick work of peeling back his undershirt. Spreading her hands across his bare chest, she nipped his rib cage painfully with her small, even teeth.

"Ouch!"

"That's for ignoring me all day." She kissed the place she nipped, then nipped again.

"You are shameless!" He chuckled, feeling his body tremble as she began kissing her way across the dark hair on his chest.

"Tell me you're sorry."

"For what?"

She nipped again, only lower this time.

"Lord!" He caught his breath as her hands and her mouth grew bolder. "You realize you're acting like that redhead you found so offensive?"

"No, I'm nothing like the redhead," she said, moving back up to cover his mouth with hers. "I can't come close to her experience," she whispered. "But I don't think you'll ever notice the difference."

He sighed and completely gave up as his hand moved downward along her body in a soft caress. "Where is everyone?"

"Asleep in the wagon."

"Harlon and Corliss?"

Their mouths touched, teased, became more intense.

"Sound asleep."

Cass could not suppress the glow in his eyes as he finally rolled her over on the blanket, gazing deeply into her slumberous violet eyes with a lusty perusal. "Then I suppose I'll have to let you have your way with me, Mrs. Claxton."

He'd finally gotten her name right.

"Yes, darling." She yielded with mock subservience. "I guess you will."

17

The Maison des Petites Fleurs orphanage arrived in Cherry Grove a little before noon on Wednesday. It was a dreary, overcast morning, and a bone-chilling wind blew from the north. October had finally gotten down to business, and the earlier reassuring rays of sunshine had been violated by clouds.

As the wagon rolled down Main Street, Patience took in the familiar sight of Miller's Mercantile, and she breathed her first sigh of relief since she'd left St. Louis forty-one days ago. The journey was finally over, and the Lord had seen them safely through.

Patience pulled the team to a halt. Corliss lifted the flap, a big smile settling over her tuckered features as her eyes took in the row of storefronts. "Lordy, Lordy, am I ever glad to see this!"

Patience sighed, her own smile projecting relief. "We're home, Corliss. We're finally home."

"Praise the Lord!"

Edgar Miller was sweeping his porch, his gaze darting to the wagon every once in a while as he tried to see who the new arrivals were.

Patience saw his balding head bobbing up and down with curiosity, and she lifted her hand to give him a friendly wave. "Hello, Mr. Miller!"

Eyes widening, Edgar nearly dropped his broom when he recognized Leviticus McCord's daughter. He suddenly turned tail and shot back inside the mercantile, slamming the door firmly shut behind him.

Cass rode up beside the wagon and stopped. Resting his hand on the saddle horn, he grinned down at Patience lazily.

"You'd better raise a white flag, Miss McCord. I believe the troops are getting nervous."

Meeting his laughing eyes with an impervious look of her own, Patience firmly gathered the reins in her hands. "Very funny, Mr. Claxton."

Cass was still chuckling as she clucked her tongue and urged the team to begin moving again.

Nothing had changed in Cherry Grove. The sleepy little town wasn't much, but she knew there were a lot of good, God-fearing people residing here, people who would see to the children's physical and spiritual welfare. She saw that the Havershams still had their restaurant and that Doug Kelly still ran his saloon and gambling house. She wondered if the saloon still served as a church on Sunday mornings. The town wasn't nearly as bad as she'd thought it was six years ago. It was a nice place, actually, one she was sure that she and the children would grow to love.

Once they were settled, the children would come to know and respect Leviticus, and she and Cass could—

Her newfound enthusiasm was suddenly overshadowed by an unsettling thought. In a few days Cass would no longer be with them. He had become so much a part of all their lives that it was hard to imagine how she and the children were going to manage without him. Patience didn't want to imagine a day without him, let alone the rest of her life, but she admitted that she had no magical power to prevent him from leaving.

The wagon turned the corner, and Reverend Olson's house came into view. Patience could see Rebecca standing on a chair, cleaning windows. The parson's wife glanced up, startled when she recognized Patience driving the wagon. She quickly recovered and began tapping on the panes of shiny glass, making staccato sounds as Patience smiled and waved at her.

Moments later the door to the parsonage flew open, and Reverend Olson came hurrying out, still struggling into his coat.

Patience was eager to see Leviticus again. Though they'd corresponded regularly, she hadn't seen him in six long years. She wondered how much he'd changed. He'd always had a penchant for gooseberry pie and lemon cake, and she giggled as she pictured her wiry little father having developed a round belly and rosy cheeks.

She couldn't wait until the children met him. Patience knew they would adore him, and Harlon and Corliss would welcome the hours of companionship Leviticus would provide.

At Christmastime, he would see to it that the orphanage had the biggest, brightest, most beautiful tree in all the town. There would be apples, nuts, and oranges to fill each stocking, and the house would be bursting with the mouth-watering smells of succulent roast duckling, tasty mince pies, delectable spice cakes and—

Her thoughts wavered as Leviticus's house suddenly came into view. Unconsciously she pulled back on the reins, bringing the team to a halt. For a moment she sat dumbfounded staring at the scene before her. There was nothing there except a smoke-blackened chimney standing alone in the pile of burnt rubble.

Patience heard Corliss's sharp intake of

breath, then her awestruck "Dear God in heaven!"

The chimney, silhouetted against the gray sky, was the only thing left of Leviticus McCord's house. The rest had burned to the ground.

Whirling, Patience saw Cass riding up beside her. Speechlessly she looked at him.

Climbing off the horse onto the wagon seat, he drew her into his arms as Reverend Olson came hurrying up to the wagon.

The reverend appeared momentarily taken aback as he saw Cass Claxton holding Patience McCord in his arms. But he quickly pushed aside his astonishment and said, "Oh, Miss McCord . . . I'm so sorry I wasn't able to stop you."

Lifting her face from the haven of Cass's chest, Patience stared back at the reverend, still unable to comprehend what was happening. "Stop me?"

"Yes . . . your father . . . he's . . ."

The meaning of what he was trying to say slowly began to penetrate her numbed senses, and her face suddenly crumpled. "Daddy?"

Reverend Olson glanced at Cass guardedly. "You'd better bring her to my house. We can talk there . . ."

Patience peered expectantly up at Cass. "Cass . . . where's Daddy?"

"Come on, sweetheart." Cass lifted her gently off the wagon seat and drew her protectively against his side. "Corliss, you'll see to the children."

"Of course."

"Aaron, you drive the team and follow us back to the reverend's house."

"Yessir."

Cass mounted his horse, then reached down and lifted Patience as he would a small child, placing her in the saddle in front of him. Stunned, she wrapped her arms around him, holding on tightly. "Cass . . . Daddy . . . what's happened to him?"

Nodding solemnly at the children who were staring up at him with open curiosity, Cass reined the horse around and walked it back in the direction they'd just come from.

When they arrived, Rebecca was waiting with a pot of hot tea and a heart filled with compassion. The reverend suggested that he and Patience step into his study. Alarmed, she glanced to Cass for assurance and he nodded. "You want me to come with you?" he asked.

She shook her head dazedly. "No . . ."

For a moment he wasn't sure she could make it on her own, but he should have known better. He had come to realize that there was more to Patience McCord than met the eye.

The door to the study closed as Rebecca reached out and pressed a reassuring hand on

Cass's shoulder. "Come sit beside the fire. You must be weary."

Cass belatedly removed his hat. "Thank you, ma'am. I'd be obliged."

When they were seated, Rebecca reached to pour the tea, but Cass suddenly jumped to his feet, his tormented gaze focused on the study door as the sound of Patience's anguished cry tore through his heart.

'Please, Mr. Claxton," Rebecca urged softly. "This is very difficult . . . Later she will need you more."

Cass sank down slowly, stunned by what had happened. His blue eyes pleaded with Rebecca, trying to make sense of it all. "How . . . when . . . ?"

"Two weeks ago, in the middle of the night. No one is sure how the fire started. By the time it was discovered, it was well out of hand."

"And Patience's father? He wasn't able to escape?"

Rebecca shook her head sorrowfully. "They found Leviticus still in his bed."

Cass woodenly accepted the cup of tea she offered, wondering how he was going to get it down.

"We were aware that Patience was on her way here. That's all Leviticus talked about after he'd gotten the news she was coming. We've felt so helpless knowing we could do nothing to prepare her for the tragedy that awaited her."

Rebecca blotted her eyes. "My, how Leviticus looked forward to seeing his only child again and the children she was bringing to fill the emptiness in his life." Overcome by emotion, Rebecca tried to stem the flow of tears rolling from the corners of her eyes. "He had such fine plans, such high hopes. He would sit for hours and tell anyone who would listen how they were all going to be so happy . . . And now . . . now what will happen to all of them? Leviticus and the home they were coming to are gone. Everything is gone."

Cass's gaze traveled back to the study door as Rebecca's words drove deeply into his heart.

The children were homeless. Again.

Later that afternoon Patience asked Cass if he would take her to visit her father's grave. He said he would, and they left just after supper. Rebecca had insisted that they stay the night at the parsonage, saying that they'd all put their heads together the next morning and come up with some solution.

At the sight of the fresh mound of dirt, Patience caught her breath and turned away, realizing that she'd been praying all afternoon that it wasn't true. But it was. Her father was dead.

Cass silently drew her back into his embrace and held her tightly as her anguish overflowed, and her tears came again.

"He never really knew me," she whispered brokenly. "And I never really knew him."

She was heartbroken that Leviticus would never know how much she'd loved him, how much she'd appreciated all the love and devoted care he'd given to her. And she had never once thought to say thank you.

Was it possible for a child to fully realize how deeply and unselfishly a mother and father had given their love, never asking, but freely sacrificing whatever was required to see the child happily and safely to adulthood? What other relationship on this earth could boast of such love, such unending commitment that asked nothing in return? How strange, she thought, that children failed to understand such love until they had children of their own.

She recalled how one day she had selfishly demanded that her papa walk through snow up to his hips to buy a silly little bauble she'd decided she had to have. He'd worked all day and walked home, but at her insistence he'd trudged back out into a blizzard to do her bidding.

Hours later he'd returned, cold and exhausted, bearing a red peppermint stick and the shiny spinning top she'd wanted. She'd jumped up and down with joy in their warm, cozy parlor while Leviticus had shed his sodden clothing and Mama had wrapped a warm blanket around his shoulders. Patience could still hear the way Leviticus's teeth chattered as he stuck his feet into a basin of hot water to thaw out.

Mama had raced around the kitchen, fixing tea and liberally lacing it with brandy to keep him from catching his death, while Patience had watched the colorful top twirl round and round in the middle of the floor, unconcerned about her father's near-frozen state.

She could recall thinking she was the luckiest little girl in the world to have such a fine papa who would buy her such extravagant things. Now she knew how fine Leviticus really was, not because he could afford to buy his daughter a spinning top but because he'd loved her enough to walk three miles in the snow to purchase a silly toy that meant nothing to him but everything to his five-year-old child.

Leviticus McCord, Patience could still hear her mother scolding, *you're spoilin' that child somethin' terrible!* But Leviticus had only laughed and candidly admitted that it was true, but that he didn't care. Then he had taken Patience onto his lap, opened the family Bible, and as her chubby fingers had worried the top round and round in her hands, he'd begun to read her favorite story to her, the one about Mary and Joseph and the little Babe born in a manger.

The tears came harder now, and Patience desperately wished she were that child again.

Drawing her gently away from the graveside, Cass supported her slight weight back to the buggy that the reverend had lent them for the journey. He lifted her up onto the seat, and their eyes met and held.

"Tell your papa good-bye, Patience."

Drawing her shoulders up determinedly, Patience turned, and with tears streaming down her cheeks, she said loud and clear, "Good-bye . . . and thank you, Papa!"

She glanced back to Cass, and a radiant smile suddenly broke through her tears. "Do you think he might have heard me?"

Cass smiled back at her lovingly. "I think he heard you."

As darkness closed around them, Cass picked up the reins, and the horse began moving away, leaving only Leviticus—and the good Lord—to know for sure.

❀ ❀ ❀

"Good Lord! Look what the dogs have dragged up!" Beau Claxton stood gazing at his brother, shocked to find him standing in the doorway of his soddy.

The two brothers began slapping each other on the back, laughing and whooping like two young boys as Charity moved away from the stove to see what all the commotion was about. About the time she discovered that it was Cass, she was already being swept off the floor and tossed into the air by a pair of powerful arms.

"Cass Claxton, put me down!"

"Lordy, you're fat as one of ma's old sows!"

"Beau!" Charity wailed. "Tell your brother that I'm not fat; I happen to be carryin' another child of yours!"

Retrieving his wife's squirming body in mid-air, Beau lowered Charity to her feet, kissing her soundly on the way down.

"*Another* young'un?" Cass teased, his eyes surveying the three children looking up at him with wide-eyed innocence. "Haven't you people ever heard of moderation?"

Beau looked at Charity and winked. "Not with this woman I haven't."

"Well, control yourself," Cass admonished with a grin. "I can only stay for a little while."

"You'll stay the night, won't you?" Charity protested. "We haven't seen you for years!"

"Sure." He reached out and ruffled the youngest child's head of blond hair. "I have to get acquainted with my nieces and nephews, don't I?"

"You'd sure better!" Wrapping his arm around Cass's shoulder, Beau walked with him over to the fire. "What are you doing here? Children! Come over here and meet Uncle Cass."

Beau motioned for the children to come to him. "You remember Mary Kathleen? She was just a baby last time you saw her, and these are the twins, Jason and Jenny."

Cass grinned and shook each child's hand solemnly. "Nice-looking family, Beau."

"Thank you." Beau beamed with fatherly pride. "It is, isn't it?"

While the men caught up on the news, Charity fixed supper. After they'd eaten the thick slices of cured ham, hot cornbread, and steaming bowls of brown beans, she sensed that Cass wanted to talk to Beau alone.

Around eight, she hugged each man, then discreetly excused herself, saying she wanted to put the children to bed early.

When she'd disappeared to the far corner of the room, Cass sat staring pensively into the fire as Beau got up to wind the clock.

"So, what brings you back in our direction?" Beau asked as he finished with the clock and reached for another stick of wood to throw on the fire.

"It's a long story, but at the moment I'm trying to find a home for nine children."

Beau's hand paused in midair, and he grinned. "Nine, huh? Your women all catch up with you at one time?"

"No, my women didn't all catch up with me at one time," Cass mimicked.

"Whew!"—Beau's brow lifted curiously—"we're a little touchy, aren't we?"

Cass supposed that he was, but he was tired and he had to get the children settled somewhere. Phebia had cried for two days, wanting the home she'd been promised.

"I'm in one hell of a mess, Beau."

Beau's eyes met his brother's solemnly. "You're serious, aren't you?"

"I'm serious."

Beau sat down to give his full attention to whatever was bothering his brother. "All right, I'm listening."

Cass took a deep breath, then began to talk of his recent journey from St. Louis, of the orphanage, the children, and the fire. He was candid about everything except Patience McCord and her forcing him to marry her six years ago. That was too humiliating to admit, even to Beau.

"Why would *you* agree to escort a pack of orphans to Cherry Grove?" Beau wondered aloud.

"I did it as a favor."

"For those old people you mentioned—Harlon and Corliss?"

"No, it wasn't for them. I agreed because the woman who runs the orphanage was in a bind," he mumbled.

"Really!" Beau stared into the fire thoughtfully. "What's her name, and how good-looking is she?"

"That didn't have anything to do with it," Cass shot back defensively.

"I'll bet!"

"Seriously, Beau, it didn't. I ran into their wagon outside of town on my way to—on a trip I was taking. They hadn't gotten two miles out of town, and already they were stuck in a mud hole. When I stopped to help, the woman made me see how desperate they were for a man to help them make the trip to Cherry Grove. Well, I couldn't just ride off and leave them stranded, now could I?"

"Since when?"

"Come on, Beau, you know me better than that."

Beau chuckled. A year ago it wouldn't have surprised him one bit to hear that Cass had left twelve people stranded along the road. "So you agreed to bring nine children, two seventy-year-olds, and the woman back to Cherry Grove." Beau had to wonder about that.

Cass nodded. Suddenly, he sat up straighter, his face animated. "You wait until you meet these kids—you're going to love them! There's Aaron—he's sixteen—and Payne—he's fourteen. I've been teaching them all about hunting and women! Then there's Jesse, Doog, Bryon, Joseph, Margaret Ann . . . Wait till you meet

Margaret Ann—you won't believe this child. She thinks she's thirty years old—and you will too once you talk to her—but she's only six. Then there's Lucy and Phebia. Phebia is three and still sucks her thumb, although we've all been trying like hell to break her of it. And then there's Joseph who's as cute—"

"Whoa! Wait a minute!" Beau glanced up expectantly. "Are you *sure* these aren't your kids?"

"Of course they're not my kids, but lately I've been thinking it wouldn't be so bad having a couple of my own," Cass admitted.

Beau thought he detected a defensive note in his brother's voice. "Ma would insist you marry first."

Cass sighed. "I'm aware of that."

"So, you were bringing the kids and the old people and the woman from St. Louis, and when you got here, you found that the house that was meant to be the new orphanage had burned down?"

"That's right. And I've looked everywhere for the past two days to find a house large enough to serve as an orphanage, but there just isn't anything." He had debated about taking them all back to St. Louis to give them Josiah's house, but with winter coming on, he realized that Harlon and Corliss would be in no shape to make the return trip.

Beau seemed pensive as he thought about the problem. "I can think of only one fire that's happened around here lately, and that was Judge McCord's house over in Cherry Grove—you remember him? He had a daughter named . . . what was it? . . . Patience, that you had that run-in with at Miller's Mercantile one day."

Cass blinked. "Seems like I do recall meeting her."

"You *recall* meeting her!" Beau hooted. "Why she about knocked your—"

"I *said* I remember Patience McCord," Cass interrupted tersely. How could he forget her? It wasn't enough that she'd been on his mind; now she and her nine kids were in his heart.

"I just asked." Beau had never seen Cass so edgy.

"Look, I might as well tell you because there's no way I'm going to be able to keep it from you: Patience McCord runs the orphanage. I said I would help her get the children to Cherry Grove safely."

Beau cocked his head wryly.

"It's the truth."

"How many guns did she have pointed at you?"

"None!"

"All right, all right, you don't have to take my head off!"

"I need your help, Beau. Now let's stop mess-ing around and get down to business. I'm running out of time."

"How can I help? I don't have a house big enough for three kids, let alone nine!"

"Then you're going to help me build one."

"You and me? Build a house that big?"

Cass nodded. "And however many men I can hire to help us. Patience needs a home for those kids, Beau, and I'm not going back to St. Louis until I know they have one."

"Well, I'll be damned!" Beau said softly. He was beginning to wonder just what Cass's main concern was—the kids or Patience.

"You can be anything you want!" Cass grunted irritably as he reached inside his shirt pocket for a cheroot. "Just have your tail end in Cherry Grove first light tomorrow morning."

18

With the help of Beau, Aaron, Payne, and the twenty additional men that Cass was able to hire, the house was completed in two weeks. It took five men alone to build the fireplaces.

And what a glorious house it was. Fifteen rooms, seven fireplaces, five spacious bathrooms complete with claw-footed tubs for bathing, and the most modern, up-to-date kitchen conveniences Edgar Miller could have shipped from Hayes on such short notice.

The house even had running water piped straight to the bathrooms and kitchen, provoking the envy of every housewife in Cherry Grove.

Cass wouldn't let Patience see the house until

it was almost completed. But her excitement and enthusiasm surpassed even the children's, so late Saturday afternoon he borrowed the reverend's buggy and drove her out to the building site.

The orphanage was situated just outside of town on thirty-five acres of prime land. The house was built in a grove of towering oak trees, providing cool breezes in the summer and a sturdy windbreak in the winter.

The horse's hooves clopped up the winding drive as Patience's hands came up to cover her mouth. She tried to keep from squealing when she saw the magnificent sight spread out before her. The house was as large as a palace!

Cass grinned as he watched her grow speechless in wide-eyed wonder. "I wanted it be larger, but the men told me that would require several additional weeks to complete, and I figured that Rebecca and the reverend couldn't stand the strain."

Having thirteen unexpected guests for two weeks couldn't be pleasant, Cass had reasoned, especially since four of the children were either ill with chicken pox or coming down with it.

"Oh, Cass, I've never seen anything like it!" Patience exclaimed, her eyes alight with joy. "It must have cost a fortune!"

Cass reined the horse to a stop in front of the house, and they sat for a few moments, admiring the carpenters' craftsmanship. The dwelling was superb, both in quality and construction. It had two stories of wood and stone, with tall columns supporting the sweeping verandas.

"The men will finish up the stonework by late tomorrow. The remainder of the furniture will be here Monday, and we should be able to get you moved in on Tuesday morning," Cass said simply as he set the brake and stepped out of the buggy.

"Oh, it's lovely . . . simple lovely . . ."

He turned to lift her down but instead held her suspended in the air for a moment, his dancing eyes meeting hers teasingly. "Is that all you can say—that it's lovely?"

She smiled down at him affectionately. "How about, thank you, Sir Galahad." For indeed she thought he was the noblest knight in all the land.

Cass shook his head, indicating that she needed to do better.

She shook her head inquiringly. "No?"

"No."

"Then perhaps a kiss from the fair maiden?"

"Perhaps you know one?"

"Sir"—she dropped her gaze demurely—"I *was* one, until Sir Galahad rode into my life." Her mouth dipped to brush his lightly, and Cass could feel the thunder of his heartbeat.

"I guess I should apologize, fair maiden. I don't know what came over me," Cass said, his voice becoming husky with desire. The last two weeks had allowed them no time alone, and he'd discovered that he had missed his sweet temptress. "Can you forgive me?"

"The fair maiden not only forgives you, but longs for more," Patience whispered.

"Come here, my little seductress." His mouth took hers and she responded. With a sigh she melted against him, refusing to admit to herself that they were spending their last few days, maybe hours, together.

The house was so close to completion. Once he had her and the children comfortably settled, she knew he would be gone, leaving her with only a memory to ease her aching heart.

Their lips parted, and he let her slide the rest of the length of his body. The intimate motion left them both breathless with wanting.

"I believe you were interested in seeing the house?"

"Oh, yes . . . I can hardly wait."

Tucking her against his side, he led her up the steps leading to the circular veranda.

"Cass, has Reverend Olson ever said anything to you about why we're together?"

"No, but I've noticed that he and Rebecca have exchanged a few inquisitive looks."

Patience and Cass shared a good chuckle as they imagined the kindly minister's confusion. Though the reverend had presided over their hasty vows six years ago, neither Cass nor Patience had expected him to think their marriage would last.

"I suppose I should sit him down and explain what's happened," Cass conceded.

"I think you should." Patience looked up at him and grinned. "Then come and tell *me,* because I still can't understand it."

"Someone will have to explain it to me first." Cass had lain awake nights, wondering how he'd suddenly found himself so entangled with Patience. They shared an easy camaraderie now, one that he knew he was going to miss.

They opened one of the two large doors and stepped into the front parlor. Long, elegant windows lined the room, bringing in the light from the east. A huge fireplace to lend warmth in the winter centered on the west wall.

Patience's hands flew up to cover her mouth again as she viewed the mammoth room. "Oh, my . . ."

"Come Christmas Eve, I want Aaron and Payne to cut the biggest, nicest tree they can find," Cass told her. "When they bring it home, I want you to make it a night the children will always remember. They can string popcorn and berries and make chains from colored paper. I'll send some of those tiny candles they can put on the branches, but you'll have to watch and be sure that they don't burn themselves. And be sure to make Phebia take a nap that day, so she won't be so cranky that she can't enjoy it. And have Jesse and Doog hold Joseph up to the tree, so he can get his share of the fun and—"

Patience laughed delightedly. "Cass Claxton, I never dreamed you were so sentimental!"

Cass grinned sheepishly. "Christmas is a special time for family. I want this year to be the best the children have ever had."

They walked toward the kitchen holding hands. Patience was taken aback when she saw the long work counters, the two ovens in the walls, two cookstoves, three sinks, and a colossal-sized icebox to keep the milk, butter, meat, and vegetables cool.

"I've never seen such luxury," she murmured, her eyes taking in the rows and rows of copper-plated pots and pans hanging over the cookstoves.

Taking her arm, Cass led her to the window and pointed to a large structure still under construction behind the house. "That's going to be the washhouse. I wanted it to be away from the main quarters so that you and Corliss won't be bothered."

"Bothered?"

"I've arranged for three women to come in four times a week to do the wash."

Patience turned, flabbergasted. "For how long?"

"From now on."

"But Cass, I can't afford to pay three women to do our wash!"

"I know you can't, but *I* can. There'll also be a couple of men who'll do the yard work, two who'll keep you in wood, a man who'll supply fresh meat year-round. Three local farmers will keep you in fresh vegetables, milk, eggs, and the fruit in season. Sadie Withers and Wanda Mitchell will be coming in daily to do the cooking so that you and Corliss won't have to work so hard. I've arranged for you to have unlimited credit at Miller's Mercantile, so you can buy staples and the children's clothing and shoes. Use it. I've also spoken with the doctor in town, and he's been instructed to forward any bills pertaining to the orphanage to my offices in St. Louis, including those incurred by Harlon and Corliss and yourself. You'll also be receiving a sizable check each month for any incidentals you might need." He paused and lifted his brow inquiringly. "What have I overlooked?"

She gazed back at him in awe. "Your sanity! I can't accept such generosity."

He drew back, affecting a mock bow. "I'm not bestowing all this on you, fair maiden. I'm giving it to the children."

"Cass . . . I don't know what to say. Your kindness is overwhelming, but—"

Cass took her arm again and guided her to the next room. Their footsteps echoed hollowly across the gleaming pine floor as they walked. "No *buts*. You should know by now you're not going to win an argument with me."

"Ha, ha! Aren't you the dreamer!"

The dining room came next, large and airy with space enough to seat fifty guests. "The children will be needing the extra room for all the friends they'll be bringing home over the years," Cass explained.

An adjoining room with back-to-back fireplaces looked out over a meadow, providing the children with restful surroundings to do their schoolwork. Next to it was a medium-sized study where Patience would transact business pertaining to the orphanage. The room had a smaller, more intimate feeling, with a cozy fireplace tucked into one corner and four large windows across the south wall.

To the left, a separate wing housed Patience's and Corliss and Harlon's bedrooms.

Cass suggested that they view Patience's quarters after they'd taken a tour of the upstairs.

Escorting her up the long, winding staircase, Cass then led Patience down the hallway, where they peeked into each of the bedrooms the children would occupy. Every room was large, bright, and cheerful. Patience could just visualize the looks of astonishment on the children's faces when they saw their new home.

Patience thought her heart would burst from

happiness. There was only one thing to mar her joy: the knowledge that Cass would not be there to share it with them.

"Now I'll take you to see the best part," he said.

"There couldn't be more."

"Ah, but there is."

They went back down the stairway, arm in arm. At the bottom Cass turned her in the direction of the wing he had left for last.

"I thought you might enjoy having the bedroom on the left, though you're free to choose any one you want."

He paused before a closed door and gave her a wink that threatened to make her heart stop beating. "For some reason, I'm partial to this one." He reached out, turned the handle, and the door swung open.

Patience was unprepared for the sight she found. The four-poster bed, the armoire, the chiffonier, and the dressing table were made of the finest, richest walnut. The draperies, the bedspread, the pillows, the fabric on the settee in the adjoining sitting room, the chaise longues, and the numerous chairs scattered about were all done in delicate shades of lavender and blue. Lush baskets of ferns hung in the corner windows where the last rays of daylight shone through the windowpanes. Outside the window was a large pond where three graceful swans glided on the peaceful water. Patience's eyes took in the small dressing room, a closet the size of a room, and the private bath with handles and faucets shaped in the form of swans.

The room was so beautiful that she felt tears welling in her eyes.

Cass leaned against the doorway, viewing her emotion with tenderness. "The lavender reminds me of your eyes; the blue warns me how much I'm going to miss you and the children," he said softly.

Not daring to look at him, she kept her eyes fixed on the swans and said in a broken voice, "You're leaving, aren't you?"

"First light, Wednesday morning," he verified softly.

"Must you go?"

"Patience . . . I warned you this would happen."

"I'm not trying to stop you . . . I just wish you didn't have to go."

"There are times I wish I didn't have to either, but I do." He wasn't sure if he *could* love one woman after so many years of running from them. But he knew that what he was feeling for her must come powerfully close.

Swallowing the lump crowding her throat, Patience turned, smiling. "Then we don't have much time, do we?"

"No." He drew her into his arms, his eyes growing dark with his need for her.

Placing her hands on either side of his face, she closed her eyes as he pulled her to him, his lips skimming over hers in something more provocative than a kiss. Suddenly he drew back as he felt the salty wetness begin to slide down her cheeks. "What's wrong?" he probed gently.

"I'm sorry. I'm doing exactly what I promised I wouldn't do."

"Going weepy on me?"

"Yes."

Stemming the flow of tears with his thumbs, he asked softly, "But why are you crying now? I haven't left yet."

Her heart was in her eyes. "You've brought me here tonight to say good-bye, haven't you?"

He sighed, tenderly drawing her head back down to his chest. "Yes. It's not easy for me, Patience, but I'm just not ready to settle down. Can you understand that?"

"Yes." Patience understood, but it didn't make it any easier for her.

For a long moment they said nothing; then he gently tipped her face up to his and kissed her. Her breath fluttered unevenly through her lips to his, "I never knew it could hurt so bad."

"What?"

"Loving you."

"Please, don't make this any harder," he whispered raggedly.

Tears ran unabashedly down her cheeks. "I'm afraid I'll never see you again."

His breath was warm and sweet against her mouth. "I won't ever be very far away from you."

"Oh, Cass, how will I ever let you go?"

They sank to the floor, holding each other tightly. Soothing her hair from her forehead, he touched his lips to her nose, her cheeks, then her mouth. It was the first time he had taken such infinite care in loving her. It was as if he wanted to memorize every inch of her, the texture of her silky skin, the scent that she'd bathed in, the knowledge that she willingly waited for him.

"I can't seem to stop wanting you," she confessed. "Is it always like this?"

"Yes."

He drew back as if there was something more that he needed to tell her. But words failed him, and he shook his head wordlessly, burying his face in the haven between her breasts.

Trying to control the tears that rolled silently from the corners of her eyes, she tenderly soothed the top of his head, sharing his agony yet lost in her own.

They clung to each other, needing to assure each other that everything would be all right, that first light on Wednesday morning would never come. But Patience knew it would and he would then be gone, never to hold her in his arms again.

Cass lifted his eyes to gaze at her, realizing that torture could be exquisite.

She smiled through her tears, cupping his face between her hands gently as she sought to ease the hurt and confusion she saw in his eyes. "We have so little time. I don't want you to ever forget me, Cass Claxton."

"Forget you?" His gaze grew even more tender. "Can a man forget a sunrise or a baby's smile?"

She felt his fingers skim down the front of her dress, releasing buttons so that he could find her. His mouth returned to take hers with heat-soaked passion as they rolled over on the floor. Her body began to respond wherever he touched her, the response becoming more eager, more anxious as his hands took on a renewed urgency. There was nothing soft, nothing gentle in what they brought to each other now. His caresses drew her upward, filling her with a deep, searing need. She could hear his sounds of pleasure as his mouth took hers with a building passion.

Her breath caught as he tore at her dress with a primitiveness he had never shown before. He was ravaging her, and even as he realized it he could do nothing to prevent it. He wanted her, had to have her.

They began to kiss with reckless abandon.

His mouth worshiped, devoured hers as he tried to say her name but couldn't. His clothes fell away; then the remainder of hers followed; and they became mindless with desire.

He rolled on top of her, and they were no longer aware that they were breathing.

"Don't leave me," she whispered fervently.

"No, let me go, Patience. You have to let me go . . ."

Soft sobs engulfed her as he passionately sought to ease her sorrow.

But Patience knew it would take more than kisses to erase his memory. She would never lie in his arms again, never feel the touch of his hand, never know the joy of his crooked smile.

She couldn't lose him, an inner voice screamed helplessly, and yet she knew she had, as he masterfully drew her into a sheath of satin-coated oblivion, muffling her sobs with his kisses. Come Wednesday morning, he would ride out of her life, forever.

19

In the end she had no choice but to watch him leave. Wednesday's dawn was as bleak and cold as the cloak of loneliness settling around Patience's heart. The first snow of the season was beginning to sift down in fine, powdery flakes as Bryon, Joseph, Lucy, and Phebia huddled around her skirt, their eyes openly indicting Cass for desertion as he went about saddling his horse. Even Margaret Ann had shed some of her sophistication as the knowledge that he was actually going to leave them began to sink in.

A cold wind whipped the tails of the heavy sheepskin jackets that Cass had recently purchased for the boys as Jesse, Doog, Payne, and

Aaron stood by, anticipating his departure with stony silence.

After delaying as long as he could, Cass finally found enough nerve to turn and face his accusers. The forlorn faces he found waiting weren't encouraging.

He cleared the sudden lump in his throat and adjusted his hat, settling it lower on his forehead, carefully avoiding meeting any one particular gaze. "Well, guess that about does it."

Corliss offered him the sack of food she and Patience had prepared earlier. "Just some chicken and biscuits—won't last long, but it'll be more appetizing than jerky."

"Much obliged, Corliss. I appreciate it." Cass tucked the food away in one of the saddle bags. "I talked to Harlon earlier, but tell him I said good-bye again."

"Shore will . . . You take care now, you hear?"

His eyes softened. "I will, Corliss."

"How long will it take you to return to St. Louis?" Patience asked, finally stepping forward.

Cass was forced to meet her gaze, though he didn't want to. They had said their final good-byes toward dawn, and it hadn't been easy. "Ten, twelve days . . . Depends on how good time I make."

"You could sell your horse in St. Joseph and

take a boat the rest of the way," she said. "It'd be faster."

"No, I don't mind. I need the time."

A faint smile touched her lips in an effort to make it easier for him, because she realized that he was hurting as much as she. "You take care of yourself. The weather looks like it doesn't plan to cooperate."

"I will." He gazed down at her, wondering for the thousandth time if what he was doing was right, and he came up with the same unyielding answer: He just didn't know.

"You'll write?" she whispered as her bravado began to slip.

"Yes . . . You do the same."

"Of course."

Turning to face the children, he looked at the faces he had grown to love, fighting the building emotion that was pressing heavily against his chest. "You kids mind your elders."

There was a combined mumbling of "yessirs" before Phebia buried her face in Patience's skirt and began to cry.

Reaching out, Cass lifted her into his arms and forced her to look at him. "You're a big girl now, Phebia, and big girls don't cry."

Tears of misery rolled silently out of the corners of the child's eyes. There were many things the three-year-old couldn't comprehend, but Phebia sensed that Cass would no longer be there to patch her small hurts and make them better.

"You want to pinch my nose?" he bantered lightly.

Phebia shook her head no.

"Will you give me a kiss before I go?"

She nodded. Cass removed the thumb from her mouth, and she leaned over and pecked him on the mouth.

He winked at her. "Not bad. With a little practice, you'll be breaking some man's heart before we know it."

Margaret stepped forward shyly to offer him a kiss. She was joined a few moments later by Lucy. God, he loved these kids, he thought as he held on to the three small bodies tightly.

Phebia suddenly backed away and extended Marybelle to him. Cass grinned and obediently gave the chosen one a kiss. But Phebia emphatically shook her head. "Marmarbelle go with Papa," she said firmly, extending the doll to him again.

Cass lifted his brows, stunned. "You want me to take Marybelle?"

Phebia's face broke into a radiant smile. "You Marmarbelle's papa!"

Gazing at her lovingly, Cass nearly broke down. "You sure you don't want Marybelle to stay here and live with you?"

Phebia shook her head again.

"All right. I'll be a good papa to Marybelle." Cass stood and carefully tied the doll onto his saddle horn.

Openly shaken now, he turned and knelt down to hug Joseph, then Bryon. Rising to his feet again, he shook hands with Doog and Jesse. "You boys behave yourselves."

"Yessir."

"Yessir."

He could feel his eyes beginning to water as he reached out and clasped Payne's hand in his tightly. "I'm depending on you to keep the smaller ones under control."

"I will, sir."

"You see that you do."

And then it was time for Aaron.

Aaron's eyes remained stoically fixed straight ahead as Cass, too overcome by his deep feelings for this young man, simply reached out to squeeze his thin shoulder. Then he turned and walked blindly to his horse.

"Cass."

His foot paused in the stirrup as he heard Patience's voice.

"Yes?" he answered without turning around.

She was suddenly by his side, her hand gently on his arm, silently willing him to turn and look at her.

But he steadfastly refused. Keeping his head

down, he said in a voice growing gruff with emotion. "Patience . . . let's just get this over with."

Wordlessly she pressed an envelope into his hand.

Recognizing the significance of the long, legal envelope, a blanket of pain suddenly covered his features. The divorce papers.

"These are the papers I promised you. All they need is your signature," she said softly. "I signed them a few days ago."

For one fleeting moment Patience thought he might relent and stay with her, but the moment was brief. He swung up onto the saddle, tucking the envelope inside his jacket dispassionately. "See that you write."

Her eyes reaffirmed her love for him, told him that she would always love him. "You do the same."

He kicked his horse in the flanks, and the children stood huddled against the driving wind, watching him ride out of their lives as simply and as uncomplicatedly as he had ridden in.

❁ ❁ ❁

"*Mon chéri,* I do not know what has gotten into you!" Laure Revuneau paced the floor of Cass's study, wringing her hands with frustration. "I did not hear from you the entire time you were gone. And now that you're back, you've been ignoring me for weeks."

Cass sat at his desk, staring out the window at the snow coming down in a heavy blanket. A sense of depression, one that had plagued him since he'd left Cherry Grove ten weeks before, was with him again.

Crossing the room to drape her arms around his neck affectionately, Laure sighed. "You have not made love to me since you returned. Have I done something to offend you, *mon chéri?*" She nuzzled his neck invitingly.

Cass pushed back from his desk, hoping to remove himself discreetly from her embrace. He didn't know why, but Laure no longer held her former appeal. In fact, no woman did. He had begun to compare each one he encountered with Patience, and it annoyed him. "You haven't done anything wrong, Laure. I've just been busy lately." He stood and walked to the fire and picked up the poker.

She followed him, her mouth curving in a provocative smile. "You are not so terribly busy now, *n'est-ce pas?*"

He studied the fire, realizing that the time had long passed to be honest with her. He had told her nothing of Cherry Grove or Patience McCord, and he didn't plan to. But he also realized that he had no plans to continue their relationship. "I'm sorry, Laure." He knelt to poke the fire. "I'm leaving for Atlanta within the hour."

She was stung by his rejection. Her startled

face was suffused with disappointment. "You're leaving again?"

"I'm sorry. I'm afraid my business has suffered since I've been away, and I will be traveling often in the next few months."

"But . . . *mon chéri* . . . what about us?"

He straightened, turned, and his eyes met hers steadfastly. "I think you would be happier if you sought more reliable companionship."

Lifting her head proudly, Laure realized that she was being dismissed. It was a compassionate dismissal, but nevertheless it had become apparent over the past few weeks that he no longer cared for her. She knew she could plead with him to change his mind or she could accept his decision with the grace befitting a lady of her stature. She chose the latter because she sensed, though she hadn't the vaguest idea why, that this decision had not come easily to him.

"If that's what you want," she said.

"Laure . . ." He sounded tired, discouraged, and she heard a familiar note of despondency creeping back into his voice as he sighed. "I wish to hell I knew what I wanted."

A tap sounded at the door as Laure gathered her ermine cloak and prepared to leave. "Perhaps you will reconsider when you return from Atlanta."

"I won't reconsider."

Laure opened the door to find Mozes waiting.

She turned back to Cass and smiled bravely. "I do not give up easily."

Cass lifted the corners of his mouth in a wan smile. Then he winked. "Take care, Laure."

"I shall, *mon chéri.*" Her eyes softened perceptively. "Whoever she is, I hope she deserves you."

Mozes stepped back to allow Laure room to exit. When she was gone, he walked into the room as Cass turned back to the fire.

"Another letter has been delivered, sir."

Cass glanced up expectantly.

"Again it's postmarked Cherry Gro—"

Mozes didn't get to finish before the letter was snatched from his hand as Cass tore into it eagerly.

"Will there be anything else, sir?"

Cass wasn't listening as he strode toward his desk, his eyes hungrily roving over the piece of paper.

"Very good, sir." Mozes closed the door, grinning. He had no idea what was in Cherry Grove, Kansas, but it had to be something special.

Seating himself at the desk, Cass began hungrily reading Patience's neat handwriting:

Dearest Cass,

I hope this letter finds you happy and well. The Christmas tree fit in the window just as beautifully as you predicted it would. Aaron and Payne took the smaller boys, and they scouted the woods on Christmas Eve looking for the perfect pine to cut.

That evening we placed the lovely candles on the tree, and the children strung popcorn and made chains from the colored paper you'd sent them. When they were finished, the tree was truly a magnificent sight.

Aaron and I took turns holding Phebia and Joseph to the top of the tree so they could place Baby Jesus in the manger. Joseph was so proud after we gathered around the tree later that night, when I opened the Bible to read to them about the angel appearing to the Virgin Mary, telling her she had been chosen to be the mother of the Christ Child and how Joseph and Mary had made the long trip to Bethlehem only to find no room at the inn.

For days afterward, our Joseph was quite adamant that he had a wife named Mary and that they had journeyed to Bethlehem on a donkey, where they'd developed bad head colds because they'd had to sleep in a stable.

Corliss and I finally got the children to bed and asleep by midnight, only to be up again before five. The older boys were ecstatic over their new rifles, and the girls simply adore their dollhouses. Of course, Bryon and Joseph thought their bicycles topped everything. Where in the world did you find such silly contraptions?

Well, I must close and get to bed. Tomorrow Doog and Jesse are in a spelling bee at school. Can you imagine that?

We think of you every day, and your name is mentioned quite frequently in Margaret Ann's prayers.

Respectfully Yours,
Patience McCord

❁ ❁ ❁

The first buds of spring were just bursting open on the oaks when Doog came running up the drive, waving a letter in his hand.

"It's here!"

Patience dropped her sewing, and children started flying out of every door. Making her way carefully down the steps, she prayed that it was news from Cass.

"Is it from him?"

"Yes!" Doog answered.

When Cass's letter was in her hand, Patience closed her eyes and held it close to her heart for a moment, imagining that she could smell his familiar scent. Of course she couldn't, and at the children's indignant insistence, she ripped into the letter and began to read aloud:

> Dearest Patience, Harlon, Corliss, Aaron, Payne, Doog, Jesse, Bryon, Joseph, Margaret Ann, Lucy, and Phebia,
>
> Please do not take in any more children until I can acquire a longer pencil.

Patience paused to glance up sheepishly. "He's silly, isn't he?"

"Read us more," Joseph demanded.

"All right." She went on:

> I have been traveling for many weeks now, and I am very weary. At times I think I will sell everything I have and retire, but after a good night's rest, I change my mind again. Hope you children are minding well and keeping up with your homework.
>
> Take care of yourselves.
>
> Love,
> Cass

Margaret Ann frowned. "Is that all?"

Patience sighed. Cass couldn't be accused of being long-winded. "That's all."

❁ ❁ ❁

Dearest Cass,

Is it ever hot! If we owed someone a hot day, we could have paid him back a hundred times lately. The temperature has soared above one hundred for days, and the children are getting cranky. Aaron and Payne have taken the smaller ones to the pond to swim every afternoon, though I had to scold Joseph again today. He chases my pretty swans until their tongues are dragging the ground.

Harlon is up and about. Feeling right perky, he says to tell you. Corliss says to tell you that she's feeling tuckered out because of all the heat. Phebia has just about stopped sucking her thumb, though she does have an occasional relapse.

I received the signed divorce papers. Thank you.

Hope you are well. I had a spell last week of not feeling so well, but I'm much better now.

We thought of you the other night at supper; we were enjoying that stew you like so much.

Take care.

Respectfully,
Patience McCord

P.S. I almost forgot! Bryon and Lucy wanted me to tell you that they've each lost another front tooth. You should see them when they grin! They insisted that I enclose their teeth—hope you don't mind.

The oaks were bursting with color as Doog came running breathlessly up the drive again.

Patience ran out of the washhouse. "Is it here?"

"It's here!"

She flew across the yard, her heart thumping erratically.

"Give it to me."

Not waiting for the other children this time, she tore into the letter, her eyes eagerly reading the words:

Dear Ones,

Since I'm in California, I decided to visit the ocean today. I sat for a long time looking out across the water, thinking of you. I was reminded of what a great distance separates us. Sometimes I worry that you don't have everything you need, and that makes me worry even more. If you should ever want for anything, you have only to ask. And don't be concerned about money. I have all we could ever need and more. I used to think money could make a man happy, but I'm beginning to realize that there are more important things in a man's life.

Take good care of yourselves—I miss all of you in a way I find hard to put on paper.

Love,
Cass

P.S. Patience, be sure that the kids have *big* pumpkins for Halloween. I mean it. I'm getting tired of you being so frugal.

Dear Cass,

The children had the biggest pumpkins in town. I hope you're happy. Do you realize you are spoiling these children shamelessly?

Take care.

Respectfully,
Patience McCord

Dear Patience,

I'll spoil the children if I want to. God, I miss you.

Cass

❁ ❁ ❁

"The old-timers are predicting at least nine inches by morning," Mozes remarked as he set a tray filled with sandwiches and a pot of tea on the study table.

Cass answered absently as he sat before the fire, his fingers folded above the bridge of his nose, staring unseeingly at the glowing embers. Patience was on his mind constantly lately. Her memory tortured him at night, and today he'd passed a woman on the street who'd reminded him of her. The response he'd had to seeing the look-alike had been mighty painful.

What was he going to do about Patience McCord? About the children?

He got up and walked to the window, where he began to pace restlessly. It had been close to a year since he'd seen them. A year. How much the children must have grown! Why didn't he go to them? How much longer was he going to feed his senseless pride that no longer required feeding, he wondered.

Regardless of what she'd done to him in the past, he could no longer deny that he was in love with her. She had changed. He had seen her change from a spoiled brat to a compassionate, loving woman. So what in the hell was he waiting for? Why did he keep torturing himself like this?

Suddenly he stopped pacing. By God, he

wasn't going to wait any longer. He was going to go after her.

His eyes caught sight of a buggy pulling up in front of the house, and he groaned.

Company, the last thing he needed or wanted. He was about to tell Mozes that he wouldn't see anyone, when he noticed a boy stepping down from the carriage.

Whirling back, Cass leaned closer to the window, his face breaking into a big smile when he recognized the visitor.

"Aaron!" Cass bolted from the window as Mozes glanced up from pouring the tea.

"I beg your pardon, sir?"

"Mozes, it's Aaron!" he exclaimed as he ran across the room and out the door.

"Aaron?" Mozes lifted his brow curiously.

Aaron was just coming up the walk when Cass flung the door open. The boy broke into a grin as Cass rushed out to engulf him in a warm embrace.

Clapping him heartily on the back, Cass exclaimed, "Aaron, what are you doing here, son?"

"Come to pay you a visit!"

Cass held the boy away to get a good look at him. He'd grown at least two inches! "Lord, it's good to see you—"

His smile suddenly froze as one possible reason for Aaron's visit crowded in on him. "Is everything all right at the orphanage? Has anything happened to Patience or one of the children?"

"No, sir, they're all doin' fine," Aaron insisted with a good-natured grin.

"Are you sure?"

"I'm positive."

Cass began moving the boy toward the house, keeping his arm firmly around him as if he might somehow slip away. "How did you get here?"

"By boat."

"Boat? From St. Joseph?"

"Yessir, I have a part-time job working at Miller's Mercantile, and I used some of the money I've been earnin' to buy my ticket."

"You didn't need to do that. I would have sent you the money to come for a visit."

"I couldn't do that, sir. Miss McCord says I need to be man enough to stand on my own two feet."

"Well, she's right, of course—are you hungry?"

"Yessir."

They walked inside the house, and Cass shouted for Mozes to bring more food. Mozes stuck his head out of the study, wondering who this young lad was who made his employer so happy.

"It's cold out there—and snowing." Cass hurriedly drew Aaron closer to the warmth of the fire.

"Yeah, but Missouri's not as cold as Kansas."

"Take off your coat and warm yourself. How in the world did you find me?"

"I asked around. You weren't hard to find."

Mozes returned with a large tray laden with food, as Cass began to fire a million questions at Aaron about the other children.

When he'd answered all of them to Cass's satisfaction, Aaron tore into the slice of steaming hot apple pie that Mozes had just placed before him.

Cass lit a cheroot and settled himself behind the desk. "Well, how have you been?"

"Real good. You remember Ernestine Parker?"

"Sure, I remember Ernestine."

Aaron grinned. "Well, me and her just might be marryin' up next spring."

"Is that so!"

"Yessir. We've been writin' back and forth, and I'm thinkin' real strong 'bout askin' for her hand."

Cass shook his head, grinning. It was hard to realize that the boy was old enough to think about such things.

"How old are you now?"

"Seventeen. Ernestine is younger, but I plan on takin' real good care of her."

Cass smiled. "Ernestine's a fine choice,

Aaron. I'm sure she'll make you an excellent wife."

"Thank you, sir. I hope she feels the same."

"Where do you plan to live?"

"In Cherry Grove. I think Miss McCord can use my help raising those kids. Corliss and Harlon are getting so old, and the kids are a real handful at times."

Cass nodded, glancing out the window, fondly recalling how there was rarely a moment's peace when the children were around. "How are Corliss and Harlon?"

"Just fine."

"And Patience?" Cass's tone softened as he turned and leaned forward in his chair. "How is she?"

"She's fine, sir. Had you a fine son a few months back."

"Oh, yeah? Well that's goo—" Cass started to lean back when he suddenly froze, his face draining of all color. He sat up straight. "Had me a *what*?"

Aaron looked at Cass directly, and his tone changed from friendly to cool in the blink of an eye. "I said, she had you a fine son, sir." After all the times Cass had told him he was to do right by a woman, Aaron found it ironic that *Cass* had walked out on Patience, leaving her to raise his child.

Cass could not find his voice.

Moving the slice of half-eaten pie aside, Aaron stood up and drew a deep breath. He didn't cherish what he had to do, but someone had to do it. "Sir, I want you to know I've thought a lot about what I'm about to say—and I know you might not be real happy to hear it, but I've come a long way to say it, so don't try to stop me."

Cass glanced up, still in shock by the news that he had fathered a son.

"I don't mean no disrespect, sir, but you've got this comin'."

"All right." Cass stood up to meet Aaron's stringent gaze expectantly.

"Say what you've got to say."

"You're a no-good son of a bitch . . . sir." Aaron struck out at Cass blindly.

"Aaron!" Cass dodged the flying fist, astounded by the boy's actions. "I've whipped men for less than this."

Aaron braced himself, fully prepared to fight. "Then you'd better get to whippin', sir, because it's the truth." The boy's face was flushed with anger.

"The truth!"

"Yessir, it is."

"You want to tell me why you think it's the truth?"

" 'Cause of what you did to Miss McCord."

"What do you think I've done to her!"

"Sir, I may not know a whole lot, but I think it's plain to everyone what you did to her."

Cass had the grace to blush. "That's not what I meant. What's all this nonsense about me being a son of a bitch?"

"You are one, sir, sure as I live and breathe."

"Why?"

Aaron kept his eyes solidly fixed to the snow falling outside the window. "You told me you'd been taught that if a man accidentally fathered a child, then he should be man enough to accept his obligation. Otherwise he was a son of a bitch."

"And you think I haven't?"

Aaron's gaze focused on Cass accusingly. "I *know* you haven't."

Cass leaned back in his chair, trying to grasp what had happened. He was quiet for a long moment, trying to muddle through what Aaron was saying. "Does Patience know you're here?"

"No, sir! And she'd skin me alive if she knew. She thinks I've gone to visit Ernestine, but I had to do this for Sammy."

Cass glanced up again. "Sammy?"

"Yessir, Samuel Casteel Claxton. I believe Miss McCord figured you might want your son named after you and your pa, seein' as how he's dead and all."

Samuel Casteel Claxton. God, Cass thought, *I have a son.* Patience had had the perfect way to trap him again, but she hadn't. She *must* have known or at least suspected that she was carrying his child when he'd left her. She'd let him ride away that day, divorce papers in hand, and never said a word.

"Aaron"—Cass's voice broke with emotion—"believe me, I didn't know . . . She never told me . . . I never dreamed . . ."

Aaron studied Cass's reaction quietly, realizing with a jolt that the news had come as a complete shock. Had he really not known about the child?

"You mean, she really never told you?" Aaron asked.

"No . . . She never said a word. I wouldn't have left if I had known . . ." Cass's eyes turned pleading. "You have to believe me, Aaron. I didn't know."

Stepping forward, Aaron laid his hand on Cass's shoulder, squeezing it reassuringly. "Well then, I think it's time you met your son." Aaron smiled into Cass's eyes, and Cass saw that the smile was no longer that of a child but of a man.

"I think so, too, son."

The expression Aaron saw in Cass's eyes reminded him of five-year-old Joseph, when he had done something wrong. "You think Patience will forgive me?"

Aaron grinned. "Shoot, yes. She's always been down right silly about you."

A proud grin spread across the new papa's face. "When's the next boat leave from St. Joseph?"

Reaching into his back pocket, Aaron drew out two tickets. "Tomorrow morning—and I'd be much obliged if you would pay me back for your fare, because I'll be needin' money when I have my own son"—Aaron flashed him an embarrassed grin—"sir."

20

The sounds of a mother crooning a soft lullaby to her child filtered softly through the room. The fire popped in the grate, and the house had settled down for the night.

Patience cuddled the child in her arms lovingly, her hand supporting the head of dark curly hair as she gazed into an achingly familiar pair of blue eyes and sang softly, "Hush, little baby, don't you cry; I'm gonna sing you a—" Patience glanced up as she heard the sound of a match being struck.

Her heart leapt to her throat when she saw who was standing in the doorway.

Cass leaned against the frame insolently, his gaze focused on the child she was holding. "Forgot to mention something, didn't you, Miss McCord?''

She managed to calm her pounding heart long enough to return his gaze innocently. ''No, Mr. Claxton, not that I can think of.''

He motioned with his eyes to the child. ''No?''

''No.''

He drew off the cigar thoughtfully. ''Where did you get the baby?''

Patience smiled. ''Oh . . . he just sort of came . . . one day.''

Cass's gaze traveled lazily over her fuller bustline. ''I'll bet.''

Patience realized that, somehow, Sammy's father had found out about him. ''Who told you?'' she asked softly.

''Does it matter?'' Tossing the cheroot in the fire, Cass walked into the room and came over to kneel by her chair. His presence suddenly filled the terrible emptiness in her heart, and she murmured a silent prayer, thanking God for sending him back, even if he didn't plan to stay.

Cass gazed down on his son, his eyes growing tender. ''God, Patience, he's beautiful!'' The child had big blue eyes and a head of dark, curly hair.

Sighing, she drew the blankets aside for him to examine their perfect creation. ''We did do good work, didn't we, Mr. Claxton?''

"We sure did!" Cass reached out and touched his son under the chin reverently. "Hi, son."

The child puckered up and started to cry, distressed that his dinner was being delayed.

Mother and father laughed, momentarily easing the tension.

"How old is he?"

"Three and a half months."

"No kidding! Why, he's big for his age, isn't he?"

"Of course." She was deliberately avoiding his eyes. She wasn't sure she could keep her emotions under control. "Samuel Casteel Claxton is going to be just like his father. A fine, strong man."

Cass leaned closer, and she felt faint as she drew in his familiar smell. She longed to throw herself into his arms and let him kiss away the loneliness of the past year, but she knew she wouldn't. Not this time.

His gaze had returned to the infant to study the shock of dark hair and arresting blue eyes. "He looks like me. Ma will be pleased."

Patience sighed. He didn't have to remind her of how much the baby looked like him. Sammy was a daily reminder of what they had once shared. "Yes, he does, and he has your streak of orneriness too."

"Mine!" he grinned, that ornery crooked grin

that tore at her heartstrings. "I'd say he takes after his mother in that department."

"Oh, now, now," she cooed as the child began to sob harder. "Is this any way to act in front of your papa?"

Cass suddenly caught her hand, demanding that she look at him. "Why, Patience? Why didn't you tell me about our son? Did you think you could keep this from me forever?"

Swallowing the lump crowding her throat, she brought the baby up to her breast to nurse. "No . . . I just wasn't sure how you would feel about it, Cass. I know you aren't ready to settle down, and a baby certainly does call for a certain amount of permanence in one's life."

Cass tried to ignore the sight of her bare breast. He struggled with the urge to touch her . . . to hold her in his arms again. "Feel about him? He's my *son*."

Patience drew a long breath, and finally turned to face him. "Yes, but he's my son too, Cass. Now, how does *that* make you feel?"

They looked at each other, their gazes locked in anguish.

"Maybe that just makes him that much more special," he admitted in a shaky voice.

"*Maybe*?" She wasn't sure what he was trying to say. Was he here to claim his son? If he was, he'd have to claim her too. She wanted Cass Claxton, and this time she was willing to fight for him. "I didn't tell you about our child because I didn't want you to think I was trying to trick you again."

"I wouldn't have thought that—"

"Yes, you would have. You know you would have."

"Well, I don't think that now," he said gently.

"Cass, I love you so deeply it's a physical ache at times," she blurted out. "I pray every night that someday you'll return my love, but I'm tired of using tricks and deceit to hold you. I'm afraid if you want your son, you have to take me too."

"I'd be grateful to have both of you."

"And you'll have to want *me* because we agree our lives will be empty and meaningless without each other," she warned, his ready acceptance failing to register with her. "I'll settle for nothing less."

His gaze traveled adoringly over her, then on to his son nursing at his mother's breast. "You'll have nothing less. I'm sorry it's taken me so long to realize how I feel, but I had to be sure—for both our sakes. I love you, Patience Claxton—so damn much it hurts."

"Well, as I say, if you ever want—" She suddenly paused, his words finally sinking in. Her eyes widened. "You love me?" she whispered.

He nodded, slowly drawing her mouth down

to meet his. They kissed for a long moment, deeply and with a hungry urgency.

"Oh, Cass, why did you leave?"

"I had to. It's taken me a year to realize what's important in my life, but not a day has gone by that I didn't know, deep down in my heart, I loved you."

"But you signed the divorce papers."

"Yes, because I wanted *that* marriage over and done with. I want us to start again. I want our love to be the ruling force this time, not manipulation. I'm deeply in love with you, Patience." His hand reached out to touch her face reverently. "I hope you can forgive me."

"Oh, Cass, if you only knew how long I have waited to hear you say you love me."

His smile was as intimate as the kiss he was about to give her. "Get used to it—you're going to be hearing it a lot for the next fifty years."

When their lips parted many long minutes later, she prompted softly, "Does this mean you're home to stay?"

"It does."

"What about your business—?"

He placed his finger across her lips in an effort to allay her concerns. "I've already consolidated a lot of my holdings, and the rest of my business can be handled from here in Cherry Grove. I'm closing the house in St. Louis, and I've arranged to have Mozes brought here to help with the children—if you have no objections."

She gazed back at him, her heart overflowing with joy. "No, of course I have no objections, but Cass . . . are you sure it's me you want, or is it because of your son that you've changed your mind?" She had to know for sure.

"I want you, my love, and my son . . . and my nine other children."

"Oh, Cass . . . are you sure? The children will be overjoyed. They love you as much as I do . . ." She paused and smiled, drowning in the familiar blue of his eyes. "Well, almost as much."

"Woman, I've never been more sure of anything in my whole life—and don't start arguing with me." His lips pressed, then gently covered her mouth.

"Then each and every one of us is yours," she said a moment later. "You don't mind being hog-tied and branded?"

"Not by you."

He reached out to pull her and the baby onto his lap as Sammy grunted and began struggling to keep his supper from disappearing again.

"Hey, kid, me and your ma are getting married—not in the middle of a road at the point of a shotgun, but she and I and our ten children are going to plan the biggest, rowdiest wedding this old town has ever seen!" Cass told his son. "I want the whole world to know she's mine, and she's going to stay mine for the rest of her life!" He paused and grinned engagingly at his son. "What do you think about *that,* Samuel Claxton?"

Sammy Claxton burped.

Cass and Patience laughed delightedly as they began kissing again. "That means your son thinks *that* sounds just grand," Patience clarified.

Cass winked lovingly at Sammy's mother. "So does his papa."

❁ ❁ ❁

Cass stood at the bedroom window, looking down on the activity, shaking his head with amazement. The orphanage was decked out in its very finest. Greenery and colored ribbons adorned each room, and the smell of fresh-cut flowers filled every nook and cranny.

The parlor was filled with tables stacked high with gaily wrapped presents awaiting the bride and groom's attention.

A magnificent eight-tiered wedding cake kept Corliss and the women who scurried about the kitchen busy trying to keep the children's fingers out of the icing.

There had been a solid stream of buggies arriving for the past hour, with people alighting from the carriages in their Sunday best to witness the exchange of vows between Miss Patience McCord and Mr. Cass Claxton.

A knock sounded at the door, and Patience swept into the room like a bright ray of sunshine.

"Hello."

Cass turned, a smile surfacing on his face when he saw her. "It's about time you got here. Come here, woman."

She went willingly to him, and his arms encircled her, one hand at the small of her back as they exchanged a long, thorough kiss.

"Patience, please! I can't make it through another four hours," he whispered, completely miserable now.

"Oh, it will be more like six hours," Patience told him solemnly.

"Six hours?"

She nodded.

He began drawing her toward the bed purposefully. "There is no way on earth I'm waiting *six* more hours to make love to you. I've already waited over a year. Enough is enough!"

She laughed, gently thwarting his efforts to wear her down. "You promised."

"Promised what?"

"You promised we could have a real wedding night."

"I'm a man in love—I can't be held responsible for what I say," he excused himself. His mouth captured hers again relentlessly.

Patience wasn't buying his sad story. She laughed, pushing him away firmly. "But you're a man of your word."

"Our wedding night is going to be real," he coaxed as he drew her back into his arms persuasively. "Real long, real passionate, real unforgettable, real—"

"*Real* real, with the bride coming to the groom unsullied."

"Patience." He shifted to one foot tolerantly. "I seem to recall a time when you were not half as worried about your virtue."

"But I didn't have to be." She pecked him on the mouth affectionately. "That was when I was married to you," she reminded him.

"Well, hell! You're going to be married to me again in another hour."

"I know." She rubbed against him, pressing her lips to his throat. "Think about that while you're waiting for the ceremony to take place."

He groaned, pulling her to him tightly, hungrily crushing his mouth against hers. Scooping her up in his arms, he started for the bed.

"Cass."

"No."

"Cass!"

"Don't argue with me."

"Your mother, brother, sister-in-law, and family housekeeper have just arrived," she gasped laughingly. "They're waiting to see you."

She felt the enthusiasm suddenly draining out of him. "Damn!"

Rubbing her cheek against his, she hugged him tightly around the neck. "You need to have a little patience, my love."

He groaned painfully. "That's what I've been telling you."

❁ ❁ ❁

There was a lot of back-slapping and hugging as the Claxton family was reunited.

Cass drew his mother, Lilly, into his arms and held her tightly. He hadn't seen her for more than five years.

"Now where are all my grandbabies?" Lilly turned to Cole's children, engulfing them in big grandmotherly hugs.

"Ma, you better ease up," Cass warned. "You still have my ten to go."

Lilly threw her hands up in despair. "Lordy, lordy, I always said you'd be the one to turn my hair gray!"

Willa, the family housekeeper who'd been like a mother to the Claxton boys, was there, beaming with pride as she swept Cass into her arms and gave him a big kiss.

Wynne was standing by, eager to talk to the lothario who had jilted her at the altar nine years before.

"I can't wait to meet the woman who's finally

snagged you,'' she teased, going into his open arms.

Cass grinned as he good-naturedly drew Cole's wife into a tight embrace. ''Wynne, sweetheart, look at it this way: If I hadn't have left you standing at that altar, and you hadn't traipsed all over the country looking for me, why, where would my brother be today? In the arms of one of those wild, wicked women—''

Wynne poked him soundly in the ribs. ''All right, all right. How many times do I need to say thank you?''

Cass laughed and knelt down to greet his nieces and nephews. ''Jeremy, look how you've grown—and your sisters, Tessie and Sarah!'' He stood up again, shaking his head with disbelief. ''Boy, they make you realize you're getting old, don't they?''

Cole was suddenly forced to sidestep as Doog, Jesse, Bryon, Joseph, and Lucy came hurtling down the stairway. ''Damn, did school just let out?''

Cass threw his head back and hooted. ''No, those are just more of mine!''

Cole looked at Wynne and grinned. It was hard to imagine Cass with a wife and ten children!

Beau and Charity arrived with the children, and the hugs and kisses started all over again.

''You're expecting again!'' Wynne exclaimed.

Charity nodded, her eyes sparkling with happiness. "Beau says it's a boy this time, for sure!"

"It'd better be, I've sure worked hard enough on it," Beau teased, giving his wife an adoring squeeze.

Events began to go by in a blur. Greetings were exchanged, and Cass grew more nervous. He kept anxiously dragging his watch out of his vest pocket to check the time.

When he was sure he couldn't wait another moment, the music suddenly sounded the wedding march, and Cass straightened his tie, took a deep breath, and stepped into place next to Aaron and Payne under the wide arch of greenery in the parlor.

Phebia had reclaimed Marybelle, and she carried her as she came walking down the stairway first, dressed in a little replica of the bride's outfit. She entered the parlor hesitantly, scattering rose petals along the pathway while sneaking an occasional suck on her thumb.

Margaret Ann and Lucy followed, wearing circlets of fresh flowers around their heads, and dressed in long lavender-blue gowns.

Jesse, Doog, Bryon, and Joseph came along next, spit-shined and polished in their new blue suits. Corliss followed carrying Sammy, who didn't care one bit for all the commotion. The latter group didn't have any official role in the wedding, but it had been agreed by all that the ceremony should be a family affair.

And then the moment Cass had been waiting for finally arrived.

Patience came down the stairway, a vision of loveliness in her ivory bridal gown.

Cass's eyes locked with hers as she walked slowly toward him, supported by Harlon's steady arm. They smiled at each other, savoring the heady moment, anticipating the hour they would be back in each other's arms forever.

Reverend Olson performed the ceremony, and this time he didn't have to prompt the groom to accept his vows, or kiss his bride.

In fact, the guests were beginning to wonder if Cass was ever going to stop kissing her.

Patience finally broke the heated embrace and covered her face with embarrassment amid the sound of loud applause.

Wine began to flow, and the wedding cake was cut, though the groom seemed a bit too eager to dispense with the ceremonies and be on his way with his bride.

The guests crowded around as Cass lifted his glass, his eyes overflowing with love as he made the first toast to his bride. "Here's to our first happy year of marriage." He winked, then leaned over and whispered in Patience's ear. "One out of seven's not bad, is it?"

She laughed and kissed him this time.

"Well, little brother," Cole said to Cass as they caught a rare moment alone a few minutes later, "I guess I worried about you all these years for nothing!"

Cass gazed lovingly at his new bride, who was busy trying to excuse herself in order to slip away. "Yes, she's something, isn't she!"

It had taken a considerable swallowing of pride, but Cass had finally told his family about his earlier marriage to Patience and how he'd come to love the children of the orphanage as much as he loved his own son. He'd had to. Lilly had nearly fainted when she'd found out he had ten children.

Beau drifted over to join his brothers. "I guess Patience will do in a pinch, but have you two *really* looked at my Charity? Now, gentlemen, there's a woman!"

"Hell, men, Wynne's got your women beat, hands down!" Cole stated flatly.

Beau and Cass both turned to give him a dour look.

The three brothers suddenly exchanged identical devilish winks. As far as they were concerned, they *all* had done all right.

Samuel Claxton Senior would have been right proud of his sons.

Elaine Coffman captured readers' hearts with her first historical romance, MY ENEMY, MY LOVE. Don't miss her next historical romance, IF MY LOVE COULD HOLD YOU, available from Dell next month.

WEST TEXAS, 1880

There were only two trees in the town of Two Trees, Texas, and both of them were in Miss Charlotte Butterworth's front yard.

That was probably why a wild bunch of cowboys rode in a dust cloud into her yard and picked the larger of the two elm trees as the place to hang Walker Reed. When the dust settled there were six men in all—five to administer justice, one to receive it.

And it was such a nice yard, too—fastidiously kept, just like the white frame house it surrounded. The house, a respectable-looking one-story dwelling, had a rather sleepy aura about it late that afternoon just as the sun was sinking behind the elm trees and dappling the shrubs and flowers that drooped from the heat.

Behind the house was a sparse little garden braving the intense heat. There, too, everything was neat and orderly; two rows of okra, two of black-eyed peas, one of yellow squash, and farther over, running along the fence, were the trailing vines of tomatoes.

Inside the neat clapboard house Charlotte Butterworth, whom everyone in Two Trees affectionately called Miss Lottie, was in her kitchen, checking on the progress of a vinegar pie baking in the oven of her brand new Champion Monitor six-hole stove. The sudden pounding of hoofbeats mingling with the deep-throated boom of voices coming from the road in front of her house startled Charlotte, catching her off guard, and she slammed the door on her new Monitor harder than she had intended. She was immediately thankful she had decided on the vinegar pie instead of the Robert E. Lee cake, which would surely have fallen flatter than a fritter when the oven door slammed.

The sound of shouting drew closer. It was probably those rowdy Mason boys chasing another scrawny coyote and trying to corner the terrified animal inside her fence, just as they had done last week. The week before that it had been a half-starved rabbit. A woman living alone had to maintain a constant vigil or find herself taken advantage of. That, and the need to protect her flowers from being trampled again, caused Charlotte to drop the two pot holders she was holding into the proper drawer and close it with her hip. Then she dusted the flour from the front of her white apron, overlooking the smudges on her nose, and headed for her parlor. Removing her spectacles, because she never let anyone see her in spectacles, Charlotte marched to her front windows and peeped discreetly—because she had been taught that a lady always peeps with discretion—through the only lace curtains in the whole county, to see what all the ruckus was about.

Her gaze crossed the planking of the wide front porch, going over the trailing coils of Carolina jasmine tangled in the porch rails and winding around gimcracks, to see five mounted cowboys from the Triple K ranch. And just as she had feared, they were trampling her snapdragon bed. That brought a sputter of outrage to her lips, but before she could act on her sputtering outrage she saw that wasn't all they were doing. They were securing a lariat to the sturdiest branch of her prized elm tree. That in itself was bad enough, but to her horror, Charlotte Butterworth discovered—locking her eyes upon the lariat looped over her tree and following it backward—that there was a most displeased if not downright unhappy stranger attached to the other end.

"Dear Lord," she whispered, "they're going to hang the poor man!" Charlotte decided a hanging was none of her affair and was about to turn away, when it suddenly occurred to her just where they were going to hang him. "From my tree!" she said, as if not believing it herself.

Her mind teeming with thoughts about what was going to occur in her front yard made Charlotte stare, white-faced, at the man's dark hair. Even from her window she could see it was matted with what looked to be blood and caked with sand. His clothes, or what was left of them, were torn, and his blood was seeping through a dozen rips. It looked as if he had been tied behind a horse and dragged for some distance. It was quite obvious he hadn't come willingly, but what was one man against five?

She saw his hands were bleeding and raw and tied behind his back. With heart-quickening alarm, she watched as his fingers clenched and unclenched, the muscles in his arms straining until the blood vessels stood out prominently against the strain to break his bonds.

But it was the stranger's face that held her attention, and she watched him for long moments, absorbing the masculine beauty of his bronzed face—the high cheekbones gleaming with sweat. From the side his nose was straight, his chin strong and powerful. When his horse danced nervously under the rope hanging along his flank, the stranger turned and Charlotte saw his eyes were a deep, dark blue, chilling in their intensity, hard with determination. In spite of his impassive expression, she had the feeling his pride was hurt. It struck her immediately that the man looked ruthless, defiant, and quite capable of violence. Yet there was an aura of integrity about him. The man might be many things, but criminal was not one of them. Something in the proud way he held his head, the straight line of his back, the clenching of his jaw, the way he did not grovel and beg or speak one word to save himself—all proclaimed his innocence.

Charlotte was reminded of another time and another place when she had watched in horror as someone innocent was murdered. Only that time she had been a child and confined, unable to help.

Charlotte Augusta Butterworth stood

watching from behind her lace curtains, her blue eyes fixed upon the stranger. A pain thrummed in her head, and there was a thickening lump in her throat where her hand rested.

She had never seen a man hanged.

And she wasn't about to see one hanged today either—not if she had anything to say about it. After all, that was her tree they were using, and she had a right to decide if it was going to remain a shade tree or become a hanging tree.

Charlotte had easily recognized the cowboys as being Triple K hands, led by old Clyde Kennedy's youngest son, Spooner. She also recognized quite easily that the cowhands were not accustomed to lynching a man. One of the men she knew only as Bridger was nervously chewing on a small sliver of wood that protruded from his mouth. Bridger was a quiet, shy cowhand, not prone to troublemaking. Two of the hands she had seen on occasion, but could not recall their names. The Mexican she knew only as Chavez. It was to Chavez that Spooner spoke.

"Chavez, you will whip his horse when I give the signal."

Chavez nodded and pushed his sombrero back on his head, the string catching against his throat in a way that reminded Charlotte of what the stranger would be experiencing in a moment if she didn't do something. Chavez swung down and tied his blood bay to one of the pickets on Charlotte's fence. Then he moved to stand beside the rump of the stranger's horse, firmly holding a quirt in his right hand.

Spooner turned toward the stranger. "You got anything to say before we get on with this?"

The stranger, sitting on the horse, his weight resting with the tension of a coiled spring against the stirrups, didn't say anything. Charlotte saw his eyes were alert, shifting from one man to another.

His face red with anger, Spooner spurred his horse closer to the stranger, his hands reaching out to draw the noose tight around the taut cords of the man's neck. Neither man said a word, but the stranger's eyes were clear and searching as he looked at Spooner, who sheepishly turned away.

That made Charlotte's blood boil with righteous indignation, and whenever Charlotte Butterworth's blood was boiling with righteous indignation—well, there wasn't much that she wanted that she didn't get.

Mere seconds later Charlotte Butterworth stood on her front porch, taking careful aim with an M-1873 .44 caliber Winchester. She blew a hole through the star on Spooner Kennedy's Texas hat, sending it sailing off his head.

The lynching was postponed.

The blue-steel eyes of the stranger who was about to be hanged were the first to lock onto Charlotte's tiny frame, hitting her and dismissing her with a look that sent a chill through her, but he said nothing.

Spooner Kennedy, however, wasn't so polite.

"Dad-durn-it, Miss Lottie, what are you doing out here?" he said. "This ain't no place for a lady. Now get yourself back inside." Dropping from his saddle and retrieving his beloved hat, Spooner poked his finger through the neatly placed hole. "Dad-dammit!" he shouted, "look what you did to my hat!"

"You'd better be glad it wasn't your fool head, Spooner Kennedy," Charlotte answered while taking another bead with her Winchester. The words were uttered in a high treble that sounded as sweet as a heavenly chorus to the stranger. Her voice, the stranger decided, was about as close to a heavenly host as he wanted to come—at least for several years. He released a long-held breath, thinking just how close to meeting his Maker he had come. Feeling the noose tight around his neck, he realized he wasn't safe yet.

"Miss Lottie, this is no concern of yours," Spooner went on. "We've got some business to settle with this killer."

Charlotte's intense blue eyes grew wider at the word *killer*, but her aim remained steady. "You'd best be taking your business up with the sheriff, then," she said. "That happens to be my tree, and hanging a man from my tree *is* my business."

"Now, Miss Lottie," Spooner said, "you know damn well there ain't another tree over five feet tall within twenty miles of here."

Charlotte was not swayed. "Jam!" she shouted. Then again, louder this time, "Jam!"

A few minutes later a cotton-haired old black man shuffled around the corner of the house. He was in no apparent hurry, despite the urgency in the boss-lady's voice. "Jam," Charlotte said firmly and distinctly, "take my horse and hurry down to Sheriff Archer's and tell him to get over here fast. And hurry up! Don't you dawdle none, you hear?"

"Yessum."

Jam's hurrying gait was the same as his taking-my-own-sweet-time gait, so he shuffled along, rolling his eyes and staying well away from the cluster of men until he was around the corner of the house. Minutes later Jam headed down the road on Charlotte Butterworth's old piebald mare, Butterbean.

The stranger shifted his position, his eyes hard on the hands of the cowhand that held the reins to his gelding. Those shaking hands were all that stood between him and hanging. He knew if the cowboy fumbled and dropped the reins the gelding would bolt and he, Walker Reed, would be left swinging by his neck.

Walker's nose started itching. A hell of a position to be in, with his hands tied behind his back. He thought about raising his shoulder to rub against it, but any shift in his weight might make his horse more skittish, and the horse was skittish enough. The rigid line of his mouth twitched at the thought of him sitting here with a noose around his neck, concerned about something as insignificant as his nose itching.

"You have a strange sense of humor if you find hanging something to smile about," Charlotte said. "Especially when it's your own hanging."

Slowly, purposefully, Walker let his eyes sweep over the cluster of men gathered around him to rest upon the small-framed woman who'd been his salvation. "It was a smile of relief, ma'am."

Walker studied the woman's face as she accepted his answer with a curt nod. In the shade of the porch her face seemed severe—all sharp angles. But then she took a few steps forward, out of the shade of the porch. The amber glow of the late afternoon sun brought out her magnificent coloring. Her face was anything but sharp angles; and as far as the rest of her—her leanness was deceptive. A woman like that was as unexpected in this flat, desolate part of Texas as her immaculate yard, whitewashed fence, and brilliant display of flowers. She seemed to be a lot like her house—quiet, respectable, and fenced in. He was suddenly aware he was feeling a stir of something more than gratitude. She was a lovely thing—or would be if she'd release all that glorious ginger-colored hair from that ridiculous knot perched on her head.

Wearing a glossy blue calico dress, she stood there so slim and so stiffly starched that she looked fragile and delicate, but Walker was not deceived. A woman who handled a Winchester the way she did was anything but fragile and delicate. The woman intrigued him, and he wondered what was wrong with him to make him feel a stab of desire at a time when his every thought should be centered upon self-preservation. Desire, he thought, can rear its ugly head at the most damnable times.

Charlotte caught the flare of interest in the stranger's eyes and felt a flush of discomfort that left a tell-tale stain upon her cheeks. The sheer masculinity of the man was distracting. She neither wanted nor needed to be distracted. Not now. Not when she needed her wits about her.

Charlotte sighed, wondering if Jam had made it as far as the sheriff's office. Or was he meandering aimlessly along the rows of fences, wandering from one side of the road to the other, everywhere finding things to distract him and feeling quite happy to be the only idle bee in the swarm. How well she knew Jam could be fascinated just watching a caterpillar crawl up his sleeve.

All of sudden the evening stage came rumbling along the dry, dusty road that ran from Abilene to Two Trees. Hezekiah Freestone, the driver, was working the brake with his foot, the heavy leather of reins from six horses resting in his left hand and the long braided rawhide whip in his right. Just as he drew even with Charlotte Butterworth's porch, he replaced the whip and waved, as he always did, as if he were seeing nothing out of the ordinary in her front yard.

"You could at least stop!" she yelled after him, wondering how any fool could pass a hanging with nothing but a smile and a wave.

The stage passed, leaving another cloud of dust that soon settled over the six men, this time dropping a little on Charlotte as well. The stage rumbled on down the road, the wheels hitting an occasional pothole or rock that sent the wheels bouncing into the air.

At that moment Sheriff Archer Bradley rode into the yard, while Jam, taking his own sweet time on Butterbean, was still some distance behind. Charlotte had never felt so relieved. Now that Archer was here things would move right along, and she could clear this mess of confusion out of her yard.

Archer drew rein and sat there for a spell, taking in the situation. His hat of worn felt was pulled low over his eyes, and now and then a quid of tobacco could be seen moving against his right cheek. Taking careful aim, Archer spat, scoring a direct hit on one of Miss Lottie's irises. Then he wiped his mouth with the back of his hand. Archer was a man who didn't like to be hurried, and just because a man was sitting before him with a rope around his neck—well, that was no reason to hurry. A jump to wrong conclusions is what happened when you hurried, and Archer never jumped to wrong conclusions.

"Now, just what's going on here?" Archer drawled finally, not missing the look Charlotte gave him—a look that said any fool in his right mind could see what was going on.

Deciding the look wasn't enough, Charlotte spoke sharply. "There's a hanging going on here, Archer . . . or there was until I stopped it."

"With that Winchester?"

"Of course," said Charlotte. "Have you ever known a lynching to be stopped with a few kind words . . . unless they're backed with lead?"

Archer's mirth wasn't hampered in the least by his scowl. His eyes shifted from Charlotte to the stranger to Spooner and back to the stranger, who by this time was looking mighty expectant and mighty relieved.

Once again Archer took careful aim and let fly with a wad of tobacco. Everyone seemed to be waiting for someone else to say something. But no one did.

While they waited in silence, a dust-devil came out of nowhere, rattling the leaves on Miss Charlotte's two elm trees and bending the heads of her snapdragons before it tugged a few tendrils of fiery red hair out of Charlotte's carefully coiled bun and whipped them across her face, one spiraling filament sticking to the corner of her mouth. Charlotte let it be, keeping the barrel of her Winchester pointed at the white disc on Spooner's tobacco pouch that dangled from his shirt pocket. She was busy thinking that men could waste more precious time, standing around spitting and scratching.

"Miss Lottie," Archer said, "you can put your Winchester down. I'll handle things now."

"You took your own sweet time reaching that decision, Archer," Charlotte said as she turned the full power of her magnificent eyes upon him in what could only be called reproach. "Untie that man first!"

Archer nodded to Spooner who nodded to the man mounted next to him. "Okay, Jake," Spooner said uneasily. "Untie him."

Jake slid to the ground and nervously approached the stranger.

"Just a minute!" Charlotte pointed her rifle at Jake. "You go around the other way," she said, "so his horse can see you coming. I'd sure hate to have you spook his horse and hang him by accident!"

Jake stopped. "Why's that?" he said with a cocky grin.

Charlotte did not respond to his grin. "Because then I'd have to shoot you."

Jake was careful to swing a wide arc, approaching from the front. Reaching the stranger, he untied his hands. At that instant a shot whizzed past Jake's ear, causing Jake to dive for the dirt at the same time the lariat tied around the stranger's neck snapped in two.

Walker's horse snorted and sidestepped nervously. When he had him under control, Walker turned toward Charlotte, feeling much like a banked fish that had just mercifully been tossed back into its natural element. "I'm much obliged for your intervention, ma'am," he said in an accent that was neither Southern nor Texan.

At the sound of his low voice, strangely husky, Charlotte looked at him, meeting his clear gaze for a moment before she drew a deep breath, her eyes narrowing. Something about him frightened her. Perhaps it was the intensity of his look, unthinkably familiar, considering that she had just saved him from death. A shiver of apprehension ran through her, and she was awkwardly aware that every eye was trained upon her. She lifted a brow, sending him a look full of so much venomous dislike that he felt a constriction in his chest. The look was both direct and quiet—a reproof withdrawn as hurriedly as it had been sent and patently meant for him and him alone. He dipped his head ever so slightly in recognition.

Charlotte's heart stirred nervously in her chest. "Don't be thanking me," she said, "I just bought you a postponement, not a full pardon. You may hang yet. That's none of my affair—as long as it isn't from my tree."

Walker inclined his head once more, this time in a curt way, his hard glance deep and penetrating as he caught the grating edge of spite in her words. The woman had just saved his life. Why did his gratitude chafe her so? He was not a vain man, yet he had been on the receiving end of enough sultry looks and honeyed kisses from beautiful women to know women were attracted to him. That this woman would stick her neck out for him and then insult him when he expressed his gratitude both surprised and irritated him.

He studied her face, the mouth so sensitive it was difficult to believe that same mouth had spoken so sharply to him. Her manner and speech bespoke cool control, but he saw in her clear blue eyes a shadow of uncertainty and vulnerability. Something made his heart contract. Whether she liked it or not, the woman had done him a tremendous service. He was thankful enough and gentleman enough not to provoke her further.

"Nevertheless," he said slowly, "I am in your debt." He continued to watch her, studying the aloof tilt to her chin, the stiff shoulders. There was something about the hint of panic he had seen in her eyes that told him she didn't find him repulsive.

The stranger was, Charlotte couldn't help but notice, handsome in a raw, ruthless way. The man's hair had at first appeared dark; but when his hands were freed and he moved out of the shade of the elm tree, his hair seemed to absorb the rays of the setting sun and it glinted with golden highlights. He wore his hair longer than the men in these parts did, yet his face—in contrast to the assortment of beards and mustaches that surrounded him—was shaved clean.

He was different. In fact, everything about him was just a shade different. His hair was a little blonder, his skin a little browner, his eyes a little bluer, his bearing a little more regal than that of any man Charlotte had heretofore encountered. When the stranger looked Charlotte over with a stare that penetrated her white muslin pinafore and calico dress, then went right through her nainsook petticoat and linen drawers, she looked away, her eyes resting on Archer Bradley, who'd just repeated his question to Spooner.

"I said, what's been going on here?"

Spooner went on to relate how he was tending herd when he heard a gunshot. Taking several of the Triple K hands with him, he rode in the direction of the shot, finding the stranger standing over the body of a dead man, his drawn Colt still in his hand. An envelope in the dead man's pocket contained several thousand dollars and a bill of sale for three broodmares out of Old King, a famous running horse. The dead man's name was Walker Reed. He was from California.

"I'm Walker Reed," the stranger said. "I'm from California. I came out here to buy horses. The man I shot robbed me last night and took the three mares. I'd been tracking him since dawn. When I finally located him and rode into his camp, he drew on me and I had no other choice but to shoot him in self-defense. I was just about to retrieve my horses and my money when these men rode up, jumping to conclusions."

"You have any proof of what you're saying?" Archer asked, fully understanding what the stranger said about jumping to conclusions. This part of Texas seemed to him to be the jumping-to-conclusionest place he'd ever seen.

"The only proof I had were those papers you heard about, but you could wire the sheriff in Santa Barbara. He's known my family for years. He could identify me."

And he could, of course. Walker's grandfather, Richard Warrington Reed, had come to California during the gold rush. A rich vein had provided the necessary capital to buy a large hacienda and ranch from a dwindling and impoverished family of Spanish descent. Three generations of Reeds had lived there. The sheriff in Santa Barbara had personally known two of those generations. It was the two youngest members of the latest generation of reeds, Riley and Walker, that had, as youths, caused him more headaches than he cared to count. Riley had finally married last year at thirty-six. Walker, a year younger than his brother, seemed in no hurry to marry.

Archer studied Walker for a moment. "You understand I'll have to hold you in custody until the sheriff in Santa Barbara can verify what you say and positively identify you?"

Walker laughed. "Believe me, being detained in a jail is infinitely better than the last offer I had in your hospitable town!"

There was something breathtaking about the man's smile, and while Charlotte was struggling to find just where her breath had been taken, the stranger dismounted with lazy ease and approached her. "I owe you my life," he said. "It may be nothing to you, but to me it means a great deal. I'll find some way to repay you. I won't forget."

His heated gaze made Charlotte's pulse thump rapidly. Before she could snap back an angry reply, the man turned and Charlotte watched as he crossed the yard and mounted his horse. She was still staring as the men turned and quietly rode single file out of her front yard, leaving in a much more orderly fashion than they had arrived.